RISE OF A PHOENIX

SHANNON MAYER

RISE OF A PHOENIX

The Nix Series, Book 3
Shannon Mayer

ACKNOWLEDGMENTS

To my laser eye surgeon. Thanks for telling me my eyes would only take ten days to heal when it ended up taking a solid two months. My readers could have had this book a month earlier.

Get ready to be mobbed by irate readers. ;)

1
PHOENIX

The helicopter blades whooshed over our heads as we flew away from the banks of the Cumberland River, away from Nashville, away from the place where the Ikimono myst had been created and nearly brought to fruition, only moments from being released on the world. A myst that took a creature, human or abnormal, and made them into a monster that could be controlled—a veritable army ready to be unleashed on unsuspecting humans.

More than that, though, we flew away from where I'd lost my son, Bear, again. I clutched at the small diary in my one hand, the leather warm against my skin, the edges of the book rough against my fingers. The diary belonged to my dead sister and held secrets that could help me bring Luca Romano to his knees so I could put a bullet between his ears and in doing so protect both my son and myself. And it had been laid in my hand by the man sitting across from me.

In my other hand, I held my left gun, Eleanor, pointing her at Mancini. She trembled, anger vibrating from her into me. "Let me kill him," she said, her words more felt than heard. The swoosh of the helicopter's rotor blades swept them away.

"Not yet. He's going to answer some questions," I replied and she calmed somewhat, her shaking slowing.

Mancini sat across from me, an abnormal, the head of the Collective. I'd never met anyone else in the group that held the most powerful abnormals in the world. Powerhouses who were supposed to be the checks and balances between humans and abnormals. I hoped I never did meet any of them. As far as I was concerned they were all pussies, unable to keep chaos in the abnormal world from spreading, which meant they were useless to me.

Mancini, though, was the one man who hated my father almost as much as I did. Powerful and deadly, no one truly knew what he was—or what he could do. An abnormal, yes, but what kind, or with what skill set? He'd offered to help me bring my father down. But his help had come with a price I'd not known when I'd accepted working with him, a price I would have never had agreed to if I *had* known. Mancini had his man Simon kill my mentor Zee, which had then forced me to kill Simon. Someone I'd begun to trust as a friend, someone I thought was going to help me find my son.

I would not make that mistake again. I would not trust those around me fully.

"Start talking, or I'll just kill you now and throw your body into the river." I yelled the words to be heard over the rotors. I stood in the helicopter, my body swaying with the movement as our pilot swept us away from the chaos below. A massive eruption blew behind us, the flames reaching high into the sky as the last of the detonators we'd set went off within the prison-turned-laboratory that had held the

Ikimono myst. At least that venue was gone and the world was safe for a little longer.

Mancini smiled at me, the irises of his strange eyes dancing and jigging as if to a tune only they heard. I stared him down, his fucked-up pupils not bothering me in the slightest. There was no false threat in my words and he knew it. In that, we understood one another. There was no bluff in either of us.

We were both killers, through and through, and a threat was more of a promise when we spoke words of death.

He slowly held up a pair of headphones and slipped them on. Killian stood beside me on my left; my older brother Tommy sat on my right. Killian held another headset up and slid them over my head so I didn't have to lower Eleanor.

I wanted to ask Eleanor what she thought about all this, but I would have to wait on that question. She shivered in my hand as if she had something to say too. I'd talk to both her and Dinah as soon as I could. They might look like guns, but the truth was they were souls trapped inside the weapons. Weapons that could fire indefinitely, and that helped my already dead-on aim be perfect. At one time in my life, I'd thought they were neutral in their chaos, that they would work for anyone who held them. But more and more, I realized they were my guns even though they'd belonged to my sister Bianca first. They wanted only to be used by me and didn't like anyone else touching them.

Which begged the question, whose souls were trapped within them?

The headset settled on my ears and Mancini's voice clicked through.

"What do you want to know first?" he asked as calmly as if asking what I took in my coffee.

If I thought for one second that he would truly come clean completely, I'd be stupid and would deserve whatever death took me. But I *would* take what he gave for now and know that it was likely only a partial truth. Partial or not, it could help me get Bear back.

"You said my mother named me Phoenix for a reason. Spill what you know about what exactly I am." I braced my body as the helicopter tipped to the left.

Mancini nodded. "Your mother was like you, Phoenix. She was a survivor. An Ascendant. A name so unheard that it means nothing to the majority of abnormals. But she never fully realized her strength, which is why she died." He paused and his eyes narrowed slightly. "Your ability is twofold. The first is the survival aspect. From a young age, you have been placed in impossible situations. Your family being the first hurdle, your rape when you were but a child," beside me I felt Killian stiffen, "your inducement into the world of assassination, your survival against other abnormals—"

"I'm an abnormal, I get it," I said. Something I'd only just learned and admittedly was still figuring out how to handle. As a hunter of abnormals for years, I had very little respect for them. But that was changing, albeit slowly.

Mancini nodded. "Agreed, but your abilities were in a sense hidden by your natural talent to kill. The reality is it was *always* there, always pushing you toward certain decisions. I'd lay a bet that you saw it as gut instinct to make certain choices when others thought you were crazy."

I didn't so much as blink my agreement, but he went on as if I had. I'd already heard some of this from a Magelore named Vivian. This bit of info was not new to me, although I had to admit I more readily believed Mancini over that bitch Vivian.

"So, that is the first part. Surviving. We'll call that your defensive abilities. Most abnormals only have one or the other, defensive or offensive. Only the strongest have both. Your offensive abilities are unique. Not only can you produce your own type of myst, but there is another part to it as well." He lifted an eyebrow, and I nodded again but didn't tell him about the blue and purple flames I'd only just discovered were a part of me.

"What else?" Killian asked, his voice coming through the headset. He must have put a third one on.

Mancini glanced at him. "She can absorb another abnormal's ability and hold it, saving it for a later date. That will likely only come in time and with much training. The only other Ascendant I knew who could pull it off killed himself trying to take on too much of another's power."

Neither Killian nor I informed Mancini that I'd already managed to do just that. No need to hand over all my secrets at once. Killian's ability was that he could use the power of electricity and lightning, something all those descended from the Irish carried. I'd absorbed his lightning more than once and held it, then released it when needed.

"What has this got to do with my mother?" I asked, and Eleanor shivered in my hand.

I ran my thumb down her stock to calm her.

Mancini tipped his head to the side. "She was like you, but not so strong because there was no training. The more you train your body and mind to be a fighter, the more the power of a phoenix will rise. Your mother was a survivor in many ways, but I don't think she ever learned how to harness her offensive abilities. I believe her heart was too gentle for that."

Eleanor twitched once and then went still. Mancini's eyes flicked to her as if he'd seen her movement.

I lowered Eleanor and tucked her into her holster, but I never took my eyes from Mancini. "You're saying the more I train, the stronger my abnormal ability is?"

"That is part of it, yes. The more danger you are in, the more expressive your ability becomes. Your myst is doing all it can to protect you, and so it grows stronger with each threat thrown at you." Mancini's eyes narrowed. "It makes me wonder if that isn't what your father is trying to do. The more he pushes you, the stronger you become, the better tool you are to him when he grabs hold of you once more."

"Stupid on his part then," Killian said. "If she becomes much stronger, she'll wipe him and all his people out."

A chill rippled down my spine and I let my legs unlock as I slid to a seat. "He means to push me to the brink of my ability and then what? Control me? But that doesn't make sense. He never knew I had any abilities. I'm not sure he thinks I do now even." And he never would have let me go so easily all those years ago. Those words I kept to myself.

Mancini seemed to read my mind and I didn't like it. "He didn't exactly let you go, though, did he? In fact, he hunted for you for the last twelve years, and then killed your husband and stole your son, which threw you back into action with more fury than ever before. It sounds to me as if he knew all along what and who you were and has been playing the long game. It would make the most sense, agreed?"

I swayed where I was even though I was sitting, not with the motion of the helicopter but the strength of his convictions and the feeling that he might be right. Abe, my Malinois dog, pressed himself against my leg. Maybe to give me support, but maybe because he too could feel the tension that came with Mancini's words. For my father to be playing the long game, to have known all along what I was . . . I wasn't sure I believed it. Or maybe I just didn't want to. It would mean he'd planned to kill Justin, to kill Bear long before I'd ever had either in my life. He'd known that if anyone came into my life they could be used against me.

I couldn't do much more than stare at the man in front of me. I didn't want him to be right—not because of any residual feelings for my father or family, but because it meant I'd been duped all those years into thinking I was safe. That the safety I'd felt had been nothing but an illusion. I hated secrets. I hated lies. I hated deceptions. I wanted reality, no matter how cold or hard it was.

I'd rather hate my life than believe it was not the truth.

Mancini laced his fingers and set them around his right knee. His voice scratched through the headset. "The more I consider it, the more I think that might be the answer to what is happening here. It won't matter to your father if you kill all three of his guardians. He may in fact want that to happen. If you kill all three, it will spike your own abilities, making you more dangerous than the three of them put together. And because he is still immortal, you won't be able to kill him. Then he has your son under his thumb, a perfect form of leverage to control you and your newfound strength."

I glanced at Killian, needing to see his reaction to this. Because Mancini was hard for me to get a read on. His eyes being part of the difficulty, but there was almost zero energy flowing from him. I believed this was truth, but around Mancini, I didn't fully trust my own feelings.

Liars fidgeted and all but danced in their seats, their energy spiking with each word as they worked to make you believe them. Even the best liars had tells. Looking back, I could pick out Simon's, now that he was dead and gone. Though they were subtle, they were there.

Mancini had none of the tells. If what he said was the truth, then I had more to deal with than I'd ever before considered.

Killian's green eyes were thoughtful as he turned to me. "It makes a wicked sort of sense, lass. But I do have one question." He turned to face Mancini. "Why would he need someone stronger than three guardians of Hell to protect him if he's immortal?"

Mancini shrugged. "I don't know the answer to that."

A lie, that one I picked up on and a zip of glee shot through me. The acrid tang of the lie floated to me before being swept away on the wind rushing through us. "Tommy, you still have my pack?"

Tommy jerked as if I'd slapped him. "Yeah, what do you need?"

I turned so my body sheltered what I was doing. Tommy laid the pack between us and from it I pulled out the red paste I'd used on Tommy. If smeared on any injury and then lit on fire, it healed wounds and infections that would otherwise kill in seconds. But that was not what I wanted. Before Simon died, he'd put something else in my pack. The sleepy as a lamb fairy dust shit that he thought might be useful. I found the small jar with the sparkling bits and rolled it into my palm, thanking him silently. He might have been an asshole, but this stuff was going to help.

"What are you doing?" Mancini asked.

"You're lying to me." I spun around as I pressed my thumb against the edge of the jar's lid and spun it open. A gust of wind whipped the twinkling dust right into Mancini's face, and he sucked in a deep breath. I spun the lid closed and jammed it back in the pack as Mancini slumped forward to his knees, the rest of the fairy dust settling in his hair and on his face. Like he'd been glitter bombed. The thought made me smile for a moment, then the smile was gone.

"Dirty pool." He slurred the words through the headset, his body going slack against the wall behind him.

I knelt over him, careful not to touch any of the twinkling bits that had attached to his gray strands. Even as I watched, they melted into his skin and hair, sinking deeper into him. I waited until they were completely gone and then I reached out and grabbed the top of his head and yanked it back so I could stare into his face. "You are going to answer some questions now, Mr. Mancini."

He licked his lips, the tip of his tongue darting out, but he didn't say anything.

I tightened my hold on his hair. "What would my father need me to be stronger than his three guardians for?"

"Oh, that's simple. He wants to have all the perks of his deal with the devil, and none of the drawbacks. He wants you or your brat to be his personal guardian against the demon he made the deal with. That won't save him, though." The words slid from him in a rush, so fast they blurred together.

I didn't let go of his hair, just tightened my grip. "How can you be sure?"

"I know things." And then he giggled. Fuck, if he went too deep, he was going to be useless as tits on a bull.

I tried a different direction. "You had Zee killed, you tried to set me against Killian by telling me he'd killed Barron, and you have not yet fulfilled your promise of helping me against my father. Why are you helping me? Why did you give me the diary? Who gave it to you?"

He grinned up at me, his eyes at half-mast as if he were deep in his cups. "All so you can kill your father. That's what you want, right? And I got the diary from a friend of mine."

I grinned right back at him, ice forming around any emotions I might have left. My name might have been a creature of fire and flame, but the cold of death and killing had served me for a very long time.

"How were Eleanor and Dinah made?"

His eyes fluttered closed. "They are souls ripped from their bodies at the point of death and shoved into the guns. Brikoff made the guns. He was the only one who could. Tricky, and I must say I've always been impressed that it was done not once, but twice."

My guts clenched and I fought not to reach and touch the two girls. Two women trapped inside my guns . . . not just sentience given to them as I'd once thought. For years, I'd assumed their ability to talk and think was a part of the myst that had created the two weapons, even as I'd wondered if there was something more.

I let go of his hair and ripped my own headset off. I needed to speak without having Mancini hear me. And I wanted to pace. I needed to move, and yet in the small confines of the helicopter that was open on one side, there really was no room. My mind and thoughts were on fire. My guns had souls trapped in them. My father had likely known what I was all along and I'd fallen into his trap time and time again which had only served to make me stronger so he could use me. There was not a lot of new information here. Unless we got back to the deal my father made, and the demons he thought I should protect him from.

Killian put a hand on my upper arm but I didn't look at him, not right away. He put his mouth to my ear. "Lass, what are you thinking?"

I turned to him, doing the same, putting my mouth against his ear, the strands of his hair blowing across my lips. "He doesn't have much more to tell us. And he is going to cause more grief than help if we don't get rid of him." I pulled back and looked at Killian then, and he nodded.

Once more he tucked in close. "Agreed. But he's a hard one to kill, believe you me. I've tried." He gave me a half grin. From my other side, Tommy shifted so I could see him. He was my brother, but he'd also been one of my tormentors in our early years. I'd been the child of the second wife to Romano, the only one born to the family without any abnormal abilities. (Besides Gabe, but he was dead, so he no longer counted in my mind, even if I had been the one to kill him.) Tommy had his own set of abilities that could tip the balance in our favor.

Tommy stood and approached us, his eyes fogged with worry. He put his hand carefully on my lower back to balance himself in the center of the helicopter. He leaned in close so he could be heard.

"I could steal his memories. We'd know then what he was really thinking," Tommy said. His face had zero scars from his ordeal with the Shadow, and even his eyes were back to normal. Which was saying something since they'd been gouged out of his skull by his own hands in the throes of the madness the Shadow induced. And I knew what that madness could do; I'd felt the Shadow's power beat against my own skin. That red paste had healed him back to good as new. Again, I had to give Simon props for that, even if he was dead by my hand.

I shivered and he patted my back as if to soothe me. I fought not to roll my eyes. It was a little late to suddenly play the considerate big brother. "Any backlash for you, though?"

Tommy shook his head. "No. I'll stuff the memories where I can't see them."

I frowned. "You mean you'd have them forever?"

"Yeah, that's the deal. Myst must have balance. For every action, there is an equal and measurable reaction. The memories aren't really taken or wiped out, like they say. They stay in the person's mind, just buried to a point where most don't find them again, not unless they really go searching. So, after I see them, I have them, and I do all I can not to look at them." His eyes flickered and I saw the level of fear he was attempting to keep from me. The twitch at the edge of his dark eyes, the tightening at the edge of his jaw. He didn't want Mancini's memories. I wouldn't want them either.

But for Bear . . . for him, I would throw anyone into the fire, including my brother. I grabbed the headset and slid it back on, adjusting the mouthpiece as I turned. "There are better ways to make someone talk. Mancini, why do you really want Luca Romano dead? Or should I have Tommy here take your memories?"

As I finished my turn toward him, Mancini lurched to his feet, toward the open side of the helicopter. I lunged for him, grabbing at his suit coat, snagging the edge of it, but the headset slowed me down. He spun and smiled at me as he fell backward into open air. The coat ripped and I was left standing there with nothing but a piece of deep blue cloth that fluttered in the wind.

Still smiling, his body swept away and behind us, but I felt like his laughter chased me. I stood at the door, my fingers gripped into the edge and stared as he fell from the sky, his shape indiscernible from any other speck. I stepped back and slid the door shut, turned and looked at Killian and Tommy. They both had headsets on.

"Guess he really didn't want to talk. I'll catch up to him later," I said.

Killian laughed and shook his head. Tommy just stared at me. "You don't think he's dead?"

I snorted. "No. If he thought he wouldn't survive, there is no way he'd have tossed himself out. He's not fucking stupid, and we'd be idiots to believe he would die so easily. Romano isn't the only one playing a long game, well hidden."

Tommy turned to Killian and asked where we were headed. I let the words wash over me because my mind was busy elsewhere.

The thing that tugged at me, though, was why would Mancini have gone to all the trouble to get Noah to bring him to me, to give me the diary, to tell me about my abilities and about my guns, only to balk when it came to the big question. Why did he really want Luca Romano dead? Or was it more than that? Or was it just the diary? I slid my fingers over it, feeling the worn edges again. I didn't even look at it, but I knew it was *possible* that it could be that important.

The only thing that was obvious to me was that Mancini wanted to use me as his weapon to get rid of my father. But what reason could make him unwilling to speak of it?

I finally let myself slide into a bench seat, the one where Mancini had sat, and actually relax. Though, even that wasn't the right word. Maybe rest was a better one. I needed to rest after what I'd just walked through, after what I'd just done. There would be no relaxing until Bear was back with me. And the fact that he was alive meant I would not stop until he was at my side once more. Abe let out a long low whine and pushed himself between my knees so his nose was pressed into my belly button. I rubbed his head with one hand, absently.

His breath was hot through my shirt, reminding me he

was there, even if he wasn't vocal like the other men who surrounded me.

I closed my eyes and let myself go over what had happened at the jail-turned-laboratory. For the first time, I'd tapped into my abnormal abilities, all the way to the core, and used them to destroy the Shadow, a guardian of Hell. Not something I would have ever thought I could do, and yet there it was, and I'd survived.

Yet again. Between Mancini, Vivian, and my own experiences, I couldn't deny the truth of the survivor defenses. I would embrace them as my own.

I rubbed a hand over my face and leaned back so my head was against the paneling of the helicopter. My eyes stayed closed as Killian sat next to me, the line of his body warm against mine.

"Hello, Lad," he said. I cracked an eye as he gave Abe a rub between the shoulder blades. "You stick close to her."

Abe snorted and rubbed his face against my thigh as if to say, What do you think I've been doing?

I let myself lean into Killian, just a little bit. Not enough that anyone watching would be able to see it, but enough that he took some of my weight.

"I'll keep my eyes open, Lass," Killian said through the headset. "Try to rest."

"Where are we going, again?" I blinked up at him even as a massive wash of fatigue worked to close them against my will.

"We'll head to a safe house not far from here, a couple hours. Then we'll make a plan." He didn't touch me, other than offering his body for me to lean on. Didn't tell me not to worry, or that we'd get Bear back. None of that. He knew I wasn't looking for anything other than a partner to get my son away from Romano. And yet he was there beside me, helping me through it when he didn't have to.

"We'll take care of this mess," he said softly, barely heard through the headset.

We . . . there was that word again. I wasn't sure I liked it, wasn't sure I disliked it. For now, though, his help would be a godsend. A partner I didn't want, but knew I needed to get through this shit storm I faced. With each passing second, I could feel it looming larger, coming for me faster. I closed my eyes again and sleep swept over me between washes of the helicopter's blades.

DREAMS. *I HAD BEGUN TO HATE THEM FOR THEY HELD MY FEARS and my hopes and dashed them both. So even while I knew this was a dream, I also knew it held something more, some piece of information I needed to be aware of that my waking mind refused to see.*

"Bear?" I called for my boy as the scene around me slowly came into focus. He was only ten; there was no way he would survive with Romano. I'd at least had my mother and Zee looking out for me at that age. Bear had no one. Not even me. My heart twisted with that shitty truth.

There was no answer from him and the fog that surrounded me faded, revealing a dusky landscape of flattened buildings and expansive desert all around.

"This is not Kansas anymore, Toto." I glanced to my side looking for Abe but he wasn't there either. I frowned and took a step, a click sounding under my foot.

I leapt to the side as the landmine went off behind me, sending me ass over head. The only thing that saved me was my abnormal ability. The survival instinct that had kept me alive so many times before. Before I even knew it was a part of me. But this was more than that. The mine should have shredded me to pieces even if I leapt off it.

A warning then of what was coming?

The scene shifted and went from dead silent to a roaring war zone in a matter of a single heartbeat. The ratta-tat-tat of rapid fire weapons, of mini-guns, and the massive concussions from landmines and hand grenades alike. The screams of dying men, the calls of their leaders as they were pushed into battle, in a language I didn't know, but I knew the cadence. My hands went for my own guns and I found neither.

I searched my body. Dinah and Eleanor were not there.

I was truly on my own for the first time in I didn't even know how long. I should have been more afraid than I was.

I crept forward, searching the area for something to use as a weapon, to find Bear because I knew without a doubt he was somewhere here in this war zone. I blinked and I was in the middle of the battle, no longer on the edges. Bullets zinged by me, the resounding boom of something larger went off over my head, and after the concussive ringing in my ears eased, I saw him. There on the far side of the red zone was Bear, pinned down by fire, his hands over his head as he lay flat on the ground.

I bolted toward him, ignoring the way the bullets whipped by me, ignoring the pain as they slammed into my limbs, back, hip, shoulders, ignored them until I fell at his feet.

He jerked away from me, staring up at me, his face twisted with anger and even hatred, emotions I'd not thought I'd ever see on his sweet face.

"You lied to me. You never tried to save me."

I SNAPPED AWAKE AS WE DROPPED FROM OUR CRUISING altitude, the air pressure popping my ears. Abe scrambled to keep his footing and I pulled him up beside me on the bench seat, looping an arm around him as he trembled. Almost like he'd been in the dream with me in spirit.

"Bad dreams?" Tommy asked me from his spot across the way.

I nodded and ran a hand through my hair. "Yeah. Was I talking?"

"More like yelling." He grimaced. "Bear is a good kid, and he's stronger than all of us. We'll get to him in time."

I nodded. "Yeah, he is. He's better than any of us too."

Tommy laughed. "That isn't so hard, to be better than us, I mean. We were all assholes."

A part of me didn't want to let him back into my life. He was my brother by blood, but my enemy by the same blood. The better sense in me said not to soften, to keep the hard exterior up. But I couldn't help it. I still wanted something that resembled family. Even if it was royally fucked up. My lips twitched. "Yeah, *you* were all born assholes. I had to learn to be an asshole."

"Learned, or born to it, your son isn't like that. You did good with him, Nix." Tommy gave me a nod and then he frowned. "I always hoped you wouldn't get sucked back into this life."

My heart gave a funny twitch. "What made you turn on him?" Him, as in our father, Luca Romano.

"He . . ." Tommy winced as if pained, "he raped my wife and then she killed herself."

Everything in me lurched because I knew the pain of losing a spouse all too well. "I'm sorry, Tommy."

"Me too." He shook his head. "I thought I could protect her because I was his favorite, you know? But he knew how to hurt me, and when I refused to go to the Middle East for him, he tried to force me."

The Middle East . . . there had been rumblings about

powerful abnormals there even when I was still in my father's employ. Was that what my dream had been about, the Middle East? What had Romano wanted from Tommy's visit there?

"Why didn't you want to go there?"

His sigh came through with a crackle over the headset. "Guy named Shaitan holds the power there. He's a total power-hungry shit that makes Dad look like a child in the playground who can't figure out how the swings work, and this Shaitan was the one who made the playground. I tried to tell Dad he was messing with darker forces than just a damn abnormal. He wouldn't listen. I think he planned to try and marry one of us boys to one of Shaitan's girls."

"Shit," I muttered. "After I was gone, then, this all happened?"

"Yeah."

"Did you end up going?" I felt Killian stir beside me a split second before he got up and headed to the cockpit to check on the pilot, but more likely to give us some semblance of privacy, even if the headsets were still transmitting to everyone. The man could nearly read my mind, and while I appreciated it at times like this, I wasn't fully sure I liked that he knew me so well already. It made Killian dangerous to my health in more than one way.

Tommy waited for Killian to go, then he fell back into his story. "I went, when he threatened my wife's life. I knew he wasn't bluffing. We all know he doesn't bluff. And he's done it before, killed the spouses of those who pissed him off."

I startled. "Whose?"

"Zee's wife," Tommy said. "Her name was Alma, and she tried to get Zee to leave Romano's employ. At least, that's what I understood."

My heart lurched with more than a wisp of green jealousy. I hadn't known about Zee's wife.

The killing of spouses was not new to me, even if the loss of Zee's wife was. Our father had Justin, my husband, killed in a car accident that was anything but an accident. Bear and I had been in the truck with him, and while I'd been injured, Bear had been snatched away before he knew I'd survived, or I knew he had. He'd been taken, and I was left believing he was dead for nearly six months before I found out the truth.

I frowned, pushing my own feelings aside. Abe curled in tightly so he lay across my lap, all eighty pounds of him. I stroked my hand through his fur. I made myself go back to the important information. "And when you were gone, that's when he raped her?"

My older brother shook his head. "No. He waited until I came back, like the asshole he is. I was home a week, and I walked in on him with her. She was crying, tied to the bed, begging him to stop. He rolled off her and I shot him. You know how that goes. No bueno."

I nodded. I did know. Our father had made a deal with the devil. We'd thought for so long that the deal only entailed him gaining power, prestige, and money, but there had been an additional bonus. He was no longer mortal, and wounds that would kill anyone else didn't even register on his radar as a damn scratch.

"And, after that?" I prompted.

Tommy shrugged and stared at his feet. "He took my gun from me, turned it around and held it to my head. It scared her so badly, Whitney was never the same after that. I tried to help her. I tried to get us both away from him but . . . the Hider I employed wasn't like Zee. He didn't have the ability to keep us Hidden for more than a few days before the shaking sickness took him. I had the money to pay him; he just didn't have the ability he'd claimed."

I kept my jaw clenched tightly for a moment. There were no words I could offer. "After that, after she killed herself, that was when you tried to stop him?"

He blew out a slow breath. "I reached out to a few low-level contacts I had in Mancini's employ. Noah was one of them, and he was nervous to let too much show, but I knew I had him from the first day. He said he knew the man who was married to my sister, to Bianca. I never believed she was dead, you know. She was too fucking smart to die easy."

I nodded. "That was the trail I laid. I let Justin believe I was her. Simpler that way. Zee hid my tattoo, and that was that."

Tommy snorted. "You didn't want your husband to know you were the abnormals' boogeyman?"

It was my turn to snort, deliberately mimicking him. "Something like that. I wanted a normal life. Can't have that if your partner thinks you might off them in their sleep, or if he's wondering just how many people you've killed." Justin had thought the Phoenix was a monster, and maybe he was right. I didn't want to burst the bubble on the life I'd created.

"What happened to Bea?" Tommy asked, and it was my turn to sigh softly.

"I found her dead in her room that weekend you all went to Miami for business. It was just the two of us. I heard her cry out. I went to investigate and she was dead on the floor. There was a note for me and in it she begged me to hide her body."

Tommy frowned. "Why would she want that?"

I shrugged. "I don't know. I just did it."

His jaw ticked. "You were a better sister to all of us than we deserved."

I blinked a couple of times before I responded. "I think we were all fucked over, coming from Romano."

Tommy barked a laugh. "There is that. Surprising we turned out as well as we have."

My eyebrows shot up. "You think we turned out *well*? What mirror have you been looking in lately?"

Laughter crept up my throat and I let it out, and Tommy joined in. Maybe for the first time, I felt a connection with one of my siblings other than a passing indifference or, worse, outright hatred.

The helicopter tipped to the side and began a descent, the blades slowing.

I frowned and grabbed a handle over my head and Abe curled his front legs around my thighs, digging his claws into the far side. The blades should not have been slowing, this wasn't like a plane making a landing.

"Killian?"

"We got problems," he yelled back. "You're making nice with your family, and mine . . . well, mine has just shown up to the party."

I reached around Abe, tucking my arm under his belly, tight behind his front legs. "Hang on, buddy."

He let out a whine and pushed his nose under my arm, hiding his face as if he at least knew what was coming. I yanked a harness on around me, tangling it with Abe in the hopes we'd both make it through.

There was a moment of absolute quiet as the engine of the helicopter flicked off and electricity crawled over the metal, creeping toward me and Tommy. I took one look at him and grabbed a parachute from my side and flung it at him as the helicopter flipped sideways and the door clicked open. We spun hard, he stumbled toward me, and his hands jammed against my sides, pushing Dinah and Eleanor against my ribs. They squawked and I shoved Tommy with the parachute.

"Jump!" The engines flicked on as suddenly as they'd gone off, and we were thrown hard to the right as if a giant fist had slammed into the metal. My last thought as the lightning crawled over my body, as Abe howled for all he was worth, was that I didn't think I liked Killian's family any more than I liked mine.

2

Crashing metal, the howl of my dog, the loss of oxygen as I tried to pull all the electricity away from Abe and take it into myself.

Bits and pieces of the fall from the sky flicked through my mind like chunks out of a movie. The rotor blades slowing, Tommy flipping out with the parachute, Killian leaping to cover my body with his own.

And then the electricity as it had slammed through us, knocking me out no matter how hard I'd pulled it away from Abe.

Abe.

"Assholes." I groaned the word as I came fully around, my hands searching for my four-legged companion. His fur was as soft as ever, but I felt nothing moving under it. Panic set in as I scrambled to get myself out of the straps. "Abe."

His body was limp as I got myself unbuckled and went to my knees beside him. The helicopter was on its side, the open door buried in the ground, my knees pressed into grass and dirt.

"Abe, don't do this to me." I took his long muzzle and

lifted it to my face but there was no warm breath escaping his nose.

"Here." Killian pushed me aside and his hands crackled. "It'll help or it won't." He put his hands on Abe's side and a pulse of electricity jumped through him. Once, twice, three times.

My jaw ached from holding it so tightly. I knew we were wasting time. I knew that whoever had downed us was waiting on us to come out and face them, or maybe they thought we'd be dead.

And we were trying to save my dog. But he was Bear's dog, and I just couldn't let him die without trying to fight for him.

Abe sucked in a breath and groaned, his tail thumped once and I couldn't help the rush of air that escaped me. "Don't do that, Abe!"

His tail thumped again and he tried to lift his head.

Killian looked at me. "Lass, you be okay?"

I nodded and the pains in my body finally made themselves known, from the bruises on my back to the sharper pains in my ribs where Tommy had fallen against me. "Alive."

At least we were on the ground and not still in the air. That was something. "Abe, stay." I rubbed a hand over his face and he closed his eyes, not fighting me on my command.

I pushed to my knees and looked around us as my hands went to Dinah and Eleanor. "Ladies?"

"Here," Dinah said softly. "Are you okay?"

"Bruises only," I said, and already those bruises were healing. Points for learning about being an abnormal and tapping into the power. Go me.

"Eleanor?" I reached and touched my other gun. She

didn't answer. I looked down to see the butt of a gun sticking out. But I didn't even need to pull it to know it was not Eleanor. I yanked out the look-alike Berretta.

"Eleanor?" I spun on my knees, searching the area. The scene hit me hard—Tommy had fallen into me, jamming both guns against my ribs . . . "Tommy, you piece of shit!" I shot to my feet, shaking.

"What happened?" Dinah asked, panic in her voice. "Where is Eleanor?"

"Tommy snatched her when I pushed him from the helicopter." I growled the words, anger and fear making my movements hard and fast despite the fading bruises.

Killian stood beside me. "Why would he take Eleanor?"

I closed my eyes, thinking about the possible reasons. Tommy had been working with Noah, who'd been working with Justin. Tommy had to know what would kill Romano, and maybe part of that was Eleanor. "Because he believes she can kill Romano. Fucking moron." Some of my anger leached away. Tommy wasn't trying to hurt me. He was trying to kill Romano. And that could be forgiven. Maybe. As long as I got her back.

I had no time to guess at how right or wrong I might be because the helicopter jerked around us. I lifted Abe and moved to one side, keeping my feet on the ground. The helicopter lifted into the sky once more. As it went, the helicopter righted itself, chunks of grass and dirt falling through the air. We scrambled to keep out of the way from the shifting metal frame.

Fuck, I did not need to crash-land again.

Killian dropped a hand on my shoulder and tugged me close. "Listen to me. My family are not only capable of lightning, though that is the power held by the strongest of us. They are weather controllers—all of them."

Of *course* they were. That explained the way the helicopter had fallen in such an orderly measure even after the blades had stopped moving. I felt around inside me, looking for the pool of lightning that I suspected would be there. My lower back rumbled with it, ready to use. "Dinah, you ready?"

"I wish Eleanor were here, but I'll do all the killing you need," she growled.

I adjusted Abe in my arms so I could pull Dinah from her holster and switch her to my left hand. "Sorry, but I need you here."

She shivered. "I understand."

I was faster with my left, and my right hand was a good place for another kind of weapon. One that was just a simple gun.

The helicopter jerked suddenly as if it would come crashing down on us and we both stumbled to the side. A move to literally put us off balance, clever, but also a serious dick move considering this was Killian's family.

"Going to take more than that to make me like them," I said.

"Let me try and talk them down." Killian tightened his hand on me. "If it goes sideways, you'll know."

I snorted. "Sure thing." I laid Abe at my feet.

Through the dust stood a semi-circle of seven people that ranged in age and size, from a tiny woman who could be no more than five feet at best, to a man well over seven feet with flaming red hair and beard.

But it was the woman in the middle who was our problem, and I knew it the second my eyes locked with hers. She had enough of Killian in her facial features that I was betting she was his mother, or maybe older sister. Hard to say with the agelessness of her face. Her eyes were wide, and though I couldn't see the color, I guessed green like Killian's. Those eyes narrowed when I didn't blink or look away.

Score one for me, I'd already pissed her off.

Killian stepped out in front first, from the shadow of the helicopter. I followed him, staying behind and to his left.

"Mam, what be going on? That is no way to welcome the son home who is your bread and butter." Killian spread his arms out, showing he had no weapons, his Irish accent thicker than I'd ever heard it. I, on the other hand, brought Dinah up and held her with both hands, sighting down his mom in the middle of the group of seven.

Her long blond hair flying around her face, her feet lifted off the ground as she floated toward us. Impressive, I suppose, but I'd seen scarier. And if she could only control the wind, then she wasn't as strong as Killian, which should work in our favor.

I kept Dinah on her. "Hold."

"I'm ready," my gun whispered back to me.

"Killian," his mother said, her voice soft and lilting with an accent that made Killian's seem mild, "we told you that we didn't want you causing trouble. That we liked the status quo. But here you are, tangling with things you would be better off ignoring. Like that one there." She flicked a hand at me and I smiled back.

"Not causing trouble, Mam. Just chasing down the bad boys to give them a spankin'." Killian grinned, and I wondered if it would work on his mother.

She frowned and the wind whipped around him, picking him up. His hands went to his throat.

That was sideways enough for me.

I squeezed Dinah's trigger as I stepped to the right. I hit Killian's "Mam" in the shoulder, spinning her backward. Killian fell to the ground, but I couldn't look at him. The other members of his family rushed us and there was no time to second-guess.

I did my best to hit them in non-lethal, but debilitating places. Knees. Shoulders. Hips. Feet. Hands. Not pretty, bone-crushing, but at least they'd have a life after I was done with them—

Lightning arced from the sky and slammed into me, throwing me backward, my back arching so hard, I was sure my head would touch my heels. I didn't fight the current. I let it slide through me, let it pool under my skin, gathering it even as it stole my breath and tried to stop my heart. Mancini's words replayed back to me that an Ascendant like me had taken in too much power from someone else, and it had killed him.

But I could feel it in my belly that if I didn't keep taking it, the electricity would stop my heart.

A split second before I knew it would be too much, the current stopped.

I hit the ground and lay there a moment, doing all I could to remember how to breathe.

"Killian, we don't like your choice in women," his mother said with a voice filled with anger.

Damn it, *everyone* thought we were fucking each other. I sucked in a hard, pain-laced breath and sat up.

"Fuck you." I flicked my hands at the group, sending the electrical current I'd pulled in from both the helicopter and the last blow back at the Irish folks. They could dish it out, but could they take it?

The blue lightning danced out of me in six perfect streaks that slammed into each member of Killian's family at the same time. They were blown back, flipped three or four times each and at least thirty feet away from us, and then *finally* there was blessed silence.

I deliberately didn't take out his mother.

I pushed to my feet, wobbled and made my way to Killian while his mother watched with big eyes, her lips tight with anger and pain. I kicked him in the leg. "Get up and tell your mother I'll kill her if she doesn't fuck off right now."

Killian rolled to his knees and then stood. I didn't try to brace him. Didn't give him my hand. We needed this to be clear cut—we were not a couple; this was a business arrangement we had and nothing more.

Not to mention, I didn't want him to look weak in front of his family.

"You are not Irish," his mother said. I turned only my head toward her, lifting Dinah as I did.

"No shit. And you are not a very nice mother." I glared at her.

"You have a child?" She arched an eyebrow.

"I do." I stared back at her. "And let me tell you, a mother who tries to choke the life out of her own son? If you were on fire, I wouldn't spit on you."

"My son has been a thorn in my side for many years," she purred.

I didn't like that she used the same words for Killian that my own father had used for me. Which made me wonder if there was a connection, and those two pieces slid together. "You're working for Romano, aren't you?"

Killian jerked beside me as if I'd shot him. "Mam, tell me you haven't defected to that piece of shit?"

She smirked. "The pay is far better, and the man is a beast between the sheets."

I had Dinah up and pressed to her temple so fast, her smirk was still on her face. "Killian, say it."

His mother looked past me. "He won't. He be soft, like his brothers."

I laughed softly. "Wonder why he brought me, then? I'm the bitch Romano made."

Her eyes slid to me and I smiled at her as I let the emptiness of my killing blood float through me, let the darkness that was death in my world rise until it filled me and I felt nothing but the trigger under my finger and the pulse of my heart and hers. Her eyes were as green as I'd thought they would be and they widened as her smirk slid from her face—finally.

"Who are you?"

"Who do you think I am?" I whispered.

Her throat bobbed. "I can guess. Romano said you be traveling with Killian, but I didn't believe it. I thought you be dead. The Shadow—"

"Is nothing to me. Besides, the dead rise from time to time. You should know that, living in this world." I pressed Dinah a little harder against her temple. "Killian, what do you want to do with her?"

He stepped up beside me. "She'll go to Romano, and that's if she doesn't try to take us down on our way."

I couldn't look at him, but I heard the indecision in his voice. There was some love still there for his family. I did not have that connection with my own surviving parent, but I understood. I dropped my hand, she smiled, and I shot her in the belly.

The boom rattled around us, Dinah howled with laughter, and Killian's mom clutched at her wound, her eyes widening as the blood spread and slid over her white shirt. "You..."

I shot her again, a little higher, closer to her diaphragm.

"That should slow you down," I said. "And maybe you'll

think twice before fucking with either of us, yes?"

She fell backward, her eyes rolling as she passed out. I stared at her and the wounds that were already healing. Maybe I'd been wrong about how strong she was.

"That won't hold her back for long," I said. Killian didn't move from beside me and I didn't dare put Dinah away. "Where to now?"

He snapped out of his daze. "This was our destination. I'd planned to come home for a bit and recharge, to gather the things that we could use. None of them were supposed to be here." Killian's voice was oddly detached. At least, for him.

I nodded. "They'll be out for a bit, I think, but we don't have a shit ton of time. We could grab what we need and go if the place is close enough."

He nodded. "Aye, let's do that."

I went back to the helicopter and picked Abe up, sliding him over my shoulders so my hand could still be free to go for Dinah if need be. He grunted and let out a fart as the pressure on his belly increased.

I wrinkled my nose. "Glad to see everything is working."

We started away from the still-unconscious bodies and the passed-out, bleeding-out woman who was his mother. "What's her name?" I asked.

"Ellen."

"Nice meeting you, Ellen!" I gave a half-hearted wave back at her as we walked away. From the corner of my eye, I saw Killian smile.

And that did a funny thing to my heart that I squashed immediately. I focused on the moment at hand. "What about Bobby?"

"Didn't make it," Killian said. "They killed him as soon as they took control of the wind around the helicopter."

Bobby was—had been—Killian's pilot. I didn't like him, but if we had to fly something else, he would have been handy. Especially seeing as he had four arms, notwithstanding the one I'd broken at the elbow. Three was still better than two.

I took a good look around and blinked a few times. We were on what appeared to be the back lawn attached to a giant-ass mansion that made the home I grew up in look like a white trash potato shack.

"Shit, you grew up here?"

"Nah, I grew up in Ireland." Killian shook his head. "This be the home me mam wanted forever."

"How the hell did she manage this?" I looked at him, saw the look of chagrin cross his face and then got it. "Shit, you got it for her? You paid for this for that woman who just tried to kill us?"

He shrugged. "I was stupid for a long time when it came to me family. Traditional Irish are tightknit, even if they don't always get along. You fight, you drink, you make up. Then you do it all over again the next day."

I blinked a few times. "Sounds lovely."

He snorted. "Yeah, well, I stopped funding her life a few years ago. She killed someone close to me, and I realized I was fooling myself. My family was never going to be what I thought they were. But I can't seem to cut the ties with them that I should."

"Remarkably, I do understand that realization. Mine just came a few years ahead of yours."

He glanced at me. "Yeah, you'd be one of the few who would get it."

I did not like the warmth that flushed through me with his words. We understood each other; that was not a bad thing in a working partner. That was one good thing about

Killian. For being the head of an Irish gang, he was damn honest. I valued that more than I wanted to admit, even to myself. That was more than I could say for my ex-partner, Simon.

I grimaced at the thought of the chameleon who'd killed Zee, and almost killed the man beside me. I'd trusted Simon and been fucked over for that trust. I didn't want to make that mistake again, but . . . Killian made me want to make it, as stupid as that was.

Which meant that as much as I wanted to trust Killian, I had to reserve judgment. I had to keep something of a barrier between us so I wouldn't be pulled off guard, so I wouldn't be blindsided when he did something that would hurt me or someone I loved. Or . . . if I had to kill him at some point. My heart tightened on that thought with a pain that I normally reserved for my worries about Bear.

But damn it, Killian had brought Abe back without question, without saying we needed to leave him behind. I didn't want to believe that he was so devious as to be working me over that hard.

"How long do you think they'll be out?" I motioned back the way we'd come.

"Thirty minutes, tops. Plenty of time for us to gather up the goods and get out." We were at the back of the house now and Killian pulled the door open for me. I lowered Abe off my shoulders and he took a wobbling step and then another. A working dog at heart, he had his nose up and scenting the air immediately.

He trotted through the door, his nose lifted as he sucked in the smells around us. No growls, so that was good. I followed him through and dropped a hand to the top of his head. "Good to have you back, buddy." I scratched his ears and he gave me a soft woof.

We'd almost lost him at the jail-turned-laboratory. He'd been injected with the Ikimono myst and had been turned into a true freak show of a monster. We'd managed to get the antidote into him and many of the other abnormals that had been injected, but there were some that were still out there roaming around, causing god only knew what kind of havoc. I'd leave that to the human police to manage. I had bigger fish to fry.

I shook my head at the size of the place. "Killian, where to?"

"Here." He moved past me, his hand brushing against my hip to direct me to the right.

My jaw ticked, but I didn't tell him to not touch me. Damn it, this was . . . I didn't know if it was good or not. I just knew any distraction from getting Bear back into my arms wouldn't be helpful and could potentially cost Bear his life.

I drew a breath to cool the sensations flickering through me. Later, I would deal with Killian and these feelings after Bear was home with me, safe and sound.

"This is a larger version of my stash at the pub, or it was last I was here," Killian said. We were in a hallway that stretched the length of the house, by the looks of it. Dark polished hardwood floors clicked under our feet, echoing the length of the hall. Abe stuck close to my left side, pressing against me here and there for reassurance and stability.

He was a good boy, well trained, but seemed to be struggling with some of the aspects of what we were doing. Explosions, fire, and sudden bursts of fighting were hard on anyone, never mind a four-year-old dog who'd only recently been inducted into this world. Trained for it, yes, but living it was different. Having his heart restarted couldn't have helped either.

"I need to find a place to drop him off," I said. "He isn't going to be much help if I have to carry him, and with his injuries he needs to heal."

"Let's get out of here first," Killian said.

I gave a quick nod and kept a hand on Abe's back, steadying him. I hoped we wouldn't be in this world too much longer. This was not where I wanted Bear to grow up, to have him always wondering who was going to try to steal him, or wondering if he wouldn't survive the day. I shook my head at myself. No, none of that was acceptable. There had to be a better way.

Killian opened a door on his left and I followed him through. The room blinked to life and for a minute, I just stared. It was a bathroom big enough that some houses would fit within it.

"The shitter is where you keep your weapons stash?" I arched an eyebrow at him. He reached past me, his face drawing close enough that I could smell the hint of something on his breath that made me want to taste it. Licorice, he smelled like licorice.

The click of the lock reverberated in the tiled room as he turned it.

"Yeah. Last place people look for guns is in the shitter."

I couldn't help the laugh and I pushed him away from me, moving until I was in the middle of the room with my back to him. My heart rate was up and the flush of desire tingling under my skin like the brush of his electricity was too much. Yes, this was getting much too intense, I was going to have to do something about it. "Killian."

He was there at my back, his hands on my upper arms, his mouth near the side of my neck. "Phoenix."

"Not now, Killian. I feel it between us, and I get it. Fuck, I *do* get it, but not now." I turned to face him, but took a step back. "I *cannot* be distracted. And I can't afford for you to be distracted either. We both need to be on our A game."

His jaw ticked. "And if we both die before we finish this? What then?"

I frowned. "Well, if anyone dies it'll be you. I'm the survivor, remember."

He spluttered, his eyes popping wide and his jaw dropping.

I laughed at him. "Killian, I'm joking. But do you see? Even this banter between us? It's not like me. I don't joke with the men around me. You . . . you bring something out of me I thought was gone forever. I laugh with Bear. I tease him and he teases me and I love him with everything I am. He has my soul and I never wanted more. I didn't expect or even want to find a partner who could do the same." Well, shit, I'd just pretty much admitted he was a partner in more than a work sense. Damn it, I hoped he didn't notice the slip-up.

"Was Justin not a partner to you?" He tipped his head and took a step toward me. I couldn't move. Damn, I needed to move away from him, but I couldn't because I wanted what he had to offer, all of it. The strength and power in him, the understanding of exactly who and what I was, and the fact that he didn't judge me for it. He didn't condemn me for my past, for what I'd done with my life, for my family. He didn't shy from the dark in me any more than he shied from my hands that had killed so many.

"Justin was a good man, far too good for me. Even in his lies, he kept the dark from me, which is why he ended up dead," I said softly as Killian's hands slid down my arms to my fingers, lacing them together.

"Am I not a good man then?" He gave me a half smile

and I struggled to breathe as those damn green eyes twinkled at me, secrets and desire filling them.

"You're a very, *very* bad man," I whispered.

He leaned closer. "I know. But you are a very bad girl. And I like it. I like all of you, Lass."

Shit, shit, shit, this was not what I needed. Well, maybe it was, but not right then. "After, Killian. You can have all of me after, but if we start this now—"

He drew a slow breath and tightened his hold on my fingers. "After may never come, no matter how you look at this. And I don't want to miss anything. I don't live for tomorrow, Lass. I live for today."

I bit the inside of my cheek and nodded. "I know. But Bear will always come first. Even after all this."

He grinned and tugged me hard against his chest, still just holding my hands. "I'll take second place to Bear." The air between us danced on my skin and did rather bad things to my body, making me ache in ways I'm not sure I ever had before.

"One kiss," he begged softly as he dipped his head.

One kiss would do me in, I knew it. I jerked away from him. "No."

He laughed. "Ah, Lass, it does me body good to see you so affected. At least I know I'm not swinging for the fences for nothing."

I twisted around and glared at him, then swept my hand toward his crotch and his obvious hard-on. "You aren't exactly keeping things subtle either."

He shrugged. "It's been a long time since a woman has called to me like this. And never one who didn't have Irish singing in her blood."

I shook my head and went to the sink. I flicked on the cold water and splashed it on my face. "Where is the stash?"

I had to get this back on the right path or we were going to end up fucking in the tub, in the shower, on the floor . . . I shook my head clear of those thoughts.

Later. We'd deal with this later.

"You weren't far off when you said the stash was in the shitter." Killian laughed as he walked to the toilet and lifted the lid on the back of the tank. I moved to see what he reached for. Inside the water tank was a handle that he gripped and twisted. A screeching groan rasped behind us and I spun around to see the tub slide to the side, revealing a set of stairs that disappeared into darkness.

"Fancy."

"No one else here knows about it, at least, last I knew." He put a hand to my back and gave me a push. "Hurry, it's on a timer to close after us."

"Abe." I snapped my fingers at him and he heeled slowly to my side. It was only then that I realized he'd not been upset about the back-and-forth between Killian and me at all. Not a single peep out of him.

"You're supposed to be protecting me, Abe," I said as we hurried down the dimly lit stairs.

Behind us Killian laughed. "Maybe he's not much into protecting your virtue."

I snorted and shook my head. I had to agree, there were better things to protect than what was left of my virtue, if I'd ever even had it. More likely Abe was just exhausted. His panting breath echoed in the chambered space. 'Round and around we went, the air cooling as we dropped what had to be close to fifty feet.

When we stepped off the stairs, I couldn't stop my eyes from widening at the sight in front of me. A stash was one thing, but this?

"What the hell? Are you Batman?"

3

BEAR

My vision was foggy as I was carried from the airplane to the waiting vehicle. The hot, humid air of Nashville still clung to my skin even though that was hours ago, maybe even days. I felt like the leftover humidity should have warmed me, but it didn't. I couldn't stop the shivering, as my body shook beyond my control to the point of spasms. Rooster carried me easily, and he glanced down at me as we made our way across the tarmac and a hot wind blew over my face.

"Kid, you going to puke again?"

I closed my eyes but didn't dare shake my head. "No." I managed to whisper the word without biting my tongue. I wasn't sick, though I wished I was. No, it was worse than that; I was poisoned.

And now I was dying. I could feel it happening as my body shut down around me.

Soon enough, I would be with my dad in Heaven. At least I wouldn't be afraid anymore, or alone. Rooster grunted, then lowered me into whatever vehicle was next. I didn't care. I couldn't think about what might happen. I was too trapped inside my own head with what I'd seen and just lived through.

I could still see my mom fighting creatures that looked as if they'd been raised from the depths of my darkest nightmares. I could still see a man get eaten alive by wolf-hybrid dogs, could still see the Shadow as he grappled with my mother as she fought to get to me. I groaned and curled tighter around my middle as the horrors stuck themselves to my inner eyelids.

To save my mother from the monsters, I'd set off the sprinkler system. Which had been full of an antidote for the Ikimono drug, which had made the monsters in the first place. Some of the antidote had gotten into my body—how could it not with the water spraying everywhere?

Having the antidote without having been first injected with Ikimono was what was killing me, and every part of my body knew it. At least I'd saved my mom.

Rooster cleared his throat beside me. "Romano, the kid is getting worse."

Luca Romano was my grandfather, and he'd not only stolen me from my parents, he'd tried to have them both killed. While my father *was* dead, my mother was not. She would come for me. I knew she would. She was the Phoenix, after all. Which meant I just had to hang on a little while longer. Maybe she would be able to fix what was wrong with me. My hopes were dashed only a moment later.

"There is nothing I can do about it. And I still have his mother coming, so I will use her to bargain with Shaitan. Pity, the boy had promise," Luca said. I forced my eyes open, something ticking at my brain.

"Do you have any Ikimono?" I blinked at him, though it was an effort as were the words.

He frowned down at me. "Yes. I plan to get production going elsewhere. Why?"

"Give me the injection." I whispered the words, not sure why I said them. It was like a part of me had taken over that I didn't know.

His eyebrows shot up. "Actually, that's quite brilliant." He flipped open his suit coat and reached inside to pull out a vial of something. "Rooster, pass me the kit there."

There was the shuffling of something and then a medical kit was handed to Luca. He opened it and pulled out a needle. "A survivor, I like that about you, Bear. A good trait to have in our world."

My teeth chattered and my heart began to slow, the beat of it erratic, which made me gulp for air. "Hurry."

He didn't speed up at all, just kept up his monologue. "In our world, the strong are the survivors. The brutal are the kings, the powerful mold the world. I'd like to think I can show you how to be all three. Since you come with one of the traits I most desire, this should make the rest of your teaching easier."

The vehicle hit a bump, and I rolled to my back, gasping for air, my heart slowing further, the blood in my veins sluggish. I closed my eyes and waited. There would be no hurrying Luca; he would either inject me in time or he wouldn't.

Rooster's big hand wrapped around my wrist. "Shit, give him the needle, boss. His heart is slowing."

"You like him now?"

"He's a damn tough kid. A sight tougher than I would have thought. But even he isn't indestructible, no matter who his mother is."

That was more words than I think he'd ever spoken in all the time I'd known him. Pain rocked through my middle, my muscles spasming, and my legs and arms flung out wide without any instruction from me. I tried to suck in a breath, to get air into my lungs, but there was nothing. My chest had contracted and there was no opening it.

This was it. I was going to die and my mom . . . tears leaked out the corners of my closed eyes. My mother would think I was dead again, only this time, it would be real. I was dying and the man who was my grandfather sat over me with something that could save me and he was doing nothing. Nothing at all.

A tiny spurt of anger flickered deep in my belly, a flame that curled and heated its way through my nerve endings. With my eyes closed and my heart stuttering to a stop, the flame grew larger, the heat waking me.

Shouting erupted around me and then the sound of several guns going off, and then a weight slumped onto me and a warm, wet liquid trickled over my neck. Blood, I knew it was blood without seeing it. Rooster was dead. It had to be him because my grandfather was immortal.

Why they'd fought, I didn't know. I only knew that my mind was fully aware even while my body slowed second by second, dying inch by inch.

In desperation, I reached for the flame I could see inside me. Purples and blues, it reached back and brushed down my arm to pool in the palm of my hand. I clenched my fist around it, dragging its heat deeper into me.

"Damn it," Luca snapped. "Heart stopped." His hand pressed against my neck and then was gone. My heart had stopped? "Too late, Bear. Again, pity. But I can't be dragging bodies with me. It would look bad when I take over Shaitan's home." There was a rush of air against my skin and Rooster was pulled off me.

Then I was grabbed by the hand and tossed through the

air, my body still shaking as it fought the antidote even though my heart had quit. I tumbled through the air and then hit something lumpy—Rooster again—and rolled off him.

The lack of oxygen, the lack of my heart beating, it swelled over me and I fought the darkness as it came.

And then the flames I'd grabbed raced around me, lighting every part of me on fire, stealing the last of the oxygen from my lungs and burning away everything.

My world was on fire and it felt as though the heat would never end, and yet . . . it felt like that was not a bad thing.

I tried so hard to open my eyes, and when I did, a figure walked toward me out of a bright shining light. I squinted my eyes and stared, because I had to be wrong, it could not be him. He was dead.

"Dad?"

And then the darkness swept over me again.

4
PHOENIX

The underground room Killian took me to was a massive cave under the house. The edges of said cave were rough with stalactites hanging here and there just over our heads. I reached up and touched one, the stone cool and damp against my fingertips as if plugged into a water source over our heads.

Somewhere in the distance was running water, either a stream or an underground creek, by the soft rushing sound of it. I didn't like the idea of being underground with a big-ass mansion and possibly water over our heads. What if the water eroded the underpinnings of the mansion? That was not how I wanted to go out.

The footing was pavement, smooth and perfectly flat, and it stretched to the edges of the cave. Abe walked in front of me, his nose up and his tail wagging slowly as he scented the air. I almost wanted to do the same, something in the air tickled at the back of my head. Like something I'd smelled before.

"Not Batman, no. But I think he had the right idea." Killian strode in front of me. "This is my backup. I knew the pub would get hit first, and my mother—being the bitch she is—would fight to the death for this house."

I snorted. "You mean you bought her the house because you knew she would protect it? A built-in guard dog . . . very clever."

"Thank you." He half turned and winked at me. "I bought this house because of this cavern below it. I had the paperwork that had been filed regarding the dangers of such a structure below a house covered up and had everything fixed within a few months with contractors I trusted. Then I stockpiled everything I thought I would need given a variety of scenarios, and gave the deed to Ellen. She never knew this was here." He looked around us with a smile. "And I can tell that no one has found it since I was last here. Nothing is moved, no footprints in the dust."

It made sense, and I understood then why he tried to stay on good terms with her. Although, I suppose that was blown all to hell now courtesy of me. Funny enough, I didn't feel bad for it.

Killian strode toward a sheet-covered vehicle and yanked the dusty material off. A big black Humvee stared back at us. "Not exactly inconspicuous," I said.

"No, but it will get us where we need to go, and then we can switch out vehicles for a minivan if you'd like."

I frowned, not taking the bait for his joke. "It's all metal. Kind of a bad idea with the electricity floating around, don't you think?"

"Aye, it would be normally. But I have the seats wrapped in a thick rubber as well as the floorboards. It's safer than anything else if my family wakes before we're gone. With our timing, it's going to be tight. They may not know where this is, but they'll be looking hard and they're good at digging up secrets when they know there's one to be found.

They'll follow us to the bathroom and then . . . it will only be a matter of time." He moved away from the Humvee to the part of the room that truly drew me.

Weapons as far as I could see. "Dinah, I need to pick a partner for you."

She'd been remarkably quiet since Eleanor had been taken. I tapped my fingers against the left holster she sat in. "Dinah?"

"Yeah, I know. Aren't we even going to try and get Eleanor back?"

Ah, so that's what was going on. I kept a hand on her. "Yes. Tommy is going the same direction as us toward Romano and Bear, which means at some point we will cross paths and then I will get Eleanor back. Okay?"

Her answer was quiet. "Okay. I just feel like we've lost her completely."

I didn't tell her I felt the same way. It would only upset her.

I went to where the weapons and body armor were stacked and started to go through it. I made my decisions fast, knowing I didn't have time to be picky. I found a USP .45 with a nice sight on it. Good enough, seeing as it was only a backup gun.

Killian paused with his hand over an AK-47 with an under-barrel grenade launcher.

"Just in case," I said as I grabbed the ammo for the .45 and stuffed it into one of the bags. For the first time in a long time, I wasn't going into a fight with both Eleanor and Dinah at my back. Which meant I needed traditional ammo, and a lot of it.

"What about the mini gun?" Killian asked.

"Too bulky. Much as I'd love to take it." I was in front of where the clothing was laid out. I grabbed a pair of army pants in dark green and a tank top that matched and looked close to my size. I stripped off the bits and pieces of clothing I had on, and put the fresh clean ones in their place. "Almost as good as a shower."

Killian grinned. "Almost as good as a show."

I didn't give him a response. Knowing it would only push this connection further. Over the fresh clean clothes, I pulled on a thin vest of Kevlar.

I might be a survivor, but part of that was not being stupid. I wasn't going to take a chance that a stray bullet would take me out before I got Bear away from Romano. The Kevlar fit well, and had good movement to it. Within minutes, I'd adjusted to it and it felt like nothing more than a weighed-down coat.

I threw my bag of gear into the back of the Humvee and went back to the table. "Nothing magical here. Why not?"

"What do you mean?" Killian paused in his motions and I waved at all the guns.

"No gag jam, fairy sprinkles, no myst at all. Why not?"

He shrugged. "I don't use it much; my own abilities are usually enough."

"Show-off." I turned my back on him and went down the line of gear for one last look. At the end of the stash was a chest on the floor. I flipped it open with the toe of my boot.

Inside was nothing but gold coins shimmering in the dim light. I reached in and pulled one up, holding it to get a better look at it. "What is this?" I didn't recognize the stamps on it; the language was unfamiliar to me, which was saying something.

"Druid coins," Killian said. "My forbears were druids and this was the blood money they took from the Romans."

"Gaelic?" I flipped the coin to him and he caught it in the air as he nodded.

"Yes."

I tipped my head to the side and stared into the chest. "Why keep it?"

"The legend is that the one who takes it and uses it for their own gain will have their life end in nothing but misery."

"Lovely," I said. "Can I have one?"

He laughed. "You want a gold coin?"

I shrugged and caught the coin as he flipped it back to me. "I don't want to use it. I want to hang onto it."

"Why?"

I shook my head. "I don't know. Gut instinct."

He pointed a finger at me. "Survivor. Okay, you take it with my permission. Just don't spend it."

I nodded and stuffed the coin in my front right pocket, doing my best not to blush because I was relying on an instinct that I wasn't even sure was my own. Just my abnormal ability cropping up again telling me the coin would be important at some point.

I closed the lid of the chest and turned toward the Humvee. Figures shifted through the shadows from the direction of the stairs.

Not good, this was not good in a small tight space. "Abe, *hier.*"

I yanked the .45 and Dinah from their holsters. "Killian, your family are quick to wake up."

He spun and lightning arced from his fingers in a flash of bright blue and white. The air around us snapped and crackled and the hair on the back of my neck and arms rose to the static, the smell of ozone covering any other scent I might have been picking up on.

I ran forward, firing toward Killian's family, Abe tucked

in close to me, panting hard. This time I didn't hold back. "Kill them, Dinah."

"On it," she snarled as she bucked in my hand, bullet after bullet slamming into the Irish around us. The .45 gave a harder kick, but I steadied it and kept emptying the clip, counting the rounds.

The last bullet discharged and I flicked the button to drop the clip and slammed the grip onto my hip where another full clip waited. An arc of lightning shot past my head and I spun on one foot, twisting around and down. I ended up on a knee.

"Above you!" Killian yelled and I didn't look, just pushed forward, pushing with all I had as the cavern ceiling above me collapsed. I jammed Dinah into her holster—I couldn't lose her too—and kept the .45 in my right hand, firing into the abnormals tightening around us. By my count, Dinah and I had taken out six, and two with the .45, which meant they called in reinforcements. Just how many, though, was the question. With our backs to the wall—literally—we were pinned down. I didn't know how long we would last facing this many powerful abnormals.

I rolled and ended up against a wall as the stalactite crumbled and crashed into the place where I'd been. From what I could see, Killian was still on his feet and giving as good as he got. Abe had crawled under the Humvee.

We could kill them all, but they weren't who we were here for and the odds were not in our favor to finish this without injury.

"Dinah, you still got a smoke bomb?"

"Yes. But I want to kill the nasty shit fuckers."

I nodded. "Right, but we need to move if we are going to catch up to Tommy and Eleanor."

That shut her up. I yanked her from her holster, her

inner workings clicking as they shifted from ammo to smoke. I fired once into the middle of the cavern and the smoke spread up and outward with a whoosh.

I scrambled up and ran for the Humvee. "Time is ticking, Irish," I yelled.

He met me at the armored vehicle, out of breath, a nick above his eye. "You're giving me a nickname?"

"Fits." I slid into the driver's side and Abe leapt in and over me, scrambling into the backseat without being told. I held my hand out to Killian for the keys. He handed them over and ran to the passenger side.

"Where are we going?" I jammed the key in the ignition and revved the engine. A spark of lightning danced over the Humvee and I braced myself, but to his credit, Killian was right. The lightning never reached us.

"Back it up."

I slammed it into reverse and a camera came on in the dash. Good deal. I hit the gas pedal and we sped backwards until I cranked the wheel hard, spinning us around. I threw the Humvee into drive and hit the pedal again, leaving his family behind in the smoke as we raced through the cavern.

"Just keep the speed up, don't slow down no matter what you see. It's all illusions," Killian said as he reached across me and buckled me up. I wanted to frown at him, but I couldn't look away. The cavern twisted and turned rapidly and I didn't dare look anywhere but where we were going for fear of smashing right into a wall of rock.

"Killian, how bad is this going to be?"

"Not bad. Terrifying, but not bad. Trust me," he said as he turned around and did some fancy work for Abe, lashing him into the backseat between two seatbelts. Strapping the dog in did not bode well for the end of this drive. Then he buckled himself in. "It'll be fine."

I stared out the windshield. "Trust is not easily given in my world. Last guy I trusted killed Zee."

"Have I ever lied to you?" Done with the seatbelts, he reached across and put a hand on my upper thigh. "I won't ever lie to you, Nix. You might not like what I have to say, but I will always tell you the truth."

"As you see it," I said.

"Sure. How else would I see it?"

I couldn't help laughing at him, but the laughter dried up as we turned what ended up being the final corner. A waterfall rushed down in front of us, but I could see through it. And through it was nothing but empty space.

"Pedal down, Lass." He pushed on my thigh, keeping my foot tightly to the gas.

"Fuck me," I whispered.

"Soon enough." He laughed and then we were in open space and I had to bite down on the scream that bubbled up my throat. Abe grunted as his straps tightened.

For just a moment, we floated and I wondered if the Humvee was going to sprout wings like some sort of transformer. But no, gravity caught up with us and we fell from the sky, the Humvee tipping so I was looking down into a pool of water that had to be forty feet below. Abe yelped and began to pant so heavily, I could feel his breath on the back of my neck, his straps yanking as tight as my own seatbelt.

I'd fallen further, with more metal around me, but never into a pool of water while my seatbelt was still on, never strapped in and unable to escape. I tried to relax into the straps holding me fast, knowing more damage would be done the more I tensed.

The seconds ticked, silence in the cab of the armored vehicle a weird thing that I couldn't help thinking was not unlike the silence of a tomb. Right when I thought I couldn't stand it any longer, we hit the water with a thunderous crash, the front end of the vehicle dipping down as I was jerked forward in my straps, my head hitting the steering wheel.

I didn't let that stop or slow me. My hands went to the straps at the same time as Killian grabbed them, stopping me.

"Lass, trust me. Just sit it out." He grabbed my hands and held them tightly and I stared at him. Never in my life had I truly trusted anyone. Not my father, not Justin, not even Zee, if I were being honest. They'd all done things that left me wondering at their intentions.

Being brutally honest, I'd never trusted my mother even, though I'd loved her fiercely. She'd died when I'd needed her most, but that was after years of not believing me when I told her how bad my life was. She'd left me to that life, whether she meant to or not.

Now here was Killian, holding onto me like I was his lifeline, and he was asking for something I wasn't sure I could give.

"I'm trying," I said softly. "It's not easy."

"Not for me either, Lass." His hold on me eased as we sunk under the water. "The weight of the Humvee will pull us down. There's a latching system below."

Latching? There was a clunk as we hit the bottom of the pool and then the Humvee began to move. "Pretty fancy," I said. "What happens to the engine? With water in it, we are not moving anywhere."

"There are sensors that seal off the compartment at the first touch of water above the skid plates. As soon as we are pulled out, they will slide open and we'll be good to go." He smiled and let my hands go. "I think of everything."

I snorted and rolled my eyes. "Sure, somehow I don't

believe you ever thought you'd be working with me going after Romano."

"True." He nodded. "But I always knew that someday my life would be on the line and I'd have to fight for it. I prepared as best I could putting into place as many fail-safes as possible."

I could understand that. Though, in my case, I'd let my preparations slide because I'd believed we were safe and far from the life I'd run from all those years ago.

What the hell had I been thinking? Looking back, I could see the moments I'd started to waver, to begin to think we were being watched. Justin had always soothed me, told me that it wasn't real, that it was all in my head, leftovers of my past coming to haunt me. More than once I'd started to look into something that stirred my worry, and then he'd slow me down. He derailed me, told me he would handle anything that came up.

I frowned as my thoughts whirled. It was like I'd been living in a dream, so easily manipulated. I didn't like it, and the longer I looked back, the more I saw places where it was like I had not been myself.

"Switch places with me," Killian said. "Before we're out of the water."

"I can drive," I said.

"I know, but we need to figure out where we be going next. Which means you need to tap into Genzo's memories. He might have something we could use."

I had been trying to forget that bit, but Killian made a good point, to use what we had at hand. When we'd been in the jail doing all we could to save Bear and destroy the Ikimono myst, I'd found an unusual ally in Genzo, leader of the Yakuza abnormals. He knew he was dying and as the maker of Ikimono, he'd never meant for the drug to create monsters, but to cure them. In a last-ditch effort to help us, he'd shoved his memories into my head so I could connect with his Yakuza, but also so I would have information that might help me in my fight against Romano.

I sighed and unstrapped my buckles and slid out of the seat, across the center divider and into Killian's lap. "Get going."

His hands trailed over me, but he didn't argue as we shimmied and he shifted over the middle and into the driver's seat.

I leaned back in my chair and then reached to touch Dinah's grips. "You okay?"

"Yeah. Just . . . it's weird without Eleanor. She's always been with me, right from the beginning." Her words were soft and nothing like the brassy bitch she normally was.

"We'll get her back."

Abe gave a woof from the backseat and I reached back to him, running a hand over his head, then undoing his seatbelts. My mind was on what Tommy had said before I'd pushed him out with the parachute. "Tommy was sent to the Middle East not that long ago to make a connection for Romano. He said that he didn't want to deal with a guy named Shaitan, but Romano did."

Killian shot a look at me. "You get that from Genzo's memories?"

"No, that's what Tommy and I were talking about when you went to check on Bobby." I frowned and thought about Genzo's memories, dragging them forward. They came up in bits and pieces as if they were fading even as I found them. "Shit, I don't think the memories thing was a long-standing job."

"Look through them fast then," he said. The Humvee emerged from the water as we spoke, pulled forward by the wrenching system. As soon as the front end was clear of the pool, he turned the key in the ignition and the engine rumbled to life.

"We've got a couple hours before we're clear of my family's territory," Killian said. "That should get us to Savannah."

"What's in Savannah?"

"One of the last private planes I own, and one that I kept secret from me family. We'll use it to get wherever it is we need to go. Wherever we figure on Bear being." He glanced at me and then back at the road.

I nodded. It was a good plan, as good as anything we could come up with on the fly. I just needed to pin down where Romano took my boy. Bear was only ten years old, and while he was strong, a survivor like me, with an old soul and huge smarts, he was still a child. And I was terrified that he'd gotten some of the Ikimono cure in his system when we'd spread it around the facility. What would it do to him? Kill him? Maim, twist or make him a monster? I shook my head, stopping that direction of thoughts. There was nothing I could do about it right then. I had to keep moving forward. I had to find him, that was all there was to it.

No, that wasn't true. I had to find Bear, and I also needed to find just how I was going to bring my father down.

My hand went to my pack and I pulled it open. Inside were two things that had more value than any money.

The diary of my older sister Bianca. And the code I'd paid to have broken that should give me the key to my father's death.

The code was something I'd originally thought was a list of cities that my father operated in, and the plan was that I would use it to take down his world. But it had turned out to be even better than that. My father had made a deal with the devil years ago. I'd been there when it happened. He'd gotten power, influence, and a form of immortality—that last I'd only found out about recently.

I'd shot him point blank and not even a drop of blood had flowed from the bullet holes.

But the now-decoded papers had the information I needed to make him mortal once more. Mortal, so I could put his ass in the ground once and for all.

I pulled the diary out first and flipped it open to a blank page. "You got a pen?"

Killian opened the dash and fumbled around before handing me a pencil.

That would do. I jotted down the bits and pieces of Genzo's memories, the last of them fading after just a few words. And really, they weren't even full memories, just words and flashes of places that I recognized even though I'd not been to them.

"They're gone, but I've got what I could. Not that it's much."

"Read it to me," Killian said.

I stared at the words that were my own and not my own. "Dubai. Brikoff. Shaitan. Tokyo. Denver. Seattle. Vancouver. That's it. Two names, five cities."

Killian tapped his fingers on the wheel. "Tokyo makes sense. And except for Dubai, the others are all places Genzo's Yakuza were working into, as far as my contacts knew. Shaitan . . . that's the name your brother mentioned."

That was the thing, Shaitan's name had come up twice now in matter of a few hours. I highly doubted it was a coincidence. I tapped my finger on the final word.

"What about the other name? Brikoff?"

Killian shrugged. "Russian mobster. Very small potatoes. Mostly works in liquor, and last I heard, had all of ten men working with him. He might have had something to do with Genzo, maybe as a supplier but nothing else significant."

Still, that name stuck out to me as much as Shaitan's, and I tapped my pencil on it, finally circling the name. "He's important. I just don't know how."

"Then perhaps I need to make a call. I've spoken with him before. He'll talk to me," Killian said.

I frowned at the single page, circling Brikoff's name over and over. "Tell me about him, anything, even if you don't think it would be something that would be of importance."

Killian took a breath and seemed to gather his thoughts before he went into it. "He's an abnormal, and like a large percentage of Russians, he is talented with metal, able to bend it to whatever he sees in his mind. He started out life as a blacksmith, making high-end replica swords and other weapons in between shoeing horses."

I frowned and Dinah shivered. I put a hand on her. "Dinah, talk to me."

"I don't know if I can talk about this," she said softly. "He . . . made my parts."

I whipped my head sideways to look at Killian to see his eyes fly wide open. "Brikoff made the gun?"

"Yes," she said. "He can . . . imbue metal with power."

I wondered if Brikoff had made Linx as well. "Can anyone else work metal like him?"

"Not that I know of," she said.

I wasn't sure exactly how Brikoff would play into things. I only knew that he was a key here. And that I had to figure out where he fit. Damn it, one more puzzle piece.

Abe shoved his nose forward under my arm as I flipped the diary to the first page. I skimmed the words, looking for something that jumped out. This was the first chance I'd had to so much as look at the words my sister had written so many years ago. Her inner thoughts, her secrets she shared with no one.

The first half of the journal was Bianca's day-to-day, who she met with, what tasks our father gave her. And then the entries began to change about three months before her death. She started seeing someone.

"This can't be right," I said, flipping the pages faster. All thoughts of Brikoff and how he'd made Dinah fled from my mind.

"What is it?" Killian asked.

"Bianca was seeing someone before she died." I kept skimming, disbelief propelling me through the pages.

"What's wrong with that?" Killian asked.

I looked up from the pages, horror filling me because what I was reading was in her own hand, and yet I still could barely believe it.

"She was seeing a man named Strike."

"Not exactly a gentle name but—"

"No," I cut him off, "he is my father's third guardian from Hell, and she was fucking him."

5

BEAR

My eyes were gummed together with sleepy dirt and my nose felt like it was full of snot that had been dry for days. Had I been sick? Distantly I recalled writing a letter in crayon on a plane, a letter that told me who I was, and that my mother loved me, and that my grandfather was evil. That had been in case I lost my memory to my uncle Tommy. But that . . . that was all a long time ago. I couldn't remember anything else more recent than that for a moment except for pain and . . . heat like fire. Why was I thinking of fire? And my dad . . . I was sure I'd seen him, that he'd walked toward me, that maybe had he crouched down to me even? My heart leapt at the thought of him being alive, of him somehow having come back to my life like my mom had.

I groaned as I tried to move. My limbs were stiff and it took me a moment to take in the sensations around me, the sounds and smells that were unfamiliar, the brush of something against my skin.

A light, incredibly soft blanket was on my body, and I lay on something equally soft that held me in a bit of a cocoon.

"Kid, you awake?"

I lifted a hand to rub at my eyes, dislodging the gunk enough that I could open one of them. Rooster leaned over me. Bodyguard, belonged to my grandfather. My grandfather had tossed me aside, thinking I was dying. That I was no longer useful. His brown eyes were gentle, though, and I clung to that image.

Apparently, I'd made it through. I scrubbed at my eyes squinting against the grit that fell away.

"Where are we?" I asked, my voice hoarse and raspy

"Well, you got your wish. You're free of your grandfather." He grunted and sat beside me, the chair creaking under his weight, groaning as if it were going to give way. He wasn't fat, but he was big, pretty much solid muscle.

I pushed up to my elbows. "What happened? Why are you still with me?"

"You were dying, kid, and I . . . I tried to help you." He shrugged and looked away. "Romano shot me, and then pushed us both out of the car. No doubt he thought the desert would finish us off. Sometimes his ego gets the better of him."

If my eyes could have bugged out, they would have, but I didn't have the energy even for that. "But we're both alive."

He shrugged again. "Both of us are abnormal, kid. It's going to take a lot more than a single bullet to kill either of us. He forgets that because he thinks everyone is disposable, because he himself can't be killed."

I rubbed at my face, knocking off the last of the crud on my eyes. We seemed to be inside a large square tent made of a light khaki material held up on posts in four corners, with a peaked roof. Outside there was a quiet nicker of horses and the stamp of hooves. If not for the sand and rugs on the floor, it was almost like being back on the ranch.

"I've got to find my mother," I said.

"Yeah, I figured you'd say that." He twisted around and produced a cell phone from his back pocket. "Here. You can call her. See if she can come get you. Think you can keep her from killing me while you're at it?" He rubbed at his neck with one hand as if he were imagining a noose or something.

The fear in his voice was heavy and I knew why. My mother was the Phoenix and was very worth being afraid of, from what I understood. She'd been the boogeyman for the abnormal world long before I'd been born. I wasn't afraid of her, of course, but that was different. I was her son and I knew she loved me. Unless she thought I really hated her. My heart gave a funny bump inside my chest as if it were trying to get out. The last time I'd seen her, I'd told her I hated her. I'd done it to save both her and me in the moment, but would she understand?

I swallowed hard, trying to push the new fear aside. "You tried to save me. She won't kill you." I took the phone and hit the power button. I had to believe she would come for me still. "She was with Killian the last time I saw her. Do you think they might still be together?"

Rooster scratched at his chin and gave a small nod. "If they're both still alive, yeah. I wouldn't put my money on Killian—slick Irish prick that he is—but your mom should be alive still."

My throat tightened as an image of my mother laid out, bleeding, not breathing, raced through my mind. I could see it all too easily, but once more, I pushed the awful thoughts away, not wanting to think about that possibility. I stared at the small screen, dredging up the last number I remembered, the one I'd seen flash on Killian's phone when he'd handed it to me to talk to my mom. Carefully I pushed the buttons and hit call.

The phone rang twice and then someone picked up.

"Who is this?" a voice growled.

I recognized him right away. "Uncle Tommy? Why do you have my mom's phone?"

"Holy shit, Bear? Where are you? Are you with Romano?" His voice lowered into a whisper.

"No, he threw me from the car. I think he thinks I'm dead." I shivered and clutched the sheet around me. "Where are you?"

"I'm going to come get you. I'll put a tracer on the call, okay? Don't hang up."

I nodded even though he couldn't see me. "You got out of the jail okay, then?"

"Your mom pulled me out. Even healed up my eyes," he said softly.

Warmth spread through my chest. Of course she did. She might seem tough to everyone else, but I knew her and she would never leave him there if she could help.

"The tracer is on, don't hang up." Tommy repeated his instructions. "Is Romano close to you?"

I looked to Rooster and he nodded, waved at me to tell Tommy what I knew.

"Not far, I think. He was talking about a meeting with Shaitan, though it likely wasn't a meeting Shaitan wanted," Rooster said.

Before I could feed that information through to Tommy, there was a screech on the other end of the line that made the hair on my neck stand up. "Tommy, are you okay?"

"You motherfucking piece of shit! How dare you steal me from Nix! Your mother was a whore and she should have tossed you in the river the second she shit you out!" A woman's voice echoed down the line as Tommy tried to shush her.

"Listen, you are part of the equation. *You* are the one meant to kill Romano. He'll never expect me to shoot him with you."

"I did shoot him, you idiot! Phoenix shot him in the jail with me!" she screeched, and I just stared at the phone. What had Uncle Tommy stolen from my mom besides the phone? And why? Why wouldn't he just help her find me, help her deal with my grandfather?

"Shut up!" Tommy roared, and then the woman's voice was muffled like he'd put his hand over her mouth. "Kid," he breathed hard into the phone, "I've got your coordinates. I'll be there as quick I can, just sit tight and stay out of trouble."

And then he hung up. I stared at the phone. "I don't think he's going to make it through this."

Rooster nodded. "He thinks he can take out the big man on his own. That's not smart. Stealing one of your mom's guns ain't too bright either. They don't like other people."

I blinked up at him. "My mom's guns . . . are people?"

"Nah, but they can talk. And that was one of them you heard. Eleanor, I think." He tipped his head toward the phone.

I didn't know how to react to that. I stared at the phone. "I don't have any other number for my mom."

Rooster held out his hand but I didn't give him the phone. He rolled his eyes. "Kid, I'm not taking it from you. You got nothing to put it in." He laughed at me, his head shaking. Almost like we were friends.

I looked down at my body and the sheet over me. I was naked under it except for a thin pair of shorts, no pockets. But the shorts weren't even mine. "Where are my clothes?"

"Burnt off as far as I could see when I came to. You got a nasty sunburn on your ass while you were at it." He laughed again, and I didn't want to laugh with him because he'd been one of my jailers. But for now, we were on the same side, and I let the laughter flow, slowly at first and as rough. All was good until I remembered where the flames had come from exactly.

I choked on the laughter and stared at my hands. "The fire is *in* me, isn't it?"

"Well, you are an abnormal, kid." Rooster leaned back in his chair. "Nothing to be afraid of. You just learn to use what you've got to survive. And considering who your family is, that's going to be an important tool. You'll outlive a lot of people you know."

I looked at him. "You never hated me, did you?"

His eyes slid to half-mast. "Nope. You were just a job. You don't hate your jobs. You take care of them; see them through to the end. I'll do right by you yet, kid." He rubbed a big knuckle over his even bigger nose.

I slid my legs around, setting my feet onto a deep red and gold woven rug. "I'm guessing this isn't your tent then."

"Nope. Belongs to a desert sheikh. Name of Shaitan," Rooster said. "Scary dude, but he took to you like a man takes to a puss—I mean, he took to you right away. I didn't have much choice and knew that we were going to need some help to get out of here alive. Just play it cool with him and I think we'll get through this."

I liked that Rooster spoke to me like an adult, like I wasn't just ten years old. Then again, I'd been through a lot in the last six months. I sure didn't feel like a kid anymore.

"I thought you said my grandfather was meeting with Shaitan?" Fear spiked through me, but Rooster shushed me.

"Romano used his last guardian, Strike, to boot Shaitan

out of his own home. That's what I meant by what I said. Shaitan is not our friend, but he isn't our enemy either. We just have to play it cool. Got it?"

I stood on wobbly legs and pulled the slippery sheet around my body like a toga. "Got it."

Rooster didn't stop me as I made my way to the flapping doorway and pushed it open to peek out. The sun was brilliant and I was forced to close my eyes.

"Ahh, I see the young master is awake." A smooth, cultured voice with a light accent I couldn't place spoke to me as though we were longtime friends.

I opened my eyes and blinked to see a man striding toward me, and for a split-second, I wondered if this was who I'd thought was my dad, but no, I'd never mistake the two of them. This man had long black hair that curled at the edge of his shoulders, and wore a well-trimmed beard that came to a neat point. He was lean, his limbs moving with a grace that made me think of the large hunting cats near the ranch, and that image was only accentuated by the loose clothing he wore. Dark pants and top, and he had a scarf around his neck, but I could see a tattoo curling up the side of his throat. It looked like a flame before his movement covered it again.

"Did you save me?" I asked.

"No, you saved yourself, young master. You have a name? Your manservant would not tell me. He's very loyal to you. That's a good thing to have in this world." He stopped in front of me, his energy swirling around him so intensely that I almost took a step back.

My eyes narrowed ever so slightly. Why wouldn't Rooster have told him my name?

I dug my toes into the sand. I thought about what Rooster had said, to play it cool.

"I'm Bear. Thank you for taking us in."

He gave me the slightest of bows from the waist, tucking his hand over his middle. "I am Shaitan, the leader of this tribe, young Bear. Anyone who is an enemy of Luca Romano is a friend of mine. In your sleep, you screamed at him that you hated him." He smiled at me, but I knew there was no true friendship in the gesture. What would he do if he knew I was Luca's grandson? Kill me most likely, or try to use me the way Luca had tried to use me against my mom.

"Right," I mumbled and ducked my head. "I phoned my uncle. He's coming to get me so you won't have to keep us here very long."

"You phoned someone without my permission?" he snapped and my eyes shot to his.

He glared down at me.

I found myself glaring back, my body tensing. "No one said I had to have permission. I don't belong to you."

His lips twitched and his eyes sparkled with humor. "Strong. That's good. Though, I knew that when I saw your fire."

I felt the blood drain from my face, my skin cooling. "You saw . . . my fire?"

"That is what saved you." He pushed past me into the tent and I followed, stunned by the change of direction of the conversation.

"How did it save me? I don't understand." I tightened the knot holding my sheet around my body.

Shaitan turned and raised both eyebrows. "As far as I understand it, you carry the flames of the Phoenix within you. We have other names for that fire, but that is what you would recognize it as, yes?"

I *didn't* recognize what he was saying, but I nodded, my throat tight. "And that flame inside me . . ."

"Burned off whatever poison was in your system. You might still have died if we had not come across you and your man because the desert is a harsh mistress, but such as it is, you are alive. You have great luck, I think. But again, that comes with the Phoenix." Shaitan went to a table I'd not noticed before and poured himself a drink. My mouth ached for water and I went over without being invited and poured myself a drink too.

"Camel milk," Shaitan said as I took a gulp. "It has great healing properties."

I would have drunk filthy water at that point, my body so craved fluids. I gulped the cup down and went for a second, but he put his hand over mine.

"Not a good idea. You need to let it rest in your belly or you risk bringing it all back up."

I took a few steps back and stared at the man who likely held my life in his hands. I hated the feeling that once again, I was forced to trust someone I truly didn't.

I stared hard at him. "What do you want from me? I don't think you saved me out of the goodness of your heart."

"Ah, now we are to it. Like a grown man, you get straight to the crux of this." He sighed and put his cup down. "We hoped that when the Phoenix came, he would be full grown. We did not realize we would find you as a child. In some ways, that is better, as I can train you, mold you. You can help me rule the desert."

I swallowed hard but kept my mouth shut.

He went on. "We know your fire is what is needed to kill Romano and the demon that controls him. They have caused me far too much grief."

"That sounds too simple," Rooster said. "I've known the man for many years and a simple fire won't be enough to take him out."

Shaitan turned and looked Rooster over, his body tensing. "You are one of *his* men?"

Rooster nodded slowly as if he were realizing the error of his words the same as I was. I didn't think it was a good idea to admit a connection to Luca Romano. Nothing about this was a good idea.

Romano had taken Shaitan's home as his own somehow . . . Shaitan did not seem like a man to allow for much wiggle room on loyalty.

A blur of dark clothing and dark hair was all I saw as Shaitan leapt at Rooster, riding him to the ground which should have been impossible. Rooster outweighed Shaitan by a lot, but he buckled as if he'd been hit by a truck. Shaitan's hands went around the big man's skull, fingers digging into his face as if his flesh and bones were putty. There were no words or screaming or anything. Rooster didn't so much as cry out as his facial bones were crushed under the strength of the other man's hands.

Rooster jerked once, twice, and then was still before I could so much as take a step to try to stop what was happening. I didn't like Rooster, but I also knew he had tried to save me from my grandfather. Too little, too late, but he'd tried, and that had to be worth something.

Far better than a death like having your face caved in by a madman's bare hands.

Shaitan sat hunched over Rooster, his body heaving as if he'd just run a mile at top speed, blood dripping from his hooked, clawed fingers. "His memories show him guarding you. Why was he guarding you? He belonged to Romano, did you also belong to him?" He turned his face so just the edge of one eye was showing, glittering a dangerous red that was no natural color. "Who are you to that son of a camel?"

I could too easily imagine those fingers digging into my

own skull, cracking it and opening my mind wide to him both literally and figuratively. Fear snapped through me and I bolted, energy flowing from a reserve deep within me. I went straight for the flap of a door.

"Stop!" he yelled after me. I just kept on moving because there was no way I was going to let him get his hands on me. The sheet trailed out behind me into the heat of the desert. I couldn't open my eyes to the brilliant sun. I ran without direction, letting my feet guide me, praying that it would be enough. I stumbled hard once in a rut and then was up again, the light still keeping my sight from me. I was running blind, using only my sense of sound and touch to guide my feet.

I could hear him behind me, running after me. "Stop! I command you to stop!" The wind picked up, a swirling storm that tugged at me, drawing me back toward him.

But I didn't stop, and as I hit another dip in the ground, my foot snagged against something hard, and I was thrown forward. I put my hands out and they pushed through the flap of a tent as I fell into it, through it maybe was a better word. The light faded as I slammed into the ground flat on my belly. The wind rushed out of me and I lay there gasping like a fish. I blinked rapidly, and found myself staring up at a woman who was hidden behind layers of cloth. Only her eyes showed above the edge of a veil.

Violet eyes rimmed with black makeup made them seem brighter, deeper. She bent down to me. "Is Shaitan scaring you, little one?"

I managed to get a breath in. "He killed my bodyguard."

Her eyebrows shot up. I grabbed the edges of my sheet and rolled so that I could look at the doorway. No one came through, but I could see a pair of feet on the other side of the flap. "Why doesn't he come in?"

"Because he is afraid of me," she said as she moved around the tent, gathering things. "All men are afraid of me. As they should be."

I swallowed hard. What had I gotten myself into this time? Out of the frying pan and into the open flames was what my dad had said about situations like this. I bit the inside of my mouth, thinking about how to get out of here.

"My uncle Tommy is coming for me," I said.

"Is he now?" She turned toward me, a smooth wide, cream-colored bowl in her hand, steam rolling from it. I hadn't even seen her mixing anything but the smell that slipped from it was heavenly. My mouth watered.

"Child, do you know that I am the desert witch? No one enters my tent without my permission and lives." She lowered herself to her knees in front of me. I couldn't guess how old she was, maybe my mom's age. There were no deep wrinkles around her eyes and her body seemed slim under the layers of floating cloth, but it was honestly hard to tell, and I didn't dare take my eyes from hers. She lifted a hand, her wrist covered in bracelets that tinkled and chimed.

"I didn't know." I spoke the truth. "I was running blind."

"Ah. So, the desert spirits led you to me?" She blinked a few times. "That explains it. Shaitan tolerates my presence because he knows what I am capable of. Like so many men, he fears a woman of power. But I believe you are in danger if you stay with him. His war with another demon will soon implode on us all."

I nodded. "I agree."

She lifted a hand to the side of her face and lowered her veil. I looked away, vaguely recalling something about it being improper to see a veiled woman's face. She laughed lightly. "So proper. You may look on me. Consider it an honor for one such as yourself. A man child."

I turned back slowly. She was very pretty, and I almost blurted it out.

She laughed again. "I see you have strength and you have fire in you. Who is your mother, young man?"

I frowned, wanting to tell her, the smell of the broth overcoming some of my better senses. "I don't know if I should tell you. Some people hate her, or fear her, and they want to use me against her."

Her eyes fluttered to half-mast and she tipped her head to one side. "Ah, I see. Another powerful woman then. The child of a powerful woman is a both a weapon and a curse to the one who has borne him."

My frown deepened. "I am *not* a curse."

"Perhaps not, if you have the strength to protect yourself. You found your fire in the desert, your near death awakened it to you as is so often the case with those like yourself."

Her words touched a truth inside of me and I nodded. "Yes, I think so. I thought I saw my father. He's dead, though."

She smiled. "Those who have passed will sometimes come to us, to show us the way back to the living if it is not our time."

My shoulders slumped.

"Perhaps I will teach you a little so you can protect yourself. All powerful women are sisters, and I would see your mother survive. If she is who I think she is, she has it in her to change our world. Or, at the very least, cleanse it of some of the evil it carries."

"You . . . you're going to help me?" I stared at her, hope burning through me. Everything about this woman screamed danger and yet . . . unlike the sheik, I knew in my belly I could trust her. A calm sensation floated through me. Yes, this one I could trust, at least for now.

From outside the tent, Shaitan snarled and said something in a language I didn't understand.

The woman stood and strode to the flap, flipped it open, and the earth around us rumbled. She spoke softly and the ground quieted, but again, the words were lost to me as they flowed in a foreign tongue.

"What did he say?" I asked as she came back and sat once more in front of me.

She smirked. "He thought he could intimidate me. I told him to be gone by the setting of the sun or face my wrath, and yours."

My jaw dropped. "I have no wrath."

Her smirk turned into a wide smile, her violet eyes sparkling with what could only be called joy. "Not yet, man child. Not yet, but you will. And when you do, your enemies will tremble in fear at your feet as they tremble at mine."

6

PHOENIX

Killian drove us to his secret airport outside Savanah, Georgia, while I read my sister's diary. Twice, actually, seeing as the diary was not that long, and not all that detailed. A part of me was grateful since it had chunks about her sleeping with the man she fell in love with. The man she knew as Strike, my father's third and final guardian from Hell. There was nothing about the deal our father had made with the devil, not even a subtle hint. So why the hell had Mancini even bothered to give it to me?

I gritted my teeth against the frustration of not finding anything useful and snapped the book shut.

"How exactly did it start between them?" Killian asked. "You said the third guardian was reclusive and that Romano used the Stick Man and the Shadow for the most part."

I nodded. "And he didn't use them that much when I was around. He leaned on me mostly." I opened the diary and paged through to find the entry I wanted. "Bea says she was snooping through Romano's bedroom and that is where

Strike found her. I knew him as Pain, but he went by both names, to be fair. He grabbed her and she just knew that he was the one for her. That it flooded through her." I shook my head. "But Bianca was never the love-struck kind of woman. She was a hardass with only one thing in mind: taking over Romano's business one day. She even told me once she would run it far better than any of the boys and planned to take over as soon as she could."

Dinah snorted. "A monkey could run it better than your brothers."

I agreed but didn't respond to her. "What I can't figure out is why Strike killed her? If Strike took Eleanor from her and pulled the trigger, the question is why?"

Dinah shivered in her holster. "Maybe she knew she was going to die anyway. Maybe Strike loved her enough to help her die with some sort of dignity."

I frowned and cast a glance at Killian. Dinah's words were far too detailed to be just a guess. Killian arched an eyebrow at me as if he suspected the same thing.

I dropped a hand to my gun. "What exactly do you know about Bianca's death, Dinah? You were there. I know you were because I retrieved you from under the bed."

"I can't tell you," she said. "Part of the spell that put me in this gun makes it so I can't reveal certain things. What I can tell you is that Mancini was out to kill Bianca. She'd turned him and his advances down and he was furious. Strike knew it too."

"That's why you blamed him for her death?" When I'd met with Mancini before, when he'd told me he'd help with taking out Romano and getting Bear back, Dinah had freaked out. She'd screamed that he'd killed Bianca and I'd almost shot him for her outburst.

"Yes. He manipulated her just like he's been manipulating you," she said. "She didn't want this life for you, Phoenix. She wanted you to be safe."

I sighed. "As wonderful as that is—and it is wonderful that she cared for me—there are no safe places anymore. Not while Romano is alive."

"I know." She sighed. "I know, but that doesn't mean we can't try, right?"

Which brought me back to the other papers, the coded ones. Like the diary, I'd not had more than a second to look them over.

I pulled them out from where I'd tucked them into the back of the diary. Two sheets with a list of things that were part of what was needed to make the final blow on Romano. The items that would create a spell that would undo his immortality and allow him to be killed. I skimmed the list, frowned and read it through twice more.

"Killian, listen to this. The ingredients list is long, and you have a part in it, but it's the method of creating the spell that I can't get over."

"Lay it on me," he said as he parked the Humvee at the edge of the airstrip.

"Melt the ingredients using the fire of a Phoenix, melt them down then dry them thoroughly and grind them into a powder. Mix the resulting fines with black powder. The shell casing must be made of the finest of gold. Then it must be shocked once with a bolt of lightning to charge the bullet with enough power to kill him."

I looked at him. "It's a recipe for a magic bullet that will kill Romano. And there is no way Tommy has all this. No way at all."

"Holy shit," Dinah breathed. "Gold would melt in the barrel of any ordinary gun, you know that."

I pulled her from her holster. "But not you?"

"No, both Eleanor and I run on a cooler temp, just under the heat that would melt gold," she said. "It finally makes sense. But you're right, I don't think Tommy would have all this. Which means he either doesn't know, or he thinks that this is all bunk. I'd bet money he thinks a gold bullet on its own will do the trick. Idiot."

Her words tinged inside my head. How could she say "it finally made sense"? How could this mean anything to her?

I closed my eyes and let my mind work it over. I pulled Dinah out and cupped her in my lap. "Dinah, who created you? Who truly created you?"

She groaned. "I will try to tell you, but it may not work."

I waited quietly while she shivered in my hand. Killian looked at me and I shook my head, keeping him quiet.

Her voice was hesitant as she started to speak. "Mancini gave Bianca the way to create us. It was part of the deal. He gave her the way to make sentient guns and then when she was of age, he would get to marry her."

She cried out and there was a creaking sound as if her stock was peeling apart from the inside out.

"Shit, Dinah!"

Her parts were literally cracking under some unknown pressure I wasn't sure how to stop.

She screamed and I held her with both hands wrapped around her. I don't know what made me do it, but I reached for the fire deep in my body and pulled it up and along my arms, down and into my hands. I wasn't trying to hurt her. I was trying to melt away. . . whatever it was doing this to her. I was trying to burn away the pain.

The flames licked blue and purple, dipping into a pink color along my skin, and I ran my fingers over her stock and barrel as if smoothing away the hurt. Heat waves rolled off the metal of her body, and off my fingertips, but no smoke flowed.

Slowly, Dinah's shaking eased and her scream slid away with a gasp. "Phoenix, what did you do?"

I blinked a few times, uncertain. "I don't know. Are you . . . are you okay?"

She took a deep breath and let it out. "Yes, I think I am. I think you burned it out of me." I had the sensation she was shaking her head, or would have if she'd been able.

"Burned what out of you?" I asked.

"The curse that held me from saying everything I know."

Killian leaned across the seats and spoke carefully. "Mancini gave Bianca the information on how to make sentient guns. Which meant he knew it would take a gun like that to kill Romano. Mancini has been playing a long, long game. Just as he accused Romano of doing."

I didn't take my hands from Dinah. "Anything else you can tell me now, without hurting yourself?"

She was quiet a moment. "I think I can tell you who I am. I had bindings placed on me when I was stuffed into this gun. Those bindings kept me from telling anyone anything about me before I was this."

A chill swept through me. "You mean . . . who you were before?"

There was a hitch in her breath and then she let out a sob. "I tried so hard to protect you, because your blood is part of the recipe in that list, and I *knew* Father had to die. I knew he had to. He is evil, Nixi. *Evil,* and I was trying to keep us both safe and then Strike told me what Father was going to do to you. That he was going to have you killed because he thought you were a normal, Mancini is wrong about that part.

"He didn't know you were abnormal like the rest of us. And I couldn't let it happen. I had to do everything I could to protect you, but he was going to offer your soul to the devil in place of his own, and then he was going to kill you. Because he didn't think you had any value to him. So I went to Mancini, he helped me get the guns, he told me how to put souls into them."

She sobbed on the words and they hammered into my skull like nails driven with a mallet. "The deal between Father and Bazixal . . . it's in the layers between the pages of the diary. I don't even know what it said because I knew he'd be looking for it. And if he found my body, he'd know I'd made my soul transfer into the gun."

I didn't drop her, though I was more than tempted. The shakes had me, rocketed through me over and over and I just sat there. Killian didn't say anything, didn't so much as touch me.

I swallowed hard a few times. "Are you saying . . . that you're my sister, Bianca?"

"Yes," she whispered. "I am your sister. And I'm sorry I couldn't protect you better. I tried so hard, Nixi. I tried so hard and I failed."

I closed my eyes and bowed my head, pressing it against the gun that held my sister's soul. "Bea. God, what a mess we all are."

A burst of hysterical laughter escaped her. "Well, that's obvious, isn't it? I don't know what you did with your fire. But you burned part of the curse off me, I think. I can help more now, I can speak my mind. I can help you figure this out."

I wanted to hold her close, but had to settle for putting her back in her holster. "You always did speak your mind. Right now, we have to get on that plane and we still don't know where we are going." Though I was leaning toward wherever this Shaitan was. All the evidence—minimal as it was—pointed to him. "And then we can talk some more." I paused. "Do you want me to call you Bianca?"

She was quiet a moment before she answered. "No. That part of me is gone. I'm Dinah now, there is no going back to being Bianca."

My heart began to hammer a staccato I didn't like, one that told me there was another truth coming I wasn't going to like. "You put the soul in Eleanor then?" I asked.

"She was my practice run. She knew what she was doing. She knew that it was a chance to protect you no matter what and she was dying already, and she was terrified Romano would use her against you," Dinah said, her voice careful.

"Are you going to tell me who she is?" I asked, afraid I already knew the answer. Afraid I was wrong, afraid I was right. Before she could say anything, I pushed forward.

"Dinah, is Eleanor . . . is she my mom?"

The silence in the Humvee was long enough that I thought she wasn't going to answer. That maybe it was some leftover bit of the curse that had been laid on her.

"Yes," she said softly, "Eleanor is your mom. She didn't just die, Phoenix. She . . . she *let* herself die. She could have healed the disease, but she didn't."

I couldn't breathe, my eyes fogged over, my vision blurred so I gave up and closed them. There was nothing I needed more than to move, to get my body out of the closed space of the vehicle. Abe whined at me, picking up on my distress, but he stayed where he was in the backseat.

I pushed the door of the Humvee open and stumbled out, unable to believe the truth, and yet, I knew the second Dinah had told me she was Bianca. I knew it was my mother's soul in Eleanor. I could still see the scene from her death in my head, of when I'd come home and ran to my mother's room. Gabe had taunted me as I'd arrived, said the whore was dying upstairs, and I'd run but I'd been too late.

The chair beside my mother's death bed was occupied. Bianca sat beside her, holding her hand as if she gave a shit about a woman who'd taken her own mother's place.

"Stop touching her," I snapped. Seventeen years old, I was young in so many circles but here I was the experienced one. I already had as many kills under my belt as years to my life.

"I just came to say goodbye." Bianca stood and clutched at the purse in her lap. "I'm sorry for your loss, Nixi."

"GET OUT!" I screamed at her and she moved, not fast, but she moved. I waited for her to go, waited for the door to shut before I went to my mother's side. She was gone, dead. My father had sent me out on a job, testing my loyalty to him, and even though my mom had been sick, I'd gone. She'd told me to go, that she'd be here when I got back. I slid to my knees beside her. "I'm sorry I wasn't here, Mama." I bowed my head, pressing it against her side, praying for the first time in a long time that she would take a breath. That her heart would beat again and I would be able to tell her all the things I needed to say.

That I still needed her. That I was a child still and I knew it and I was so afraid of what my life was becoming. I didn't want to be the killer I was. But there was no one left who would believe me. There was no one left to save me.

I took a breath of the hot humid air, and realized tears streamed down my face, the Savannah summer wind catching and drying them before they left a track on my skin. I rubbed at my face. "Fuck."

Dinah wiggled in her holster. "We couldn't tell you. That day, your mom was sure it was one of her last and she begged me to take her soul before Romano did."

I frowned. "Why would Romano take her soul?"

"I don't know. But I think it has to do with the deal. I think he *has* to give *a* soul to the devil, and I don't know how soon it is but he was always on the lookout. I think the soul had to be one of his own blood, or close to him. Otherwise, he would have just taken someone off the street. She was like you, Nixi. She was a creature of legends he didn't realize he had under his thumb, so . . ."

Killian stepped up beside me. "If he'd known, he would have fought to keep her alive, to use her for more than her soul."

"Agreed," I said. I understood why my mother had done what she had. I'd do anything for Bear even if it meant dying for him. I just wished I would have known that she had sacrificed so much for me.

We headed toward the private plane, and I moved on autopilot. If anyone jumped out at me, they were going to get shot. My nerves were strung tighter than a two-dollar banjo and they hummed for me to draw Dinah and start firing at something. Anything.

"Where to, Phoenix?" Killian hitched the bags of gear on his shoulders. He was not letting me get off track. "Are we going after your father, or Bear? Because while Romano may have the kid, those are two very different courses of action. We need to be sure this is the right choice." He was being careful with his words and I didn't like it.

"Bear," I said without hesitation. "I won't leave him

behind again. I thought he would be safe and I was wrong. He needs to be with me."

"It was reasonable to leave him behind before," Killian said. "I would have argued if I thought differently."

I reached to my bag for the phone Mancini had given me. Untraceable and pre-loaded with helpful numbers amongst the underworld of the abnormals. My fingers found no phone.

"Fuck you, Tommy, you stole my phone too?" I didn't remember him being so good at lifting things. I blinked and grabbed Killian's arm. "You got that number I called you on still on your phone?"

He nodded and dug it out of his pocket. "What are you thinking?"

"Tommy thinks he knows where Romano is, and where Romano is, Bear is. He can take a go at Romano all he wants. That will keep Romano busy, and we'll get Bear, and then we'll get Eleanor." I couldn't make myself call her my mom even if it was true.

Killian cleared his throat. "Phoenix. We need to talk about something hard first. Something I'd hoped you'd have seen on your own by now."

I stopped moving, the heat around us suddenly seeming to ratchet up another few notches. "What kind of hard?"

He grimaced. "You need to kill Romano, and we know how with that list of whatever it is you have there that you've been avoiding looking at." He pointed at the diary.

"I know we need to and I have not been avoiding it." I didn't know where he was going with this.

"You said it's a magic bullet needed." He arched an eyebrow. I nodded. "Then you need Brikoff. He can pull this shit off in no time. Once we have ingredients, we need that

Russian to finish this off to make the bullet. Magic and metal. That's his jam. We need him to make it right."

"We don't have anything yet." I could feel my ire rising. "Why is this a hard choice?" He wasn't going to go there, was he? Fuck.

He rubbed a hand over his face. "I think we should get it all done before we go after Bear. Getting Bear first is your heart talking, Lass. I need your head in the game if we're going to actually save the boy."

My jaw dropped and my anger spiked along with the shock. "Are you fucking kidding me? My head is always in the game, Irish, *always*!"

The way his lips tightened said it all. He didn't think my head was in the game. "It's not smart to go at Romano when we *know* we can't kill him. You're not going to get more than the one shot at him, Phoenix. Let's make it count."

I didn't think I could be any angrier. And then Dinah spoke up.

"I hate to agree with him, but I think he may be right. I think we need to look at this like any other job, Nix. Not that it's your son waiting on you."

I jerked Dinah from her holster and threw her at Killian without any thought. He caught her easily and I strode away from them both, back toward the Humvee. "Then you can be his fucking gun, Dinah."

"Lass," Killian called after me.

I didn't say anything, because there were no words to define the emotions swirling within me. Anger, hurt and mostly . . . chagrin that burned all the way through my belly and to my back along my spine.

I got into the driver's side and turned the key, backed the armored vehicle up and took off. I needed time to think, to clear my head.

My throat was tight and I struggled to breathe around the lump in it. I was a mother first, and my instinct was to go after Bear. To save him and bring him home. He'd been without me for too long and there was no way he wasn't wondering where the hell I was, why I hadn't come for him.

But there was another instinct at war with that of a mother. The one of a killer, the one that knew Killian and Dinah were right even though I hated every part of that truth in that moment. I hit the brakes and the Humvee slid to a stop in a cloud of dust and spitting gravel that tinged off the sides of the vehicle. I didn't know where I was and I didn't care. I slammed my fists on the steering wheel as I screamed, tears streaming down my face. Every breath burned as I sucked it into me because the truth cut through me like nothing else could.

Killian and Dinah were right.

That truth tore what was left of my heart and soul to shreds. In order to save us and find us all peace, I had to leave Bear at the mercy of the evil and danger around him, trusting he would still be there when I finally found him.

The sobs were part anger, part hurt, and they drained me of the emotions as surely as if I'd turned a faucet on.

I waited for the heaves and the hiccups to subside. I wiped my face, found a water bottle, and then a cold nose stuffed into the back of my neck and a big warm tongue gave my skin a swipe. I reached back and curled my face into Abe's neck, drying the last of my tears. "I'm so sorry, Abe. We can't get him, not yet."

He gave a snort and pushed harder on me, and I clung to him as I pulled my shit together. We needed the bullet. Then we'd get the kid out.

The kid.

Not Bear.

Not my boy.

The kid.

That was how it was going to have to be if I was going to walk away from going after him again.

"This is the last time," I whispered, almost a prayer. "The last time I walk away from you, Bear."

7
___

I made my way back to the small airport to find Killian sitting on the tarmac, his back against the stairs that led up into his private jet.

"Abe, let's get this kid home." I opened the door, went around and opened the back door for him. He hopped out, grunted and then limped alongside me.

When we got close to the plane and Killian, he stood and offered me Dinah back. I took her without a word and stuffed her—harder than necessary—into her holster.

There was not going to be any of this "you were right" shit.

"Where is Brikoff?" I asked.

"I called in a favor while you went for a drive," Killian said. "Funny enough, he's in your home state."

"New York?" I frowned. "Why there?"

Killian shook his head. "No, I meant Wyoming. Fly fishing from what his people said, out of a little town called Jackson Hole." The coincidence was not lost on me, which meant that Brikoff was there for something other than fly fishing. But what the fuck was he there for? Jackson Hole was overly religious and had very few abnormals to be dealing with. Maybe he just wanted a break from the madness of the abnormal world.

"How long is he there?" I asked.

"Two weeks, and he got there three days ago," he said.

I tapped a finger on my thigh, thinking, but I wasn't left to it very long before a high-pitched bell went off.

I tensed until Killian dug out his phone and answered it.

"Aye?"

Watching his face, I knew without a shadow of a doubt, he'd be an excellent poker player. Not so much as a twitch passed on his features.

"Aye, here, talk to her." He handed me the phone as I frowned at him. Who the hell would be calling me on his line?

"Sis."

"Tommy." I breathed his name and the anger came roaring back through me. "You fucking shithead!"

"I'm sorry I took your gun," he said and in the background, Eleanor screamed obscenities at him. Another time I would have smiled, but not now. "Listen, Nix, I have everything I need and I'm going to take a go at the bastard. I have a bullet, it doesn't need all that shit that you think it does. It just has to be gold." Just as I thought, he was going in half-cocked. "Will you talk to Eleanor and tell her to shut the fuck up and help me?"

I did laugh then. I bent at the waist while the mirth poured out of me, taking all the nervous energy and anger with it. "Sure, hold the phone up."

"You aren't really going to tell her to be quiet, are you?" The incredulity in Dinah's voice was not lost on me.

"Eleanor, can you hear me?" I asked.

There was a sharp intake before she spoke. Her voice was rough from screaming. "Phoenix, I can hear you."

All the things I wanted to say bubbled up and it took all I was to hold them back and just keep it short. "Help Tommy. If he thinks he can kill Romano, then help him. But realize you are *my* gun, not his."

She snorted. "I have always been your gun, Phoenix."

I had to close my eyes to hold back the sudden tears that bubbled up. God, I was a mess. I had to get my shit under control.

"I know, you've always been with me," I said.

Killian's hand brushed against my lower back, supporting me silently, but I shoved his hand away. I did not want his touch right then, not when he'd backed me into a decision I didn't want to make. I swallowed down the emotions, burying them under my training. "Tommy, where —" Hell, I wanted to ask him where he was, where he thought Bear was, but I held off with the barest threads of self-control. "Where are the ingredients you found? I'm going to get a second bullet ready."

"Are you serious?" he spluttered. "I've got this. And I'm telling you all that herbs and lightning and blood is bullshit designed to put you on a wild goose chase. Just the gold. Like a werewolf of old, only this is a gold bullet instead of silver."

"Sure, and when he kills you because you didn't use the recipe, I have no desire to be left in the fucking dust with nothing when you already know this shit."

The sound of his teeth grinding came through the phone clearly. "I don't know where Noah put the stuff. He pulled it all together. Him and your hubs. Noah brought me a bunch of the stuff a while back."

"And you're not even using it, are you?"

"Look, I didn't think it could hurt to put the stuff in he gave me, but there were things that are impossible, that make no sense. This will be enough, it has to be." I heard the desperation in his voice. Maybe a part of him knew it wouldn't work. But the hate that was pushing him wouldn't let him slow down. I understood that probably better than anyone else.

I looked at Killian and hit the button for the speaker phone. "You're telling me Noah can get us the ingredients?"

"The herbal stuff. He told me Justin had a stash of it, so he would know where it was," Tommy said.

My thoughts raced at a rate that I knew what it meant. "And the grindings of a curse?"

"I used my ring."

My father wore a ruby ring that connected him to his three guardians. He'd given each of his sons a duplicate ring so they could have the backup if they needed it. That was what I understood, anyway.

I didn't say anything, but it didn't feel quite right to me. The rings, they were a part of this, but there was still something missing. "And the whole thing from the past?"

"I used an old photo of Dad's dad. A picture of the past. Look, I'm telling you I've got this."

Again, it didn't feel right to me. Maybe the translation was off on the deal. Fuck if I knew. I wanted to scream in frustration, but I knew that would answer nothing. "Tommy, one more question. The magic bullet, the coded paper Justin had, where did it all originate from?"

"The deal. But the deal was something I never did find. Not the original," Tommy said.

He confirmed what I suspected. "Try not to get my gun stolen or broken," I said.

"I've got this, Nix," Tommy growled. "I have to say, you're colder than I thought, not going after your boy."

"Fuck off," I snarled, all former warmth between us gone in the heat of lies and pain.

He was quiet a moment and I wasn't sure if he was still there until he took a short breath in.

"I'll kill him, Nix. I will. We'll all finally be free."

Dinah snorted. "Overconfident as usual, Tom."

"Who was that?"

"My other gun," I said. "She's pissed you took Eleanor. So am I. But I'll get her back. One way or another."

"Yeah, I don't want to keep her. She's a mouthy fucking hag." He snorted.

I hung up on him. There was nothing more he could tell me.

"He might have known where Bear was," Dinah offered, her voice a careful neutral.

I didn't answer her because my mind was spinning. Justin and Noah. Once more, things came back to the deadly game they'd been playing.

Without another word, I hurried up the stairs, poor Abe limping along behind me. I reached over and grabbed his collar, carefully helping him up the last few steps. He grunted when I let him back down and I followed him to the rear of the plane.

I wished that I could heal him the way my body healed itself at a rapid pace. Maybe I could help him out, though. Maybe I could do something to ease his discomfort. All my thoughts of sending him away were gone now. I needed him with me, the one companion who I could trust.

I put a hand on him and just kind of pushed some of my buzzing abnormal energy into him. He picked his head up, and his eyes brightened as I kept gently moving more and more of my energy to him, giving him what he needed to heal.

His tail thumped a few times and he stood, shook his whole body and gave a bark. I slumped in the seat. At least there was that. A small thing but a victory no less. I patted the seat beside me and Abe leapt up, where just moments before he could barely take a step.

I looked up to see Killian watching me. "Lass, I'm sorry."

"Don't be." I shrugged and turned to face him. "You were right. And that fucking pissed me off."

"No one doubts your love for him—"

I held up a hand to stop him. "I have to treat this like a job, Irish. We get the bullet together, we go after Romano, we get the kid. Got it?"

His eyes tightened as if I'd punched him in the gut. "Got it." He drew a breath and then spoke again. "Where are we going then?"

I stood and moved to the galley where I grabbed a paper pad and a pen. I took them back to the seat with me and started jotting notes. "We need a ruby ring. The spit of a female demon. The herbs. Gold for the casing. Brikoff. Something to do with the past. And the grindings of a curse." I tapped the pen on the paper. "Some of these don't feel right. Like there is something missing from the translation. I think," I frowned and closed my eyes. "I think that we might find some of the stuff at the house in Jackson Hole."

Killian startled. "Why?"

"Because that is where Justin would have hidden something. Especially if he thought it needed to be safe. He would have put it where it would be protected the most, right under my and Zee's noses."

"And the translation?" he asked.

I grabbed the diary. "Dinah?"

"Yeah, it's in there. The front cover is pasted together. That's where the original deal is."

I grabbed a knife from my thigh straps and slid the tip of the blade through the layers that hid the last piece of information we needed. I put the knife back and then pried the layers open with my fingers. Inside the tiny opening was a thick piece of parchment. I pulled it out, blinking several times as I ran my fingers over it.

"This isn't paper," I said softly.

"What is it?" Killian reached over and touched the "paper." "Shit, is that skin?"

"Yeah, it is." I turned the folded skin over a couple of times. "Not sure what kind, though."

"What do you mean?" Dinah asked.

"Human and most abnormal skin, mammals really, have evenly spaced pores, smallish but there, even if you shave all the hair off. This has no pores, almost," I ran my fingers over it trying to get a sense of it, "like whatever this is from, it would never sweat."

"Does it matter?" Killian checked over the panels of the plane.

"No, I guess not," I said, though in the back of my head I wondered if indeed it might matter. What if whatever this was from wanted its skin back?

I opened the "paper." It had been folded in half twice, giving four squares that easily fit inside the journal.

The words were done in . . . not Latin, as I'd assumed. Demons and Latin just seemed to me to go together like milk and cookies. "I don't know what language this is." I brushed my fingers over the words, symbols really. "I think maybe Arabic?"

Killian leaned over for another look. "I don't think it's

Arabic, but close. Same region would be my guess. We need someone who can decipher this for us."

He was right. Again. "Then we need a professor of history maybe or languages, or better yet, a linguist." I folded the paper and stuck it into the hiding place of the journal. We couldn't read it yet, and I didn't want to lose what was likely the key to figuring out all this shit.

I tapped my fingers on the journal. "I think we need to get the skin paper looked at again, and fast. Whoever translated it into the coded papers either screwed up or deliberately left shit out."

"That would mean finding someone who can actually translate it," Killian said. "Lucky for you, I have someone who might be able to help us. He's a professor of history, and an abnormal to boot." He pulled his phone out. "Doesn't hurt that he owes me a favor or two." He gave me a wink but I didn't react. Couldn't. I'd closed off that side of me and I couldn't differentiate between shutting down my love for Bear and the growing feelings for Killian. So, they all got jammed away so I felt nothing and could keep moving.

He got up and moved farther into the plane to make the call, his voice a soft murmur.

I stared at the paper, thinking when I wanted nothing more than to be moving, to have my ass in high gear and making shit happen.

"I'm sorry," Dinah said.

"Don't be. You were both right." I circled the pen around the page and the words I'd placed on it, not allowing myself back into my emotions.

She sighed. "Okay. Let's get this fucking bullet so we can get the kid and be done with all this."

Killian touched me on the shoulder as he passed by me

and headed back out the plane. "The professor can see us right away."

I stood. "Where is he?"

"Not far from Savannah."

"Convenient." I wasn't sure I liked the ease of the professor being here right when we needed him. Life rarely handed you things you needed that easily without consequences.

I followed Killian, and Abe followed me back to the Humvee. I opened the back door for Abe and he hopped in, good as new. Killian looked back at the dog, frowned but said nothing. For which I was glad. I was tired and frustrated and pissed off. I didn't need any more questions thrown at me.

Killian drove and I forced my eyes shut, forced my brain to power down. It was a trick Zee had taught me in the very beginning. To push all the emotions away, to shut them off like a light switch and let your mind float in a space of nothing. I could hear his words in my head, a mantra I found myself repeating over and over. I needed it now more than ever before.

Death is nothing. Fear is nothing. The past is nothing. I am nothing. I am death.

With those words rolling through my head, I dozed, jerking awake when the armored vehicle's engine turned off.

"You can sleep longer if you want, we're early for the meeting," Killian said.

"No." I was groggy, my head heavy with not enough sleep. I wobbled on the first few steps I took out of the Humvee and then I saw where we were. Savannah State University, if the sign on the large pillared white building was correct. I let Abe out and he glued himself to my side without being asked.

"He still teaches," Killian said, taking the lead. I took note that he had no weapons on him that I could see. My cross-body holster was visible and held two large knives—as were my low-slung hip holsters. Dinah was in the left-hand side for easy access and my now-backup gun was in the right. I looked at Killian. "I'm not giving up my weapons."

"Didn't expect you to." He kept his eyes forward.

Dinah grunted. "At least he knows you're pissed at him."

My jaw ticked. I wasn't really pissed at him, but I wasn't going to get into it. He was right, we needed that fucking bullet and we needed it fast, as in yesterday. Time was wasting.

He strode ahead of me, up the steps and through the large double doors into the university. There were very few students around and I did a slow circle. "Where are all the kids?"

"It's Sunday," Killian said. "No classes."

The heel of my combat boots clicked softly on the floor of the expansive place as I followed Killian through several large rooms to a smaller doorway on our left. He turned the handle and let himself in, and once more I followed. Abe's panting came faster and faster. Something about this place was triggering him.

The hallway was narrow and old, the walls made of plaster with just the bare minimum light overhead. I couldn't blame Abe for his growing anxiety. I didn't like the tight space either, despite the high ceiling.

"He has a flair for taking his students into the past," Killian said.

"You were one of those students?" I reached out and touched the wall, feeling the age in the building under my fingertips.

"Yes," he said. "I was his favorite student, of course."

I snorted. "Right. Favorite to see leave, I'd wager."

Killian laughed. "Perhaps."

The hallways sloped downward and then up again as if we were in some sort of carnival ride. Rather strange seeing as this was a place of learning to have it feel like a place of amusement and fear.

The hallway suddenly opened into a theatre of a room with bench seating sweeping up around us. Like an amphitheater of old, the benches looked to be made of stone and were rough on the edges. We walked out between them to the center of the room where a large wooden desk sat like a throne, and behind it an old man. Abe let out a low growl and I dropped a hand to his back, feeling the hair along his spine stand. Bad signs all around.

Bald except for a few wisps of hair sticking out, the professor had sharp eyes and I felt them on me like the pinpricks of a thousand tiny needles. Testing me.

"Killian, to what do I owe this pleasure?" His Southern accent was soft, cultured. But there was a hard chunk of iron in the old man. I knew it as surely as if I could see it in his spine.

I kept moving forward, drawn to him like a moth to the flame. "We have something for you to translate."

He nodded his mostly hairless head, and his eyes never left mine. "Well, well, if it isn't the Phoenix. I wondered when you would find your way to me."

8
___

The professor stood slowly behind his large desk and I tensed, my left hand dropping to Dinah's stock. He didn't seem to notice, but I was suddenly aware of where we were and what a shit place it would be if the professor turned out to be anything more than Killian's ex-teacher.

A large semi-underground amphitheater with only one door in and out that ran through a tight-ass tunnel was not the place to be in a gun battle.

"I suppose you think it odd that I know your name," the professor said as he came around his desk, seemingly oblivious to my tension or the low growling that rumbled out of Abe. "I shouldn't be surprised to find you with Killian, here."

"Why's that?" I asked, not moving my hand from Dinah.

His eyes, now that he was closer to me, I saw were dark blue. Like the sky right before the sun goes down completely. Twilight eyes.

The professor smiled at me and held out his hand. "Because he is a magnet for trouble."

I didn't hold out my hand. "Forgive me, but I don't shake."

"Fair enough. Your life has been far from favorable." He bobbed his head as he turned away from me. "What can I do for you? Killian said you have a paper you need help translating? Or is that a cover for something else again?"

Killian laughed. "No, just a translation, Professor."

He went back to his desk and I followed him slowly. I pulled the journal out and peeled the cover back, to reveal the pore-less skin paper. I unfolded it and laid it out on the desk as the professor sat.

He reached out and touched the paper, then let out a long, low hiss. "Skin from the back of a demon." His eyes shot up to mine. "What is this?"

"The deal between a mortal and the devil," I said. "We need to know what it says as the translation we have is incomplete." Not the whole truth, but it would do.

The professor sighed and gingerly touched the edges of the skin. "This is written in Acadian."

"That's a dead language," Killian said. The professor nodded but didn't take his eyes from the symbols.

"It is. Which makes me wonder why it would then be put in code. The number of people able to translate this properly is very small. But it looks familiar to me, let me see . . ." The professor pulled out a piece of actual paper and a tall feather quill which he dipped into an ink well. He began to scratch annotations quickly.

There was no sound except the scratching of that tip on the paper . . . that and a sudden tapping of boots on the hallway that led to us. I spun and went to one knee, Dinah raised. "Do you hear that?"

"That is Martin. Ignore him," the professor said. The footsteps continued and the space in the hallway fuzzed as if

I were looking through dirty glasses. Which I most certainly was not.

"Martin."

The heavy sarcasm was not lost on the professor and he let out a sigh.

"Martin is a ghost. He keeps me company when the students are not around."

I didn't lower Dinah. "Ghosts aren't real."

Killian laughed. "Oh, Lass, they are."

The strange footsteps picked up pace and then a cold blast of air rushed through me, cold enough that I had to clamp my teeth shut to keep them from chattering. I spun to see nothing behind me. No fuzzing of anything. No ghostly figure. Just Killian watching me, and the professor working on the translation. He was fast, I had to give him that.

The professor kept scratching with his pen and paper, muttering under his breath. "Fascinating" was the word I heard most.

I didn't want to disrupt him with any more questions about Martin. I stood and made my way across the room away from the professor and Killian to the far side and a stack of books. Dinah grumbled something when I put her back into her holster.

"I don't like this place either," I said softly.

"That's not what I said," she chirped louder. "I said this place gives me the fucking creeps."

I snorted. This from a gun who held the soul of my dead sister.

"There," the professor announced. "It's done."

Both my eyebrows shot up as I turned back to face him. "You sure you got it right?" That seemed awfully fast for translation of a dead language.

"Well, of course I did. This is the second time I've translated this particular piece. Though it was a copy before, it is the same wording on a large chunk of it. And this is different. These two marks here. A double set of stars which mean death and rebirth. Interesting, those."

I strode to his desk, put both hands on it and leaned over it to stare hard at him. "What do you mean this is the second time?"

He smiled up at me, those twilight eyes sparkling with humor. "Let me be clear. I was only asked to translate the bit about how to kill the signer of the document. So that part I didn't fuss with as much as it was quicker, but I did put it down for you."

He pushed the sheet of paper he'd written on across to me. "This is the first part, the deal itself. Go ahead, read it out loud, it won't hurt us."

I put a single finger on the paper and tugged it toward me. Abe gave a low whine in the back of his throat and that cold wind wrapped around me again.

"Fuck off, Martin," I snapped.

A laugh rolled around us and then the cold was gone. The professor nodded at me. "He likes beautiful women with foul mouths. He'll follow you, I think."

Great, just what I needed, a fucking ghost stalker. I took a breath and started to read the paper out loud.

"Herein lies the blood contract between Luca Stephan Romano and Bazixal, demon of the eighth realm of Hell." A chill went through me that had nothing to do with Martin, the frisky ghost. "Fuck."

"My thoughts, too, Lass," Killian said. "Keep going."

I swallowed hard and pressed on. "From this day forward, Luca Stephan Romano will have the world opened to his needs. Power and influence will flow to him like a river to the sea. His body will remain untouched, as though it does not age, no disease will touch him, no weapon kill him.

"For this gift," I almost gagged on that last word, "Luca Stephan Romano will give up the following. His soul, and the souls of two of his children in the proper manner, handing them over to Bazixal on the midnight hour of the crescent moon in the summer of fifteen years past the date of the signing of this paper. Soulless, Luca Stephan Romano will live for as long as the sun moves through the sky."

My throat tightened as I did the math. "That's this year."

"Shit. And the crescent moon, that's . . . days away." Killian breathed the words. "His deadline is coming, and two of his five children are dead."

"Tommy is going right to him." I looked up then. "That's one. And he still has Daniel."

"Except he thinks Daniel has value. He'll use him only if he has to," Killian countered. "He needs you. It's why he never wanted Mancini to kill you."

My eyes popped wide. "What?"

"Mancini wanted you dead after you escaped the first time." Killian shook his head. "We all thought Romano cared for you, that was why he asked Mancini to go easy. But it wasn't that at all."

"Fuck," I whispered. "He doesn't care about his own soul. And if he has Tommy and chooses not to use Daniel and I'm not there . . . Bear. He'll use Bear as a replacement for me."

My mind could barely digest what I was coming to understand about Romano, about the deal and what it meant for me and my son.

The professor leaned back. "May I suggest you continue reading?"

I blinked and looked down at the paper. The remaining

words did nothing to dispel the horror crawling through me. I swallowed once and then kept reading.

"If the price is not paid by the appointed hour, then the price will be taken at Bazixal's discretion. The loss of the power and prestige for Luca Stephan Romano will be the least of his costs on that night." At the bottom of the paper were two stars, just as the professor had said. I ran my finger over them.

I shook my head. "What could Bazixal take? Romano doesn't give two shits about any of his children, or women."

"Unless he's afraid of Hell," Killian said. "You said you were there when the deal was signed."

"Yes." I bit the one word out, doing all I could not to think of that day for so long.

"Tell us what happened. Maybe there is a clue in there," Killian prodded.

Abe pressed against me hard and I reached down for him, grabbing hold of his scruff to help ground me.

"Fuck, I have done everything I can to avoid remembering that day."

"Time to turn the tables on Romano," Dinah said. "You got this, Nixi. You're stronger than all of us."

I closed my eyes and breathed in and out slowly, centering myself as I let that one memory come to the front of my mind. Much as I didn't want to see it, the scene came clear fast, as fast as if it had happened only moments before and not years. I let the images flow though me and out my mouth as I saw them again, as if for the first time.

I followed my father toward the large mansion house on the edge of the New Orleans swamp. The rot and smell of thick mud coated my mouth. But I kept a straight face. This was one of the first times he'd let me come along with him as a bodyguard. That was a step up from straight killer and enforcer thug in my mind.

The door to the mansion was open and he strode through like he owned the place. I kept up easily, sweeping the shadows with my eyes, looking for an ambush. All I got was the cold that crept around me, like an air conditioner that would kick on to combat the heat of the swamp. Only there were no humming electrical lines or equipment. The house was dark except for a few candles lit here and there, flickering with the wind we created as we went by.

"Keep up," Father barked at me. I didn't dare roll my eyes, though I wanted to. He thought I wasn't paying attention, but if he wasn't going to let me lead I couldn't do more than trail him. Idiot.

He approached a second set of double doors and he pushed them open. The room behind the doors was lit up with candles and a large fireplace that roared with flames, the crackle so loud, I was shocked we'd not heard it through the closed doors as we'd approached.

Father went to the head of the table and the bottle of wine. He poured himself a glass and loosened his tie, then sat in the big chair, again as if the house was his.

I moved around the room carefully, sweat pouring off me from the combined heat of the summer night and the fireplace that was attempting to spit out the flames as if it had been lit with gasoline.

"How many are we expecting?" I asked as I circled around. A question I should have asked sooner, but I'd been excited to come. Like a puppy going for a walk.

"One," Father said. "You are to say nothing."

"Of course," I threw back. I was young in my late teens, green, but no fool. I knew this world well already.

I came around to his side, satisfied that there was no entry behind us. The only way in or out was through the door we'd entered and now both faced.

So much for that belief. The door slammed shut and a sharp wind raced through the room hard and fast, knocking my father back in the chair.

The fireplace groaned and the bricks around it began to shift, opening the space so it was no longer a fireplace but a wide pit the length of the table and half as wide. The heat in the room ratcheted up as the flames licked higher, reaching out for us with hands. Flame hands.

I held my ground but it was difficult. My father scuttled out of his chair and stood behind me. A part of me was proud, because I was doing my job. I was protecting him.

Drawing on Zee's training, I let the fear flow through me and didn't fight it, but used it to heighten my senses and reflexes.

"Romanooooooo." A voice boomed out *of the fucking fireplace.*

"I . . . I am here," my father stuttered and managed to move out from directly behind me to the side of the table farthest from the flames. Whatever sweat I produced dried before it could drip down my skin. I forced myself to control my breathing so I didn't end up panting like my father.

He was sucking for wind like a fish out of water.

A body stepped out of the flames, ten feet tall, heaving with muscle and flames along the limbs that were nothing but blackened flesh. "I am Bazixal. You called on me and I answered. You claim a deal and you come to make it now. Unless you have changed your mind?"

Holy shit, my father made a deal with the devil? *That was what we were here for?*

"Dad, this isn't a good idea," I said, moving toward him. My job was to protect him, which meant I had to get him out of here. Now.

I reached his side and put a hand on his shoulder. He backhanded me, catching me off guard. I took a step back, tasting blood.

"I told you not to say a word," he snarled at me.

I clamped my mouth shut and gave him a tight nod. If the fool wanted to make a deal with the devil, then I wouldn't stop him. But I'd remind him of this moment one day. That I'd tried to save him from himself.

"Here is the deal in writing." Bazixal held a piece of parchment out to my father. My father reached over the table and took the paper.

"What is this, a joke? I can't read this nonsense."

"It is as we discussed. Power and prestige and the other gifts you require for the price I require of you." The demon's voice curled around me like a constrictor. I wanted to slash at it with my knives, to drive it away from me. The fear he induced was nothing I'd ever experienced before, like I could shatter to pieces if he so much as looked at me.

As if my thoughts called to him, the demon started around the table toward me. My father moved backward, away from the man that was anything but.

I did not.

I planted my feet even though my head screamed at me to run, to save myself from the come-to-life monster in front of me. I refused to back down from this creature. Just another abnormal ready to be ended by my hands.

"I kill monsters like you." The words slid from me, ice against the flames.

The demon leaned over me, his eyes drawing mine. "You have

great fire in you, Phoenix. Perhaps one day I will taste your wrath, but not this day."

I glared up at him, holding to every bit of training Zee had given me. How to keep the fear at bay, how to stare down the monsters, how to hold your ground. My knees were locked but trembling as the demon looked me over, and it was only then that I realized the heat around us was curling up through my hair, lifting it in a wave away from my neck.

"Your price is as we discussed?" Father said, breaking the spell. "Two as well as mine?"

"It is." The demon turned from me. "Two of any flavor."

His eyes, black as night, flicked back to me. "I will take the strongest for my own, Luca Stephan Romano." Those eyes flicked and jigged, dancing as if alive with some sort of parasite.

My father pulled a knife, pricked his finger and signed the paper while I watched in horror that he would actually go through with this madness. "It's done."

The demon snapped his fingers and the paper flew to him. He looked it over and gave a low chuckle. "Done it is, and better than I could have hoped. I will send you three guardians as agreed upon, to help you in your quests for power." The devil laughed then and the sound rumbled through me, cutting the last of my strength in my legs. I had to reach out and grab the table to keep from falling.

Bazixal stepped back into the pit and the bricks around him shifted again and then the fire dropped to nothing, dead, black, cold. But the heat stayed with me for days, waking me in the dead of night with the feeling that I was being roasted alive.

I OPENED MY EYES, MY HEART RACING AS IF I STOOD IN THE presence of the demon once more. There was a brush of cold against my cheek, like fingertips trying to soothe me. I ignored Martin's attempts to get my attention. "At least, that confirms what we're seeing here." I pointed at the translation.

"It does, and it's rather concerning how well you remember it. That does not bode well." The professor sat with his fingers steepled under his chin.

I stared at him. "What do you mean it doesn't bode well?"

He laughed softly. "You remember every detail, down to your father striking you. Not good. You see, there will be some people who want to use you, but in order to do that, you can't know the truth. For that, I must take your memory from you. Mancini, as my benefactor, wouldn't want you to remember everything."

I started to ask him what the fuck Mancini had to do with this deal, but then his body began to shift, elongating and stretching upward until his head brushed the ceiling fifty feet up.

I had Dinah out and firing before the professor even completed his shift. I only knew two things. One, I couldn't let him take this memory from me, and two, I had to get that skin back.

"Killian!" I yelled for him, the professor stood between us. Abe let out a sharp bark and then he dodged in around the professor's spindly legs. He bit at the back of them, tearing the flesh and drawing a scream from the now overly tall abnormal that swayed above us. His movements reminded me of the Stick Man, of how he seemed so fragile in the thin makeup of his body. But that had been a lie, and I suspected this would be the same here with the professor.

The professor's skin was tight over his bones, stretched

and taut, and Dinah's bullets bounced off him like it was armor instead of skin.

Lightning arced up around us in the small space and the professor bent backwards, howling through clenched teeth as Killian nailed him. The crack of molars on molars was rather satisfying and I used that moment to leap toward the desk the professor now straddled. I landed on my belly, slid across and grabbed the deal and fell off the other side, rolling as I hit. As fast as I could, I was up on my feet and bolting around the side.

Something tugged at me, a cold brush. "Come on, Martin." I didn't know why that ghost had to come with me, but he did. Then again, I couldn't blame him for not wanting to stay with the professor.

There was a chuckle in my ear that I ignored as I bolted for the only exit. "Abe, *hier*!"

Abe was to me in a flash and Killian was right behind me as I sprinted through the tight, dark hall that would lead us out. Warmth trickled down the side of my face. Blood, but whose?

We burst out of the small door, tumbling over one another in an attempt to keep moving.

Abe circled around me until I got back to my feet. Killian and I ran like children running from the cranky old neighbor down the street. Only this neighbor was trying to hurt us, not just yell at us to get off his fucking lawn.

The floor of the main hall bucked and rolled as we ran across it, sending us flying in opposite directions.

I hit a wall hard and slid to the floor.

"Dinah."

"I'm here. I don't understand why my bullets won't pierce his flesh. That dirty old bastard needs to die!" she snarled.

I didn't disagree, but again I was reminded of the Stick Man. The professor looked like him; it seemed reasonable that his body might have similar defenses. "Think Stick Man! Right now, we need to get the fuck out of here."

I pushed off the floor and sprinted toward the big double doors until I realized it was just me and Abe. I spun.

Killian was pinned against the far wall, a long, narrow hand and fingers pressed to his throat. The professor's hand as he climbed through the floor. I had Dinah up and fired three times in the space of a heartbeat. Right into the professor's wrist. The bones shattered even though the skin didn't break. It was enough that he dropped Killian. "Abe, *bewache*!" I gave him the skin document, right into his mouth. He sat where he was, even though he trembled.

I ran toward Killian, sliding to a stop as the professor pushed himself farther up out of the floor, coming for us.

"Motherfucker." I growled the word, the fury of protecting someone I loved rising through me with my flames. My hands caught fire first, the blue and purple heat rising around me as the professor came at me. I lifted Dinah and shot, sending my fire through her and into the bullet like I did with the electricity.

The bullet drove into his chest, burrowing in past the hardened skin and straight into his heart. He froze as the bullet dug deeper, his twilight eyes going to mine.

"The righteous anger of a woman defending her family is a sight to behold, even in death. Beware the demon, for he will wish you to be his own."

He fell backward, his legs still in the hole he'd created in the ground, his back cracking as he dropped.

The flames around me faded and I waited until the professor's chest stopped moving.

"We are a fucking rock star team," Dinah said. "That was amazing!"

I turned toward Killian, going to a knee. "Hey, you all right?"

He blinked those green eyes up at me, confusion and then anger filling them. "Who the fuck do you be?"

9

Killian's confusion was contagious. I stared right back at him. The professor he'd taken us to who deciphered the deal my father had made with the devil lay dead behind us. But not before he'd tried to kill us both, or maybe just take our memories. It made sense that he would have that ability though, to take memories, create a world of history inside his head and then teach it to unwitting students.

And that's when it slammed into me.

"Holy shit, he took your memories." I breathed the words, shock filtering through me along with the implications.

Killian pushed up and away from me as he looked around. "Why am I in the university?"

I stepped away from him. "What's the last thing you remember?"

He hesitated, his eyes going distant as he pulled on his memories, or what was left of them. "Going to Barron's."

I squinted one eye because I didn't dare close them both, not right then. "That was right before we met for the first time, Killian." Shit, this was not going to help anyone. Least of all me and Bear.

"And you are?" He arched an eyebrow.

Yeah, this was not going to go well, but I still needed him, and I did not mean in the emotional sense, not at all. I snapped my fingers and Abe trotted to my side. I took the skin document from him and tucked it into my sister's journal and put that under my shirt. There was only one truth that might keep Killian with me now. Because there were no feelings left in him for me. I ignored the pang in the region of my heart.

"You were going to help me kill Romano. We have a way to do it." I tapped the journal. "We came to the professor for more information and then he tried to take my memory. Instead he took yours."

Killian shook his body a little. "How can I trust you? Are we fucking?"

"Nope. And stop fucking asking about it." I turned away from him, hoping he would follow. But I wasn't going to stand there and argue with him. There was not time to fix this mess and kill Romano and get Bear back. The loss of his memory was a pain in the ass, but it wouldn't change the course of what I had to do. I'd just have to go it alone.

A tiny bit of my heart reminded me that Tommy had said the memories could come back, if the one they'd been taken from searched for them, if they wanted to know what was in their past.

Nothing new there.

Again, I did what I could to ignore the pang in my heart region and banished all the thoughts I had of someday, of maybe when this was over, or we'd deal with it later. Killian had been right: there was no knowing when we'd lose each other. Or that we could lose each other without even being dead.

"Are you crying, Lass?"

"Fuck off." I hadn't realized he'd caught up to me or that there were tears sliding down my cheeks. Again, there was a brush of cold against my back. Martin then was sticking around for sure.

I made my way to the Humvee, brushing my face clear of the tears. "Can you fly for me?"

Killian's eyebrows shot up. "You hired me as your pilot?"

"It's a long story, and I doubt you'd believe it. But your pilot is dead, and we're on a time crunch to kill Romano." I let Abe into the backseat and then took a seat in the passenger side.

I wanted to deny the tears but perhaps a few had slipped out. Damn it, I did not need this shit. This emotional realization that he meant more to me than I wanted to admit was rough.

Killian slid into the driver's seat and turned the engine over. "The plane's here then?"

"Yes."

"You going to fill in the gaps, Lass?"

His use of the word Lass almost undid me. I took a breath and then spoke, filling him in on autopilot, the words just a numb recitation of what had happened so far. "My name is Phoenix. I was Romano's boogeyman. He's taken my son, and to get him back I need to kill Romano. You were helping me; my ten-year-old son saved your life at one point and you felt obligated to return the favor.

"We've got the original deal between Romano and the devil that has extended his life. We brought it to the professor to translate to make sure we got it all. Then said professor decided I remembered too much and that

Mancini wouldn't like that so he attacked us. I guess he thought you needed to have that memory of me speaking my memory silenced. From here, the plan is to go to Jackson Hole, get Brikoff working on a magic bullet, and see if we can figure out the next step from there."

Killian said nothing as I spoke, as I went through the details of the things we'd done, of who we'd eliminated, of what we had ahead of us.

I drew a breath as we reached the quiet airport for a second time.

"You expect me to come with you then, to risk my life for a kid I don't remember?"

I shook my head. "No, I expect that you will want to help me kill Romano to secure your place in the underworld as the new top dog."

I couldn't believe I was having to even have this conversation. At least he hadn't drawn on me, because I wasn't sure I could pull the trigger on him. And that was dangerous. I needed to be able to eliminate anyone who stood between me and Bear, even if that person was Killian.

"I need you to fly for me," I repeated. "Will you do that? The possibility is there that your memory could come back. If you wanted it to." That last bit . . . what if he didn't want to figure out how his memories were attached to me? No, I could not go there. I had a job to do and that job was kill one person, save a kid. That was it.

He rubbed a hand over his lips and looked at me, really looked at me as if he were trying to read something only he could see on my face. "Aye, I can do that much for you. But you can't expect anything else."

It was the best I was going to get and I shook his hand on it.

Moments later, we were on the plane, and moments

after that, in the air. I stayed in the back because I didn't want to see the distrust on his face. Distrust I hadn't even earned. I snorted to myself.

"You should just fuck him. He'd do you even now, you know," Dinah said.

I slapped a hand over her. "Shut up, Dinah, or I'll never let the lightning run through you again."

She huffed. "That's rude."

"That's a little sister knowing how horny her big sister was before, and based on previous encounters, it hasn't changed."

Dinah let out a laugh but I didn't laugh with her. There was nothing funny about any of this. I'd just lost my best ally to a twist of fate I'd not seen coming. Across from me, the seat cushions depressed and Abe watched, his head tipped to one side.

A voice whispered to me.

You aren't afraid of me.

"No, Martin," I said. "I'm not. I'd like to know why you are with me, though."

The depression shifted a little and then I had the impression he leaned forward. *You will walk into the void soon. You're going to need my help. I can see a bit of the future. You will lead me to my savior. But only if I help you survive to reach her.*

"Well, that's not ominous at all," Dinah grumbled. I agreed with her.

"Okay, Martin. I'll take it. But let's be clear, I am not your savior."

No, that you are not.

His laughter rose and faded and the air around me warmed once more. Abe gave a snorting huff as if he'd scared the ghost away.

I stood and went to the door into the cockpit. "Killian, how long to Jackson Hole?"

"A couple hours, tops."

I turned to leave and he reached out his hand, snagging my wrist. "No, sit with me, here."

There was no reason for me not to. Except that it involved my feelings for Killian, and all those did right now were frustrate me and apparently produce tears, which other than for Justin's death, I had never given to a man. But I sat and slid a headset on over one ear.

I pulled out the diary and Dinah and laid them both on my lap. "Okay, sis. Let's talk. Time to figure out what is going on with this deal, who the fuck Mancini is really after, and what the last two items on this godforsaken recipe are because I'm not sure Tommy is right."

Dinah wiggled on my lap as if getting comfortable. Abe snuck into the cockpit and sat beside me, his eyes tracking Dinah's every movement. I flipped open the diary and pulled out the three sheets I had. The original deal, the translation the mad professor had made, and the list that had come from the code breaker.

"This list of things for the bullet." I pulled *that* sheet out. "A lot of it is herbs and things like that. Things that could be found anywhere, I think, but it will take time." Which I was sure by the weight in the pit of my stomach we did not have.

"Read me the list," Killian said.

I sighed. "Dried larkspur, essence of cassava, stem of belladonna, oil of basil, innards of a desert cactus, fern leaves, spit of a female demon—that's rather specific—, Irish lightning, blood of a phoenix, grindings from a curse, a piece of the past," I paused. Then I pulled out the new translation from the professor. He'd said that he'd already gone through it once so he'd done it quickly but . . . there were subtle differences.

"This list, the one from your teacher," I ran my finger down it, "it's mostly the same except for these two. *Skin* of a female demon, a blood-soaked piece of the past."

Killian snorted. "Yeah, those be tough ones either way. How do you find something like that?"

Dinah cleared her throat. "The skin that the deal is written on. Didn't the professor say it was demon skin?"

I stared at the pore-less skin. "Yes, he did."

"So, could that be what you need? It would make sense seeing as it is the actual deal. A lot of curses and counter-curses involve taking a piece of the original in order to work properly."

"Dinah. You're a kickass smart woman," I breathed.

"Of course. It's family genetics. The women get the smarts, the men get . . . well, I'm not sure what they get out of the deal." She laughed and I managed a smile.

"They're just plain asses," I replied.

Abe shifted his face on my thigh and I put a hand on him, rubbing his ears.

"That last bit on the list, read it again." Killian adjusted something and then turned to look at me. His eyes were intense, and I had the feeling he was trying to read just what we meant to each other. I refused to give him anything but a working relationship. His memories had to come back on their own or not.

Because I wasn't sure I could lose him all the way and not feel it. So maybe this was better, for things to be over before they truly began.

"A blood soaked piece of the past," I said.

"That is specific . . . is there something from your childhood that could be soaked in blood?" he asked.

I stared at the words. Piece of the past. It niggled at me, tugging at my mind, but I couldn't piece it together. "No, nothing off the top of my head. Anything that was bloodied would have been hidden or gotten rid of to hide the evidence." I circled that bit with a finger. "I think I know, I just can't put it together right now. The grinding of a curse, though . . . that is something that I think I know."

Dinah wiggled a little. "What do you think it might be?"

"Grindings of a curse . . . it makes me think of a stone being ground down and my father's ruby ring that he had to keep the guardians in check. That ring is cursed." Maybe Tommy was right about that much. I tapped the papers, certainty filling me as I spoke the words. One of the ruby rings . . . that was going to be damn hard to get.

I folded the papers and stuck them inside the diary, then put the diary inside my shirt under the Kevlar. I picked Dinah up and stood, and almost put a hand on Killian's shoulder for balance. Or maybe just to touch him for a moment. To take a little comfort from him just being there. But I withdrew it.

I stepped out of the cockpit. The cabin was quite roomy, and there was a bench seat that would work as a makeshift bed if I wanted to lie down. Abe followed me quietly, his hip bumping into my leg here and there as if to remind me he was still with me.

"Dinah," I said.

"Yeah?"

"Thank you, for . . . everything."

She was quiet a moment. "You are my baby sister. Even though I didn't show it, I was always looking out for you. For both of us."

I lay down on the bench and Abe jumped up and settled between my knees, his head on my thigh. He gave one jaw-cracking yawn and closed his eyes. I felt the same, but I had too many questions. "Did you really love the guardian, Strike?"

She let out a heavy sigh and I put her on my chest. "Well, yeah. At least, I thought I did. For all I know, he manipulated me. He's not just good at pain, as his other name implies. He can control people through the pain receptors in their brains. Can make them believe that what they are seeing is real. I was safe if I was with him. Father wouldn't dare touch me. And that was worth it to me. Our talents together meant we had the potential to take everyone out around us."

I frowned. "Then why kill yourself?"

"Mancini. He wanted me dead because I'd turned him down after he helped me, and Strike . . . he said that if Mancini called in the hit, there would be no stopping it. This way I had the chance to live on right under his nose."

That didn't make sense. "Strike and the other guardians could have protected you."

"Not by what Strike said. He believed that if Mancini ordered it, that even he couldn't protect me. Looking back, I wonder just who he was working for. You know that the three guardians resented having to work for Father? They hated him, hated that they were under the thumb of someone they called a mewling pawn."

I snorted. "That's a good one. I'm going to use that the next time I see him."

She snickered. "He hates it when they call him that."

"So, he knows they don't like him?" I tucked an arm under the back of my head. "You think that's why he threw them at me, to finish them off? Or do you think it's like Mancini said and it's to push my abilities into overdrive?"

"Which also makes no sense. Father doesn't even know

what you are. The only one who seemed to really know was—"

"Vivian, but she's dead, which just leaves one person. Mancini," I said softly. The pieces were all there, threads and bits of a story I couldn't put together. The words just didn't fit. "Dinah, we are missing something."

"I know. It is rather galling," she grumbled.

"Hey, I have a question."

"Shoot." I smiled as she said the word and she laughed. "Though, not literally."

"No, not here. That would end poorly. Though, the last time I got thrown out of a plane we did okay," I said. "My question is, why did Zee hate you and Eleanor? I mean obviously, he didn't know who you were, but . . ."

She sighed before she answered. "I think it's because we were both so angry and the curse bound us in ways we couldn't possibly have predicted. Because I knew Eleanor before. We didn't realize she was bound by constraints, as I ended up being bound too. Zee wasn't wrong. We were egging you on to kill more. At least, back then. We both had so much pain and anger, it had to come out somewhere."

I wondered what Zee would have thought to know that the love of his life was trapped inside a gun. He'd loved my mother fiercely and he'd loved me like the daughter of his heart. I doubt he would have cared. He would have loved her still.

"You care for Killian," Dinah said with great tact. "Do you love him?"

I thought about the question for a solid minute before I answered. "Maybe. I don't know. And I honestly don't want to think too much about it until I have Bear back and Romano dealt with. There is nothing safe in this world if I love it. You saw that even with Abe. Now with Killian's memory gone, how can I explain to him everything we've been through together?"

The Malinois lifted his head, his eyes sleepy, and I ran a hand over his head. "Romano will use anything he can to try to control me. I have to take that away from him. I can't and won't stop loving Bear or Abe. I can hold back on Killian."

"Smart," she mumbled. "But you don't want to."

I shrugged. "He knows me better than anyone else in my life, maybe, except for Bear. Not even Justin knew who I was. If he had, I doubt he would have loved me. He thought I was you, Dinah. He thought I was the beautiful sister forced to run away. The beauty who needed saving from her beast of a father."

Dinah let out a sigh. "Killian's a good match for you, far better than Justin ever was."

"You barely knew Justin," I pointed out.

"But I did see what a fool he was trying to take on Romano, and almost getting you and Bear killed. Bear is my nephew, and I want to meet him for real," Dinah said.

I put a hand over her. "I want you to meet him too. Though that's going to be something of an explanation as to how he's related to a gun."

She laughed and I closed my eyes, though I didn't really sleep so much as let my body rest. Weird to think that the re-emergence of my sister—albeit in a strange form—could bring such a level of comfort to my battered heart. But I'd take it for the momentary respite it was, knowing we were far from done with the violence.

10

BEAR

I sat cross-legged inside the tent of a beautiful woman in the middle of a desert, waiting for my uncle Tommy to show up to take me back to my mom. Weird, this was too weird. Reminding me of a fever dream like when I'd been sick as a kid.

Despite the heat, a fire had been lit in the center of the tent, the flames dancing and licking upward. Sometimes I thought I could see shapes in the fire, faces of people I'd known. Twice I was sure I'd seen my mom. Shaitan had been one of the faces too.

I'd been given a pair of loose pants that tied around my ankles, and a top made of fine, light material that felt as though I wasn't wearing a shirt at all.

To be fair, I didn't know from one moment to the next if I was hallucinating, and that made it easier in some ways to accept the current state of my existence. Because if I was just dreaming, then the weirdness could be tolerated.

"Man child," the woman said softly, "we will begin now to work on your control of the fire inside you. It can both heal and harm, cure and make ill, burn and cool."

I frowned at her. "Are you really not going to tell me your name?"

Her lips curled upward into a smile that made her dark eyes sparkle. "Perhaps one day you will know my name. But not now. Not this day."

I frowned harder, my brows tight. "Okay. You know that's kind of strange, right?"

"Names have power, man child. Power that can be used to control you with the right spell." She turned and cupped her hand into a bucket of water and tossed the liquid onto the flames of the fire we sat beside. The water steamed and the scent of a sweet flower followed.

"Jasmine is a powerful flower. It opens us to our abilities when we are at the beginning of them." She wove her hands through the steam, cupping it and pushing it toward my face. I took a deep breath, knowing intuitively that was what she wanted.

The smell stuck to the inside of my nose and I drew it deeply into my lungs. The tent wobbled a little and I wondered if there was something besides the flower in the water.

"Desert witch," I said, "why are you teaching me if you don't want a man to be strong?"

She laughed at me. "Not all men are bad, just the ones who believe they are superior. They are not, not any more than I am superior to any other person. You will learn this, or you will die."

Another time that would have upset me, but in that moment, her words made perfect sense and I completely agreed. I gave her a nod, my head a little fuzzy inside. "Okay." She smiled again and I smiled back. "Now what?"

"Your fire will protect you when you are in danger. That is the first way you will connect with the flames." The desert witch pointed at the fire. "Put your hand in the flames. Your own fire will rise to protect your skin."

I hesitated. That was more than just learning how to control my fire, that was totally doing something my parents had always told me not to. *Don't touch fire, fire burns*. But I'd felt the fire inside me and I didn't doubt the desert witch knew what she was talking about. And again, this could be just a dream. I took a deep breath and thrust my hand into the fire.

My skin prickled and there was a bloom of flames that raced from my elbow all the way down to my fingertips. Blue and green; there was nothing but a pleasant warmth that made me think of my mom for some reason. As if she were there with me, hugging me. Tears prickled at the edges of my eyes as I thought of her.

"Pain?" the desert witch asked.

I shook my head. "Just . . . it makes me think of my mom. And I worry that she thinks I don't love her because I said that to keep her safe, but I didn't mean it." The words poured out of me and I snatched my hand out of the flame but the blue and green didn't fade. I lifted my hand into the air in front of my face. The connection was simple, and directly tied to my brain. Like a video game without the controller, I could make the fire bigger or smaller with a single thought.

"You are a natural." The desert witch raised her hands and waved them through the smoke once more. "It is not uncommon when a child finds their abilities early and uses them instinctively when they have been pushed to the brink."

I bit my lower lip and pulled the flames back. "So, I don't need training then?"

"Oh, I never said that. There is much you can do with

your fire. Like healing. You could be a healer instead of a fighter like your mother." Her eyes didn't so much as blink as she said those words, and I felt it in my belly that she would weigh my response.

I settled for honesty. "I don't know yet."

She shrugged. "You have time to decide."

"Can't I be both?" I shifted my legs and found myself reaching out to put my hand back in the fire, to run my fingers through it as if it were water and not flame.

"Perhaps. But it is not so easy. You will train the fire in you to be one or the other; to be both is . . . quite difficult. I am not sure if you will have it in you."

I twisted my lips and bit the bottom one as I thought on her words. I didn't want to hurt people, but as I'd learned recently, there was always someone waiting to hurt me. To hurt those I loved, and I would want to protect them. And I'd want to heal my mom or Abe if they were hurt, or Zee. I sighed. "I want to learn both."

She clapped her hands and a tinkle of bells rippled through the air. "Good, that is the right answer."

The bells faded and were replaced by the sound of an engine roaring, drawing closer. I twisted around in my spot and looked at the front flap of the tent. "Is that Shaitan?"

The sheik had until the morning to leave, according to the desert witch.

"No, I do not believe it is." She stood and went to the tent flap and peeked out. A sigh slid from her. "Man child, this is all the time you and I will have together. For now." She turned and held a hand out to me. I took it and she helped me stand. "I will oversee you healing your friend who came with you and then you must go. Our paths diverge, but they will come together again. Someday."

She stepped out of the tent and into the bright sunlight.

There was the sound of rapid gunfire and screaming and then several explosions that sent rock and sand high into the air like water geysers.

I found myself hanging onto her tighter. The wind snapped around her body, flattening her skirt to her, and it was only then I saw the bulge of her belly. She was pregnant?

The desert witch glanced at me. "Yes, I carry my daughter in secret. Her power will rival yours, man child. Remember that when you meet her as an adult."

I couldn't look away from the desert witch. "I doubt I'd ever meet her."

Her smile was genuine. "You will. But for now, you will heal your friend and . . . protector."

I looked in the direction we were headed. Rooster's body lay out on the sand, face up. His broken face—what was left of it—had been scorched by the sun's heat, nearly blackening the remaining skin. A few vultures hopped about, but they seemed reluctant to get any closer to his body.

"Shaitan killed him," I said, hesitating. "I saw it." I did not want to go nearer to his dead body.

"He injured him gravely and he will die by nightfall for the final time if you do nothing, for this is his last life," the desert witch said softly. She crouched beside Rooster as if he didn't stink, as if his wounds weren't still oozing and as if there wasn't a blitz of weaponry going on around us. I flinched as a particularly loud blast of gunfire went off close enough that I wondered how much danger we were in.

I made myself crouch beside her while my gorge rose. "What do I do?"

"Put your hands on the injury. Your flame can heal. You only have to command it to do so and give it some of your strength. This is where you must learn on your own. I can open the door; you must walk through and find the right path." She took my hands and laid them against Rooster's face. Though I wasn't sure it could even be called that anymore. Face implied eyes, nose, mouth. There was nothing here but a broken and caved-in skull with a tongue sticking out of the lower portion, swollen from the heat.

I swallowed the vomit that crept up my throat and closed my eyes. That was the only way I'd be able to do this. I thought about Rooster's face the way it had been before and about putting this face back together. About soothing away the wounds and making it so there was no more hurt. No more pain. No more wounds.

The flames on my arms heated more and more, to the point that I almost yanked my hands away from Rooster, but I gritted my teeth and held my ground. I was not going to fail at this. I would figure it out so when my mom or Abe, or anyone else I cared for was hurt, I could fix them. I could make the pain go away. So that I never lost anyone else again.

Like my dad.

I gasped and opened my eyes as Rooster sat up. His eyes were wild, but intact. His face was put back together with only a few scars from where Shaitan's fingers had gouged deeply. He reached up and touched his skin. He looked different to me, like the bone structure of his skull had changed, but I suppose that was to be expected when it came to having your face rearranged.

"Your ability will get stronger. One day you will be able to take the scars too," the desert witch said. She pushed to her feet and looked down at me. "I must go now. And you must go with the one who has come for you. That is your path; I see it. Go with him."

She turned her back on us as she raised her veil to cover the lower half of her face.

"What just happened, kid?" Rooster grabbed my arm and I turned back to him.

"Long story."

We just stared at each other. Rooster shook his head. "I was dying, for real, for the final time."

"Yeah, well, we both might die if we don't get out of here." I ducked as another round of gunfire went off around us, the sounds catching up to us as the desert witch disappeared back into her tent.

Rooster grabbed me and hauled me up. He didn't waste any more words as he all but carried me out of the range of the fire fight. As if he hadn't just been laid out on the ground.

He ran until we hit a slope of sand and then we both scrambled up it, sliding down the other side far enough that we could peek back over the edge and see what was going on.

"Kid, you brought me back, didn't you?" Rooster asked softly as we watched men shooting at each other from a distance.

I shrugged. "I'm sorry about the scars. I'm just learning."

He dropped an arm across me. In a hug?

"Kid, I'm proud of you. I'll do everything I can to protect you, even . . . even if it means dying."

A strange flush of pride raced through me. "You don't have to do that."

"I do. And I will. I'll protect you with my own body." His voice was gruff with emotion.

"You already did that. I think we're even." I wasn't sure I wanted to be responsible for his death again, even if it pleased me that he saw what I did as having great worth to him. That I wasn't just a burden to be cared for, but to be looked after because I'd helped him.

He stared out across the edge of the sand, not acknowledging that I'd pretty much just set him free from any further need to take care of me.

"There he is." He pointed at a Jeep barreling between the tents, my uncle hanging halfway out the window. A gun popped and blazed from Tommy's hand, sending smoke bombs between the tents. Uncle Tommy had come for me, just like he'd said.

I was up and running, Rooster right behind me, yelling.

"Bear, don't!"

"He needs our help!"

I slid to a stop at the base of the sand hill and called my fire up along my skin. I couldn't let Uncle Tommy die, not when he'd come here for me. Not when he was going to help me get back to my mom.

The blue and green flames blazed to life around me.

"You ain't got nothing to—holy shit." Rooster skidded to a stop behind me, but I didn't turn to him.

I thought about throwing the flames outward toward the men shooting at Uncle Tommy. I balled up my hand and tossed a ball of flames like a baseball. Only it didn't fly like a baseball but more like a rocket. The swirling blue and green flames exploded against one of the tents, lifting it off its tie downs and lighting it up in an instant.

I bit my lower lip as I turned and flung my other hand toward tents on the far side. Fear raced through me as thick as the flames that coated my skin. I did not want to be a bad guy, but I couldn't let someone else die when I had the power to stop it.

The Jeep peeled out toward me and Rooster. Behind it came a swirling wind that I was certain was Shaitan.

"Bear, douse the flames, you did good," Rooster said softly, and I let the fire go. I slumped, fatigue hitting me so hard, I would have crumpled to the ground if not for Rooster catching me. He helped me into the Jeep and strapped me in. Tommy turned in the front passenger seat and held his hand out to me. "You okay?"

I nodded. "Are you okay?"

He gave me a tight smile, one that didn't reach his eyes. "We're going after Romano. I'm going to stop him once and for all." The Jeep took off, bouncing through the ruts and rises in the sand until we were long gone from the scene of the battle. I twisted around to see the desert witch standing behind us, between the swirling wind that was Shaitan and us. She stalled him.

"You're a damn fool. You don't have everything you need," a woman's voice said with more than a hint of venom. I blinked and stared at the gun in his hand.

"Did your gun just talk?"

"Yeah. This is Eleanor." He rotated the matte-black gun around and stuffed it into a holster on his chest. "She's not happy because I took her from your mom."

"I'd rather have the boy take me than you," Eleanor snarled from her holster. "At least he's got some sense in his head."

Tommy rolled his eyes. "I know what I'm doing. The cursed bullet was only meant to throw us off. The only thing I need was a gold casing which I have, and you, Eleanor. For whatever reason, it needs to be you or Dinah who makes the final blow. That much I believe because of the heat factor of most guns."

I looked up at Rooster and he shook his head. "Don't know what he's talking about either, kid."

"Uncle Tommy, where is my mom?"

"She's coming too. We'll take care of Romano and then we can all have a beer." He grinned but I didn't smile back. I didn't think my grandfather—his father—would be that easy to kill. But I was just a kid, what did I know?

I clenched my hands into fists and shook my head. I wanted out, but I remembered what the desert witch had said. "I'll come with you, but only if you have a real plan. One I can help with."

Uncle Tommy looked at me as we bumped along the desert road. "You want to help kill your grandfather?"

I swallowed hard before I answered. "I want to make sure he doesn't hurt anyone again. Not me. Not you. Not my mom. Not Killian. He's already killed my dad. I . . . I don't want to lose anyone else."

Rooster stiffened at Killian's name. "You think Killian is worth saving?"

I glanced at him. "He kept me safe. He tried to stop Luca from taking me. And he's helping my mom."

"But he failed," Rooster bit out.

"You aren't in a place to judge," Tommy said. "The kid is right. The only way to stop Romano is to do it together."

I put my hand out on top of Tommy's and waited for Rooster to do the same. Reluctantly he dropped a hand onto mine.

"Then let's do it." Tommy tapped the driver on the shoulder. "Take us to the Grotto."

11

PHOENIX

In the dream, I stood in front of a man all dressed in black, his hair a dark brown, eyes the same shade. I had never seen him before and yet I knew who he was.

"Strike."

"You have a good set of instincts," Strike said. The place where we stood was not real, more like an empty limbo, as if the world had been stripped away from us. I suppose that was the deal with dreams, though. They could do that.

"This isn't real," I said.

"I'm taking your connection to your fire." Strike reached out and grabbed the edges of my face with his hand. "You are not tapping into your ability fast enough, deep enough. You are going to need it all to face Romano. This will speed up your learning curve."

I made a move as if to pull Dinah and shoot him, even if it was just a dream. He smiled at me. "You'll thank me later."

"Why are you helping me now?" I struggled with the words as he faded.

"I've been helping you all along," he whispered.

* * * *

"We're close," Killian yelled from the cockpit, snapping me out of my doze.

A part of me had hoped that with my eyes closed the pieces of the puzzle laid in front of me would miraculously come together. They hadn't, and now I was groggier than I'd started out. I sat up, rubbed my face and made my way to the cockpit to slide into the seat beside Killian, then put the headset on once more.

"You know Brikoff. Will you put in the call to him?"

"I suppose I was the one who found out where he was?" His eyes twinkled at me and I stared back at him. Twinkling eyes.

"Do you ... remember something?"

He leaned in close and caught my mouth in a kiss that I was not expecting. I closed my eyes and kissed him back. The heat between us had not diminished in the least. I touched his face, shocked at how much weight came off my shoulders with his memory coming back. He was right, there was no guarantee of tomorrow, and I would take what I could get. I kissed him harder and had to stop myself from pulling him out of the seat and into the back of the plane to strip his clothes from him.

As if he could read my mind, he let out a groan and slid one hand under my shirt and Kevlar, over my ribcage and onto my breast, squeezing so carefully with only the mildest trickles of electricity running from him to me. I couldn't stop the way my body responded even if I'd wanted to.

He was breathing hard when he took his lips from mine. Mind you, I was struggling for breath too.

"Bits and pieces," he said. "Enough to know you're telling me the truth."

My jaw dropped. "But..."

"I thought a kiss might jog me memory." He winked at me and I couldn't help the blush, and I didn't even know why I was blushing, only that he'd caught me wanting him. Damn it, he'd caught me good.

Killian glanced at me with his lips quirked up on one side. "So, here we go. I remember enough to know I want to keep you alive if only to see where we go from here. We get Brikoff to agree to make the bullet, check your house for ingredients and then what? Kill your father, rescue your son, and then run away to somewhere nice and quiet, just the three of us."

Dinah sighed softly. "Oh, yeah, totally dreamy and fuckable."

I had to agree with her but I kept my mouth shut, mostly because I was still thinking that same thing.

Killian snorted. "She's quite something."

I shrugged. "She was always like this, even before." I frowned, though, as his words really sunk in. "You think we can just walk away from this world after Romano is dead? Because I don't."

Killian sighed and reached across for my hand. I let him take it, relishing it more than I wanted to admit. "We can for a little while. But you're right. A vacuum in the underworld of abnormals is not good. You either become one of the bosses or you work for one of them. And you'd have very little choice as to who you work for. There is no utopia here, no chance that all the bad ones will be eliminated and no one would take their place. Romano is just the worst of the worst. There will be others."

Abe bumped up beside me, putting his head into my lap and I absently stroked his ears. "Is that why you started your gang?"

"Aye, it is. There was no safety with the Irish abnormals, just chaos and death. I knew from a young age I was going to try and harness all that power and use it to at least try and improve things. To escape in the only way, by leading my people."

"Did you know you would become a killer?"

"I don't remember a time when I wasn't." He didn't look at me, just stared straight out the window. "My father trained me young, not unlike Romano did to you. He beat me until my powers started to develop, and that's partially to blame for the strength of my lightning."

Were all the powerful abnormals psychotic? I rubbed a hand over my face. "That seems extreme."

"It's common practice amongst those with children who could develop powers." Killian did glance at me then. "Did you not see any of your siblings beaten?"

I shook my head, but already my thoughts raced into the past. "I didn't, but I saw the aftereffects. I always thought it was because the boys were fighting amongst themselves. It never occurred to me that Romano was doing it to them."

Dinah cleared her throat. "It's partly why Gabe was so miserable. He was beaten the worst and nothing came from it. He was a failure. Father didn't bother with you because he didn't think your mother had any abilities. That and you are a girl."

I looked down at her in her holster. "What do you mean?"

"Mine came on during puberty when I was thirteen.

More common in women to have that change in hormones start the shifting of powers, so I was never beaten. And it's why he believed you were without abilities," she said.

"What was your ability?" Killian asked the question, and I was glad for it.

"I dealt in illusions. I could change how people saw me, and how they saw the world around them." Her voice was thoughtful. "It meant I could get the boys in trouble easily, and I was on the path to convincing Romano to put me in charge."

"Devious," I said.

"Surviving," she tossed back. "But now that Romano knows you are an Ascendant, he's pushing you too. I'm sure of it."

"Maybe. I'm not sure he knows what I am. There is only one person alive I am sure of, and that's Mancini. I doubt he would have shared information with Romano, seeing as he wants him dead."

"No maybes," Dinah said. "It's Romano's MO—force your kid's powers to bloom, and that's enough to convince me that he's on to you, and maybe has been for a long time."

She might be convinced, but I was far from believing this was all on Romano. Mancini had a hand in some of it, that much was for sure. A thought caught me from left field. "Dinah, how did Mancini get your diary? It was in your room the night you died, wasn't it?"

"It was," she said. "You never saw it?"

I shook my head. "No. But that means someone else knew you were going to let Strike kill you."

"No one else knew. I couldn't take the chance they'd try to stop me. We planned it for that weekend when all the men were away, when it was just you and me," Dinah said. "I knew that if Father found my body, he'd have had Daniel re-animate me long enough for Tommy to pull my memories."

My jaw dropped as my brain tried to work out her words. Killian had no such issue.

"What the fuck? One of Romano's kids is a necro? Who the hell was his first wife?" He muttered something in Gaelic under his breath, but I was struggling to breathe around this information.

"Julianna was my mother," Dinah said with more than a hint of pride. Killian cursed again and I lifted both brows.

I caught his shocked expression. "Care to explain?"

"Julianna was an unusual abnormal. Her powers manifested in different ways depending on what she was threatened by. She was a true chameleon in every sense of the word. She could take on others' powers and make them her own. She was legendary; still is, I suppose," Killian said. "She disappeared a long time ago. We all assumed she was dead."

"No, just trapped," Dinah said. "And then when she had Gabe, Romano thought her ability to pass on her powers was gone. Her body died shortly after."

And shortly after that, he moved on to my mother, who had been an Ascendant too. Maybe Romano did know what I was. I changed the subject back to the original topic.

"Daniel can re-animate?" I spoke slowly so as not to struggle with the words.

"You didn't know?" Dinah seemed genuinely surprised. "I thought you knew what we all did. Or maybe I just assumed because you were our boogeyman too. Killer of abnormals."

I shook my head, unable to do more mostly because my mind was racing at top speed. "Dinah, at the Magelore's house in Seattle, do you remember what we faced? There was a re-animated crocodile. Magelores can't actually re-animate anything, only take souls of their victims."

"Right . . . oh, shit. You think Danny was there?" She let out a long hiss and Abe growled next to me.

"I think if he wasn't there, he'd been there earlier. But why?" I clenched my hands into fists until my nails bit into my palms. The Magelore had killed the croc, but the croc had bitten her nearly in half. A creature that truly belonged to her wouldn't have done that. The more I thought about it, the more I was sure it had been one of Daniel's creations. I could feel it in my gut; this knowledge that Danny had been at the Magelore's home . . . looking for something, maybe?

"Necros are bad, Phoenix, one of the worst abnormals to tangle with," Killian said. "I had to deal with one back in Ireland before I left. He wiped out my people and then raised them as an army against me. There are still stories of him floating about." A quick shudder raced through him. "Fucking monsters. They often bed the people they raise, a desire for them so strong it don't bother them that they be dead already."

Bile rose in my throat. Daniel had been the quietest of my three brothers, keeping to himself and only occasionally tormenting me. "Any idea on how to handle a necro then? Because as far as I know, Danny is still working for Romano."

"He was going to be sent out to the Middle East, after Tommy," Dinah said. "I mean, that's old news, before I died, but it *is* possible it still happened. He could still be there, I suppose."

I doubted he was still there, but interesting that there were so many pieces tying my family to the area. Not that the Middle East in itself was specific enough to get coordinates, but it was a start. I was not about to discount it.

I wracked my brain. "Let me think." Before I'd left Romano's employ, Danny had been sent on a job to acquire new places for the money to come in through. I closed my eyes, trying to see the last few weeks I'd spent at home, trying to see if there was even a hint at where Danny might have been sent. But we'd not really crossed paths; Romano had us going in different directions.

"Does it matter at this point?" Killian asked, interrupting my thoughts. "He's either there, or he's not. If he is, we'll deal with him and hope that he's like Tommy, turning on Romano."

I blinked my eyes open. Killian was right. "Easy enough in theory, but it bothers me that he was at Vivian's. *That* Magelore knew far more than she let on. I almost wish I hadn't killed her."

Killian barked a laugh and Abe woofed as if he agreed. I didn't laugh, and my thoughts turned inward.

What the hell had Danny been doing at the Magelore's home?

I had a feeling the answer was going to be beyond important. And I didn't like that I was going to have to base our next move on a hunch that involved my older brother and a dead Magelore.

12

Jackson Hole, Wyoming. The place where everything began and now here I was, looking for answers, yet again.

"How are we getting into town?" Killian asked. His words trailed off as I headed toward the pay parking lot at the airport with the crook of a finger. I took note of a few new cameras here and there, but nothing I was terribly worried about. By the time I had a vehicle secured, and someone realized it was being stolen, we'd be gone.

I led the way to a bigger truck, one with four doors and lovely shiny rims which told me it wasn't someone who worked a farm for a living. The smells of summer in the prairies washed through me as I worked on the hotwiring, the wind blowing in through the open doors.

"Damn you, Zee," I whispered as I got the wires to spark and the engine turned over.

"Who is Zee?" Killian asked as he slid into the passenger seat.

"Zee was my mentor," I said, feeling weird to have to explain who Zee was to a man who'd met him, "more like my father than the father I was born to. He always said I would come back here, that I would find my way home."

"And?" Killian prompted.

I shrugged. "The wind smells like home to me." I backed the truck out of the parking spot and headed toward the ranch. To the only place Bear had known as home, and to the place I swore I would never return to. But there was something waiting for me here. I knew it in my gut, and there was no way I could deny that my instincts had steered me right most of my life.

Killian stared out the window as we drove, taking it in. "It's pretty here. Quiet."

I nodded, feeling the strain between us again. The uncertainty. "That it is."

"Brikoff is at a fisherman's lodge on Snake River," Killian said. "Fly fishing. You know where that is?"

I answered by taking the turn that would take us to the river. The road went from pavement to hard-packed dirt road, and then in the distance, I could see the sparkle of the water as it danced along, oblivious.

I parked the truck and we got out. Abe leapt ahead of me, spinning and yipping. My heart panged for him. "He thinks we're home to stay."

"Maybe you should leave him?"

"No. He's got to see this through with me." Again, it made no sense but I went with it, this knowing without understanding. Whatever Abe's role in this journey of mine and Bear's, it wasn't done. Not by a long shot. I just wish I knew what it was.

I didn't touch my weapons as I walked but I wanted to, which told me just how on edge I was. The more I touched them, the more anxious I was about the outcome of a situation.

This Brikoff was a Russian mobster, but I had a feeling he was more than that. To be a small mobster and only have ten people working for you was one thing. To be courted by the other mobsters when you were that small was another thing entirely.

"There." Killian pointed to a thickly built man in waders out in the river, casting his fly.

"Any suggestions as to how to deal with him?" I asked as we approached the edge of the river.

"He's . . . different than any other mob boss I've dealt with," Killian said. "I can't judge how he might react. Go with your gut on it."

I snapped my fingers, bringing Abe back to my side without a word, but I pointed him to Killian.

"*Bewache.*"

Killian raised an eyebrow at my command for Abe to guard him. I shrugged out of my coat and handed it to Killian.

"Dinah, just you and I are going in."

"I've got your back." She said.

I nodded and took a step into the river. The shockingly cold water tugged at me the deeper I got, making each step an effort to stay upright. It got deeper before it suddenly shallowed where Brikoff stood.

He tipped his head. "What are you doing out here without waders?"

"Having a talk where no one can overhear us," I said.

I pulled Dinah out, but turned her so she was on display in my palm. "You made my guns."

He twisted his upper body and I got my first good look at him. Mid-fifties, his hair was bright blond so any silver that might have been there was not visible. He wore big sports sunglasses that covered his eyes, but I'd have guessed at blue. There was a scar on the upper side of his lip that pulled his mouth into a smirk. His accent was so light, I had to work to catch it.

"You think I made this gun? I have no such talent—"

"Stuff it, chubby," Dinah growled. "I bought the guns from you, and you designed them for me to Mancini's specifications."

Even in the sunlight, I saw Brikoff's face pale. "My God. Bianca?"

"Not anymore." Dinah shivered. "My name is Dinah now. But it's still my soul inside here."

He reached out to touch her. Normally I would have yanked her away but I held still. Like fly fishing, this would have to be the exact right moment for me to set the hook. He ran a single finger over her muzzle and she shivered again.

Without another word, he tipped his head and started to walk farther out into the river.

Well, that was unexpected. Killian was right about that much.

I followed Brikoff with only a single glance back at Killian and Abe. Abe sat there, his eyes glued on me but he didn't move. Good dog.

We reached a small island in the middle of the river and Brikoff turned to me. "Where is the other gun?"

"Don't worry about her," I said. I was not about to tell him that Eleanor had been stolen from me.

He shook his head, awe creeping into his voice. "I was not sure that the weapons would hold a soul so well. Dinah . . . how do you feel?"

I kept her in my palm so she could speak clearly over the rushing of the water. "I'm fine, but I need your help one more time."

Of course . . . she'd dealt with him before. I should have

asked her for help in this. His lips tightened. "You paid me, and that is that."

"Yeah, well. We'll pay you for this too," she said.

"I am no longer for hire. I am retired." He moved as if to go past us. I spun Dinah and had her back in her holster in a flash. Pulling a gun on this one wouldn't work.

"And if I told you I could give you a million dollars for one small thing? What then?"

He'd slid his sunglasses back on so I couldn't read his eyes, but his body was tense. "What exactly do you need?"

I slowly put my hand into my pocket and pulled out the coin I'd taken from Killian's trove of goodies. "I need you to turn this into a bullet for Dinah."

He reached out and took the coin, a sigh slipping though him. "This coin has been held by bloody hands. It has soaked into the metal."

A snap of cold air in the summer sunshine whipped my hair. *A blood-soaked piece of the past. Clever.*

I waved my hand at Martin, but said nothing. He was right. Brikoff pulled his sunglasses off. "Did you hear that?"

I blinked up at him. "Hear what?"

"I could have sworn . . . never mind." He turned the coin over in his hand, staring at it. "A million dollars for a single bullet. That is a great deal of money to offer without even negotiating a lower price."

"It's worth it to me to have it done right." My guts clenched at the bullet not working. At it failing, or getting stuck inside Dinah's chamber. That would kill her, what was left of her soul anyway. This would be a one in a million shot, and Brikoff knew Dinah's inner workings better than anyone. Which meant he would be the only one to make the bullet.

"I can have it ready in a very short time. You have the money?" He arched an eyebrow. I nodded.

"I have to go get it. A million is no small amount to be lugging around." I took a step back, paused and then nodded at him. "You're not the small potatoes they say you are. Are you?"

He smiled wide. "No. But it is best to let the idiots kill each other."

I snorted. "I don't disagree."

"But you are going to help it along, aren't you?" he called out to me.

"Have that bullet ready in two hours," I called back, ignoring his question. "I'll be here and I'll expect it."

I slogged through the water, the icy chill numbing my legs again while Martin's touch on my back numbed the skin there. "Martin, knock it off."

I must be close to you if I am attached to you.

Whatever he was going to help me with, it had better be soon so I could see him off with whomever he needed to be with. His savior. I snorted again to myself as I stepped out of the water. Dripping wet, I slogged toward Killian.

"He's going to do it."

Killian gave a quick nod. "And the price?"

"A lot of money. But I've got it tucked away here." I headed to the truck, calling Abe to me once more. He happily bounced along. This was the place he knew, the fresh air and the wide-open spaces. Not the tight-knit crush of city buildings or pressed down by gunfire.

Back in the driver's seat, I hotwired the truck again and we left the river behind in moments.

"Where to now?" Killian settled into the seat. "And I remember the bathroom, and our discussion there."

I almost hit the brakes, and I managed to keep my face straight. "I suppose that's good."

"You think I'm a bad man." He chuckled. "I like it."

"Focus, Killian. Fucking later."

He let out a long laugh and I smiled though it was tentative. I knew what survivor's guilt was; I'd dealt with it after I lost Justin and Bear. This was more of the same. The feeling that I didn't deserve to have any moment of relief from the crushing drive to get Bear back, to kill Romano. Smiling and even laughing with Killian along the way wouldn't stop me from doing either of those things. Even if it felt like it.

Back through town, I turned in the direction of my ranch.

It wasn't long before we crested the hill that had changed my quiet life and thrust me back into the skin of a killer. Dinah was quiet; in fact, she'd said nothing since we left Brikoff. Why? Was she worried about what he thought? Or was she upset that I hadn't thought to ask her for her help and insight?

I wanted to talk to her but I knew now was not the time. Later, we'd discuss. For now, we had a job to do.

As we rounded the last corner of the road that led into my ranch, I got my first glimpse of the house post-fire. I'd left when it had still been raging, the flames too hot for me to do anything about, and a murderer to find. There had been no thought in me then as to what would happen to the house after. Because I'd had no plans of coming back at any point.

Charred timbers stood up here and there, held up by whatever amount of cement still clung to the footings. The rest of the house lay in a crumpled heap, as if someone had pulled the pins holding it together and it collapsed where it stood.

The once rich wood was black as night, scorched, the life sucked right out of it. But all of that was peripheral. Because there was someone at the site, someone I had not expected to find here.

My middle brother, Daniel.

I stopped far enough back that there was no way Daniel could see it was me in the driver's side, not with the way the light was hitting. He stood on the rubble and turned toward us, a hand raised to his eyes but it wouldn't help him.

"Lass?" Killian leaned forward. "Who is it?"

"Daniel. And if Dinah is correct, he can manipulate the dead. As far as I know, he's still working for my father." I clenched my fingers over the steering wheel, thinking as fast as I could. "Would he recognize you, Killian?"

Killian shook his head. "Not likely. Why?"

"You get out and go have a chat with him. Find out why he's here under the pretense of trying to get him to flip to your side of things. Tell him you need him for a job. Don't engage him if he wants to fight." The plan whipping through my mind was only half formed but it felt right. Like it would be our best shot.

"Then what?" Killian undid his seatbelt, twisted, and looked at me. "Report back?"

"Yes."

He slid out of the truck and walked toward Daniel.

My brother was built slimmer than the other two boys in the family, but his hair and eyes were as dark. I just hoped that darkness didn't include his soul. I hoped for a turnout like Tommy, that Daniel had seen how corrupt and maniacal Romano was and wanted out. I hoped, but at the same time I knew that the chance was strong Daniel was still with him.

I watched with my hand on Dinah as Daniel took a few

steps toward Killian. They shook hands; Killian's head bobbed as he spoke.

"What do you think they're talking about out there?" Dinah asked.

I shook my head. "Doesn't matter unless Killian comes a running back here with a horde of the dead on his heels."

"That's why I didn't want my body to be found," she said softly. "I knew Danny would bring me back to life, or at least my body would be brought back and I . . . I couldn't stand the thought of rotting to pieces. Even if I wasn't technically there."

"That's the most you've said since we left Brikoff," I said. "You want to tell me why?"

"Strike."

That surprised me. I'd been sure it was her maker Brikoff that had set off her silence. Then again, Strike had helped to put her into the gun in the first place. But more than that, what she said next stopped me in my tracks.

"I can't stop thinking about him and . . . our daughter."

13

The interior of the truck held a heavy silence as Dinah dropped that little bomb. My ears buzzed as I stared at Killian still talking to Daniel at the site of the burned-out ranch house. I finally found my breath to speak, or at least some of it.

"Wait, what?" I spluttered. "Why wouldn't you say anything about this before?"

Dinah didn't answer so I just kept going. I sucked in a sharp breath, my heart squeezing on her words. "You had a *daughter* with the guardian?"

"It was in secret. Not even Father knew," Dinah said softly. "I went away in my fifth month, before I was truly beginning to show, and I was induced early so I could go home as soon as possible. The plan was always for me to go and get her, later."

"Later never came," I said.

"No. When I realized I was going to be killed anyway, I decided to take matters into my own hands. And because of the curse that came with this sentience, I couldn't even tell you about her."

I did something then I knew was stupid. I knew it was nothing but emotions talking and yet I did it anyway. "We'll find her, Bea." She startled when I used her real name but I continued. "After Bear, we'll find her. Did you name her before you gave her up?"

"Yes. Her name is Emerald. Her eyes were green even then." She sucked in a deep breath as if holding back more emotion than she wanted to show.

Killian turned away from Daniel.

"Here he comes," I said, ending the conversation about a niece I'd never known existed before that moment. He wasn't exactly running, but he wasn't taking his time, that was for sure.

Killian slid into the truck. "Your brother is . . . interesting."

"What did he say?" I asked as I backed the truck up slowly.

"Wait, we're leaving?" Dinah barked. "Why come all this way then?"

"Killian?" I prompted him.

"Long story short, he gave me nothing. I tried to muscle him into working for me but I didn't scare him in the least, and he's one creepy fucker. There were dead things working through the salvage of the house, digging around."

I frowned as I put the truck in park over the crest of the hill, just out of sight.

"Wait, are we or aren't we going?" Dinah asked. "I'm confused."

I ignored her and kept my attention split between Killian and the road back to my brother. "He say anything useful?"

"No, only that I should fuck off and leave him or he'd

make me one of his pets. Not real friendly-like at all," Killian said. "I don't think your family likes me."

I snorted. "Any more than yours likes me." I stepped out of the truck and he followed suit. "Killian, can you give me a charge?"

"I can come with you, Lass. No need to give you a shock." He shut the door behind him and I nodded. I wasn't here to protect him. He could come if he wanted to. Even with his memory loss, there was enough that he wanted to be at my side. That thought warmed me a great deal. I had a bad feeling about this one, which was why I'd backed the truck up. We'd need a way out after whatever happened. "Come on, Abe." I snapped my fingers and he heeled to my side.

I started down the road, Killian on the other side of me.

"Why did you back us all the way up if you were just going to walk in?" he asked.

Dinah laughed. "Because she knows that Danny has a thing about being bothered when he's working. The more times you poke at him, the more pissed he gets. He can lash out, and he'd wreck the truck just to spite you. You sent Killian in there to irritate him, didn't you?"

"Yes," I said. "The more upset he is, the worse his control will be with his dead things. When it comes to abnormals, I've never faced another that could control the dead. But with most, when the focus wavers, they lose control of their ability and that is that. And you are correct, that is why I moved the truck."

Killian grunted. "Sometimes I forget who you were before. Even without the memory loss."

"I'll take that as a compliment," I said. We were within a hundred feet away and I pulled Dinah from her holster.

Dinah cleared her throat. "I don't want to kill him, Nix. I . . . I was close with him, as close as I could be without setting off Father's radar. Danny was sweet at one point. No matter what he is now, I loved him as my brother, once."

Well shit, that was going to complicate things.

"Fine. Leg shots, to be clear, and we'll try not to kill him." At least, not right away.

I aimed down her sight, seeing Daniel's kneecap as clearly as if it were five feet in front of me, and squeezed off a round.

Daniel spun and went to the ground, grabbing at his knee. I had no doubt that this was not going to be easy. But dead things didn't like fire, and that was something I knew I could pull off.

Score one for me.

I strode forward as the things he was controlling raced out of the shambles of my house. Not just dead things, but bits and pieces of dead things. Hands mostly, some attached to forearms, some not, some with all the fingers, some down to nothing but the skeletal bones of hands.

Several raccoons, though I couldn't be sure, because honestly, without fur and missing large chunks of flesh, it was a bit harder to say. Mostly it was the way they moved with their strange hopping waddle toward us that made me think of the little masked bastards that had tipped more than their share of garbage cans. That, and the fact I knew we'd buried at least ten after the dogs got ahold of them. Beside me, Abe let out a low growl, and his back hunched. Yeah, definitely raccoons.

"How are we handling this?" Killian's voice had a bit of a catch in it. I couldn't blame him. The things coming at us were less than pleasant to look at and that was without the smell that rolled out ahead of them.

"Fry them," I said and tried to call up my fire. It seemed

to sputter inside me, unable to light. What was this garbage? "Shit."

Damn you, Strike. He'd done this to me. This was a bad fucking time to learn a lesson.

Uncertainty caught me off guard and I struggled to find the flames that had saved us more than once. What the fuck good was it to be a goddamn abnormal, freak show of nature, if I couldn't at least use the ability when I wanted to? Sweat dripped down my face. What if Strike had done what he said he was going to do and stole my ability to use my fire? Damn, this was going to make life shitty in a hurry.

Killian stepped up beside me and electricity danced all over his body. "Nix?"

"I'm working on it," I growled. Forget the fire; I'd always done things my way, without any stupid ability. I yanked Dinah and my backup gun and aimed not at the oncoming mass, but at Daniel.

"Abe, *hier, bewache!*"

Abe pinned himself to my right side and let out a long snarl as the creeping things drew closer. It was hard to take my eyes from them; the unnatural movements as they scuttled across the ground was like something out of a horror flick.

"Daniel, you do not want to piss me off. I want to talk, not kill you!" I squeezed a round off at the closest raccoon to me with my backup gun, hitting it in the head and flipping it over backward. It lay still but only for a moment.

"I think you underestimate me just like the others," Daniel called back. "You think you know me? What I'm capable of?"

Abe lunged from beside me, grabbed a hand by the dangling forearm and shook it hard enough to snap bones before flinging it away from us.

"Killian, hold things down." I tucked both guns away while Dinah gasped.

"Nix, what are you doing?" she squawked.

"Abe!" I called as I leapt to the side, going to the outside edge of the horde of dead things. They followed me, hurrying to catch up to me. That was the only advantage now: I was faster than them.

I sprinted, pumping my arms and legs as fast as I could, ignoring the fingers and claws that grabbed at my pants and boots as they scrabbled to get a hold on me. I was ten feet from Daniel when he smiled at me.

Fuck, that smile was all Romano. "You're going to regret this," he said.

I grinned back and launched myself not at him, but to the left of him, rolling my body perpendicular to his. I saw the confusion on his face a split second before I finished my spin, and slammed my boot into the side of his face.

I landed hard, rolling a few feet before I caught my momentum and slid to a stop on the debris of the house. Daniel was still standing, barely. His body swayed where he stood, his hands holding his head.

"You were always an asshole," he muttered. "Thought you were better than me because you were a better fighter."

I snorted and pushed to my feet, looking to the dead things. They'd paused in their movements, uncertain without his direction.

"No. I never thought that." I stood. "Daniel, Romano is going to kill you the second you are no longer useful. He needs two souls, two of his *kids'* souls to keep his own immortality. Tommy turned on him. Bianca was going to turn on him before she died. Gabe is dead. You can't think that you're going to get anywhere by actually staying loyal to him. He's going to hand you to a fucking demon, Daniel."

His eyes rose to mine and he stood straight. Blood trickled down the side of his head, down his neck and disappeared into the top of his shirt. "I was always the favorite, Nix. He won't hand me over. He'll give the demon you and Tommy. If that's even what's going to happen."

I laughed at him, I couldn't help it. "Nope, his favorite was Tommy. The rest of us knew that. How could you be so stupid as to believe *you* were a favorite?" Yeah. Poking the bear, this would either work brilliantly or completely throw me on my ass.

I was banking on brilliance.

His face tightened like he'd just had a lemon jammed into his mouth. "That was a ruse. I was the favorite. You killed who he wanted. But I raised them from the dead and we questioned them. You were just a cog in his plans. The dead don't argue, they just answer."

Well, that made a whole lot of sense when I looked at it that way and only confirmed what Dinah had said about why she wanted her body hidden.

I shrugged, knowing that I only had a minute if I was lucky to shut him down. "What are you looking for?"

"Same thing you are. Going to make sure no one finds it. Dad has worked too hard to have this taken from him." He grinned at me and my heart pinged a little. There were echoes of Bear in his face.

"And you would be looking for what exactly?"

"You don't know?" He barked a laugh. "Shit, you really stuck your head in the sand, didn't you? Your husband knew *everything* about you. He knew who you were and he used you to get to Romano. He didn't love you, Nix. He knew you were the Phoenix. He knew you were a killer. He worked with us for years. We just didn't know he was *your* husband.

We knew he was married. That he had a kid. That he was vulnerable."

His words could not have rocked me more. "No. That's not possible."

He nodded, his smile grim. "How do you think he was found so quickly. Killed so easily? Because we *knew* him."

"No. Romano would have gloated to me about it. He would have—"

"He *still* wants to use you. Why, I don't know since you are fucking useless," Daniel snapped, his fists tightening at his sides. "He wants to use that truth about your husband as a hammer at some point to break you, but I told him it wouldn't work. Not when you're already fucking the Irishman."

He tipped his head toward Killian who stood silent waiting with his lightning, ready to fight at my side.

"Even if everything you say is true, it changes nothing," I pointed out.

"It changes everything." Daniel shook his head and I realized he was buying himself time. My kick to the head had rattled his ability. I should shoot him now. Slow him down further, but . . . I wanted to hear what he had to say. Maybe I was being a masochist, but I couldn't pull away from it.

"You're saying that Justin and Noah worked for you?" I asked, keeping one eye on the dead things as they slowly made their way closer.

Daniel snorted. "Noah worked for Mancini all along. Justin worked for Dad." He glared at me. "He gathered all the information he thought he could blackmail Dad with and then hid it."

Killian shifted his stance, drawing our eyes to him. "You mean information of how to kill Romano."

"Yeah, that."

"Why are you telling us this?" Suspicion rolled through me along with a sense of unease. "What do you get out of spilling the beans?"

Daniel gave me a slow grin that tightened the skin on his face, making it skeletal in the fading light of the day. "Time, Nix. I was buying myself time to bring my friends to the party."

There was a rumble on the ground, the sound of hoofbeats that slid up through the soles of my feet. I spun around to see a dozen skeletal bison running for us from the far side of the ranch.

I dropped to my knees and twisted around to shoot Daniel but he was already at his vehicle. I shot anyway, hoping to hit the radiator.

"Bison, Nix. Let's deal with the bison," Killian yelled.

Damn it all to hell. I stayed on my knees, fighting with the fire inside me, all but begging it to unleash on the things that were coming for it. The more I tried, the more it slid through my fingers, which only pissed me off. That was what I needed to feed the flames—anger.

Abe started barking at the bison skeletons that were now within a hundred feet. I had seconds at best.

The other dead things lay down where they were, no longer under Daniel's control. All his power was running through the stampeding two-ton herbivores.

Killian arced a shot of lightning into the lead bison. The bones lit up from within but the thing kept moving, kept thundering toward us.

"Shit, how do we stop it?" Killian grabbed my arm and hauled me out of the way of the herd of bison as they thundered past.

We leapt to the side, their hooves slamming into where

we'd been only seconds before. They didn't slow, but spun on their hooves as they raced toward us again.

I could just imagine trying to get their bodies off the remains of the house.

"We need to lead them away," I yelled as I pushed to my feet and bolted from the house, down the slope that led to the river. That was only part of the reason. The farther Daniel was from his creations, the less control he'd have over them. That was how it had worked with every other abnormal I'd ever faced.

Down the slope we ran with the dead bison right behind us. Skeletal they might have been, but there was still weight to them, still some flesh; they were not small creatures even in death.

A horn jammed me in the back and a bison let out a bellow of triumph as I stumbled.

Dinah gave a screech that was pure frustration. "I hate necros!"

I was hit again and this time flipped into the air, ass over head so I got a glimpse of the herd as they thundered underneath me. I landed behind them and they slowed, turning back to me. So, it was just me they were after, not Killian.

"Abe, to Killian, *bewache*!"

Abe gave me a look and then raced to Killian's side. "I'm going to lead them away." I panted the words. There were some ribs broken, I was sure of it. "Get back there and see if you can figure out what he was looking for under the house."

I didn't wait to see if Killian nodded or so much as blinked a yes. I tore off, leading the bison deeper into the fields. I headed for the trails I'd run when I'd been getting back into shape so many months before. The curve of the trail ran around the side of a gorge; if I played my cards right, I might be able to lead the bison right off the edge.

I might not be able to kill them, but maybe I could slow them down long enough to deal with whatever was still at the house.

My breath came in gasps and the bison were *not* slowing as we raced through the trails. The adrenaline pulsed through me, but my fire still burned low. Whatever Strike had done to me, he'd done it well.

A bellow of the lead bison was the only warning I got. I dodged to the left as a set of horns swung through where I'd been only a moment before. I could see the edge coming up. I put everything I had into picking up speed despite the sharp sting of the broken ribs. I had to time this right or I was going to be hurting a hell of a lot more than just a few broken ribs. My death would cement the loss of Bear's soul to the demon. I could not let that happen.

I raced away from the trail toward the open ledge. Ten feet away, then five. This was it. I dropped to my knees and then spun, sliding to my belly as I turned around, my momentum taking me over the edge feet first in a shower of dust and pebbles. I stared up through the cloud of self-made dust at the bison as they picked up speed too, charging at me with their heads low. The smell of death and rot preceded them.

My feet went over the drop off and gravity took hold. I scrabbled at the dirt as I slid over the edge. I gripped the rocks, tore nails off and held my breath as my fall halted and the bison leapt over the edge of the cliff, tumbling down around me. I pinned myself as flat to the edge of the cliff as I could, holding my breath.

14

Pinned to the cliff wall, I knew it was a risky move, but there had been no choice. Daniel's connection to his dead bison was obviously stronger than any other abnormal I'd dealt with when it came to their abilities. Which meant there might not be a distance issue with his hold on them. The hundred-foot cliff was the only hope I had to slow them down long enough to get done what I'd come home to do.

Hence, the cliff diving.

My fingers gripped the edge of the dropoff, digging in and holding all my weight. Which was why a hoof slammed into my left hand, cracking it under the weight of the dead bison.

I let the scream explode out of me. Not just because of the pain but because that was my fast hand. The one I killed with. I'd injured it before, but I felt the twist of the bones cracking as the bison used my hand as a launch pad.

The last bison fell over the cliff and I just hung there by my right hand, breathing hard, not sure I could even pull myself up over the edge. My vision blurred and I fought the darkness as it crept up around me, fueled by the break in my hand, the warmth of my own blood flowing down my arm. I didn't dare bring my hand to where I could see the damage. I knew by the feel that there were compound fractures—two at the very least. Every movement of my body sent a shot of pain through my hand.

"Pull your shit together."

I stared up, blinking several times because what I was seeing was not possible, which meant I was hallucinating. "Zee?"

My mentor, gruff as usual with one eyebrow arched, crouched to stare me in the eye. "You heard me. Pull it together. I might be dead, but you've still got work to do. And Martin here is only able to reach you part of the time because the connection isn't strong."

I hung there, staring up at the man who should have been my father. "Zee, I left him. I didn't go for him first."

"Bullshit. Romano took him from you, and you're doing what you have to do to get Bear back. Don't you start wallowing in your emotions, that won't bring him home. You are the terror of the abnormal world. That has not changed. Get your head out of your heart and kill that fucker Romano."

The image of Zee faded and there was the sound of barking. Abe.

"I'm here!" I yelled.

Moments later Abe was there sniffing at my broken hand as I held it above my head to keep the swelling from going out of control. "Abe, *nein*." There was no bite to my words, but I knew that if he so much as bumped my hand, I'd lose consciousness.

"Nix!" Killian was there a split second later, dropping to

his knees. He reached over the edge and grabbed my shoulders. "Lass, this is going to hurt."

"Pull me up." I locked my eyes on his as he tightened his hold on me and yanked me up. My broken hand flopped and I blacked out as the pain crashed into me, a wave of nerve-biting agony that might as well have been one of those bison slamming into my head.

I was on my back when I came to, my hand being held over my head, and my head against someone's knees.

"Irish?" I kept my eyes closed because a rush of nausea circled through me.

"Yeah. Your hand is shit, Nix. Can you heal it? There be tales of fire being a healing thing," he said.

"I don't know." The truth galled me to say it.

"You'd better try." He didn't have to say why. I knew without having him say anything. I would lose the hand if I wasn't able to heal it on my own. Already it grew cold from the lack of circulation. The trickle of my blood running down my arm had slowed, but that was about the only good thing.

My eyes were already closed, so I let my mind go to that place in me that the fire resided. It flickered there, as hot and wild as ever. But I couldn't reach it any more than I could reach it when I'd been facing Daniel.

I whimpered, for the first time realizing that I could not fight my way out of this. That I was going to lose my hand and that was going to hurt my chances at finding Bear. Zee's words whispered through me.

Pull your shit together. Pull your head out of your heart, Nix. Your heart will get you killed.

Zee, as so often was the case, was right even in death. I focused on my breathing, slowing it until my body calmed. Every beat of my heart sent a pulse of pain through my hand and up my arm. I had to figure this shit out and there was no time to do anything but fully embrace it. Whatever belief I had that perhaps I would go back to being normal after all of this had to be banished.

The fire in the center of me did not want to be beckoned out. "I do not have time for this shit." I snarled the words as I mentally grabbed at the fire. "You belong to me. You do not belong to Strike or any other abnormal. Do what you're fucking told!"

The fire roared upward and through me, rising along my arm and then engulfing my hand in the heat of its flames. I pulled the power up through me and it took everything I had, every ounce of willpower in me to direct it. Around the flames, I could feel the compulsion that Strike had put on me and I realized it had nothing to do with the flames, it had to do with what was inside my head. He'd slid thoughts into me that were eating away at my confidence. I could see them like an army of tiny ants that marched through my brain, taking tiny bites of me, eroding who I knew myself to be.

The dirty fucker had messed with me. I pulled away from Killian and fell forward onto my elbows and knees as I called more of the fire to me. Mine, this fire was *mine* and I would use it to burn through the world if I had to, if that's what it took to find Bear. I lit the ants of doubt on fire, smiling as they curled up, smoking and peeling away from my mind until they were all gone. Strike's compulsion was shredded and every lie down to the last eaten by the flames.

The heat rose and with it the air around me lifted, floating my hair around my face as I let the fire purge me of the hold that Strike had put on me.

Slowly I stood, the flames licking along every piece of my body, warming me. I wondered if I'd burned my clothes off. If so, Killian was getting quite the show. I didn't open my eyes, I didn't need to see the fire. I knew it inside and out, and I was not going to let anyone take it from me again. This was my birthright and it would rise or fall with me.

The seconds ticked by and I let the flames die, lowering my hands. I didn't even realize I'd raised them in the first place. As the heat dissipated, sliding from me and leaving me with a faint chill, I finally opened my eyes. Clothes were still on, so that was a nice perk.

Killian stared at me from twenty feet away, wide eyes and jaw hanging open. "That was quite the show. Wanna give me some warnin' next time?"

I looked around me. The earth was scorched where I'd stood, and Killian had moved to the outer ring of that fire. I looked down at my left hand. The bones were back in place. The skin was healed but still scarred, as if to remind me of the damage done. I flexed my fingers and grimaced. The hand was tight, as if it were not fully functioning. But at least I still had it, something that had been in question only moments before. Even as I thought it, the tightness receded. I'd take it, scars and all.

"Sorry. I didn't quite know what I was doing," I said.

He grunted. "Good to know."

I snapped my fingers on my right hand for Abe and he trotted to me, totally unbothered by the fact I'd just exploded in flame, scorching the ground around me. Thank God for dogs and their unconditional connection to their people. Abe tucked in beside me, giving me a hip check as he went by.

"Not that I'm not grateful for the rescue." I started back down the trail that would lead us to what was left of the house. "But why aren't you back there digging through the rubble?"

Killian said, "I thought it best to check on you on the off

chance that your brother circled around and came after you while you were dealing with the big beasties."

I nodded my thanks.

It didn't take us long to get back to the house site and the mess there. Dead things littered the charred rubble. Rubble that Daniel had been determined to get through. I frowned, thinking about some of the things we'd learned. I pulled the journal from under my shirt and opened it. From it, I exposed the deal between Romano and Bazixal.

"Strike gave this to you, right?" I held the paper out in front of me. Dinah shivered, the equivalent of a nod.

"Yes, he did. He told me to hide it well," she said.

Which she'd done, hiding it in the layers of the cover of her journal. The other coded paper was done in Justin's handwriting with the things needed to make the bullet that would kill Romano. At the bottom of the translation and the original were two small marks that had tugged at my mind since I'd seen them. A single star drawn twice.

Killian leaned over to look at it. "That's the mark the professor mentioned."

The memory came back to me in a rush as I ran my fingers over the double stars. "It's the same two stars as on the small safe Justin had when he was a kid. He showed it to me once, not long before the accident, like it was a big joke."

I walked into our bedroom to see Justin sitting at the edge of the room with his back to the wall, a small gray metal box in his lap. The cover of it faced me, with two stars hand-scratched into it. Probably from a knife, if the rough edges spoke truthfully.

"What's that?" I strolled toward him, my curiosity piqued.

Justin glanced up at me and then back down to the box. "When I was a kid, me and my best friend each had one of these."

He tapped the edge of it, the gray metal tinging, and then grinned up at me. "We thought we could use it to share things."

I frowned and sat beside him. Inside the box were a few packages of weeds carefully labeled, a tiny bit of gold and a few slips of paper with silly words scrawled on them.

I reached in and pushed a few things around with the tip of a finger. "What do you mean share things?"

He laughed. "Well, in our infinite wisdom, we believed because we both scratched the same design into the lid, that the boxes would be linked. For instance, if he put something in his box, it would appear in mine. And of course, vice versa." He flashed me another grin. "You can imagine our disappointment the first time we tried it."

I laughed softly and pushed the lid closed. "You should show Bear sometime. He'd like that story."

He put the box to the side and pulled me onto his lap, kissing me hard.

"That . . . that was what Noah had been going after." I frowned as my memories swirled around me, teasing me forward. "The first time Noah came to my house after the accident, I didn't know it was him but . . . he stripped my bedroom and took the family Bible. But that was just a ruse, I think, something to throw me off. We're looking for a gray metal box with two stars etched onto it, just like these." I waved the paper and then tucked it away again.

I stepped through the rubble of my home, the only true home I'd ever known, and the anger in me sparked and grew.

I was going to end this chess game. I was going to bring Bear home and we were going to start again.

I could see the house in my mind's eye, the rooms laid

out, the hallways, the kitchen and bathrooms. I stopped moving, standing in what had been the center of the home, the main living room. Bits and pieces of the furniture peered through the stacks of charred lumber. I was surprised that there was anything left, to be honest. Which meant at some point, the fire trucks had arrived and put the flames out, or at least I assumed that. Maybe the town had just let it burn. That wouldn't surprise me.

Killian lifted a chunk of wood and flipped it to one side. "Unless you know exactly where he might have hidden the box, we could be here a long time. And then there is your dear brother. He could come back at any point and try to finish things."

Time was not something we had. I crouched, thinking of all the places Justin might have hidden the box containing the things we needed. "Dinah, did anyone ever come into the barn?"

"What, into our room?" She snorted. "Only you."

I frowned, turned and stared down at the barn, a thought hitting me hard. "When . . . when I came for you and Eleanor right after I lost Bear and Justin, you said it had been months since you'd seen me last."

"Right." She sounded confused, but my heart had begun to beat very fast.

"Dinah, I hadn't been into that room in years. But you said months. I just didn't think about it at the time. What did I do when I came in prior to that day?"

"Holy shit," she whispered. "You had a box in your hands. A box you tucked in behind some of the guns. We tried talking to you but you ignored us and just went right back out. Someone . . . looked like you? An illusionist like me, maybe?"

My heart wasn't slowing. I couldn't slow it because I

didn't want to believe the truth that was pouring through me. Slowly I turned to look at Killian. "I only know one chameleon. Is it possible he could look like other people?"

"Simon." Killian breathed out the name. "It's possible, and it would make sense with his other abilities."

I put a hand to my head. "But if Simon . . . was here then, months before the accident, why didn't he try to kill me then? How did he get the box from Justin and why the fuck did he hide it?"

Part of my brain tried to tell me what I didn't want to see, and that only made my anger rise. I backed off the pile of rubble.

Killian's eyes went soft and I could see that he'd come to a conclusion. "Lass. Do you not see who he is? Or would you rather I say it out loud?"

"God," I whispered. "I took his head. He killed Zee and I took his head," I whispered through the horror as it hit me just what had happened.

The pieces slid together, and even though I didn't understand every single step, I knew it. Simon was a chameleon.

Simon was Justin.

I'd taken Simon's head and in effect killed Bear's father. I spun and threw up on the burned charred bits of the home we'd lived in for more than ten years together. Laughing, loving, raising Bear. I puked until my stomach was empty of anything that resembled food or fluid.

A cool breeze brushed over my face.

Martin.

A hand touched my back.

Killian.

I thought about meeting Simon for the first time.

How he'd acted as though he loved me from the beginning. How he'd known about things I liked without asking, like my coffee. Remembering the hotel room when I'd been sick, dying, and he'd fought to keep me alive, and how I'd seen his face then, how I'd thought he'd been Justin for just a moment.

How jealous he'd been of Killian.

I didn't understand how it was possible. I only knew it was true. Simon was Justin, and I'd killed my own husband in a fit of rage.

15

I kept backing away from the rubble of my home, the rubble of my heart, and the memories of the man at the center of it. The man I'd once loved and thought loved me. I struggled to breathe around the realization that Simon hadn't been Simon at all.

Simon . . . was Justin.

Killian spoke to me but his words were a white humming noise that didn't penetrate the shock that had a hold on me. I shook my head. "I'm going to get the box. Stay here."

I needed a few minutes to clear away the buzzing going on in my brain. This was all too much and I wasn't sure I could handle what was being thrown at me. Justin. Simon. The same man? Why hadn't he told me? Why hadn't he tried to save Bear on his own if he'd known that he was with Romano? He had to have known that Bear was with Romano. There was no way he couldn't.

So many things made sense now, though. Like how Abe had always liked Simon. How he'd never once growled at him. The way Simon had found me so easily. How he'd known so much and yet acted like he knew so little. Pretended not to have done his homework to keep from letting too much slip. All of it lined up with the truth as I saw it now. Right down to the fact that I'd not been good at being able to see if Simon was lying or not, the same way I'd not been able to see if Justin had been lying or not.

"Fuck, shit, damn." I hit the side of the barn before I stepped through the door, rattling the wooden boards.

I grabbed the sliding door and yanked it shut behind me, blocking me from Killian's sight. In the semi-darkness of the barn I let myself feel everything. The anger that stemmed from the lies, but more than that, the hurt and shock. I bent at the waist and put my hands on my thighs.

"Dinah, Simon was Justin. Justin didn't die, he . . . he didn't come back to me. He ran the fuck away. He didn't really love me." I stood up as *that* realization bitch-slapped me. Justin could have come back to me, but he hadn't. And he hadn't gone after Bear either. He'd just fucked off, not bothering to come to me until I'd made my way back to New York and he'd been contracted to kill me. Probably that was a ruse too. My breath came in short gasps as I tried to keep up with my heart. It beat so fast, I was sure it was going to explode. I slid to my knees, shaking. I could barely think through the truth as it tightened its hold on me.

"He . . . couldn't have loved us. If I'd even suspected he was alive, I would have searched for him." I shook, my muscles reacting to the shock, and I couldn't stop the involuntary movement.

"Why would he do that?" Dinah asked. "Why would he leave you all alone? Why wouldn't he tell you the truth? Why wouldn't he just . . . I don't even know what to say, Nixi. I'm sorry you were married to a selfish asshole . . ."

She trailed off and I knew the feeling, because I didn't know what to say any more than she did.

"Dinah, he'd been trying to get me to fall back in love with him when I was truly myself, as Nix. But I'd only loved him when I'd been pretending to be the perfect little housewife."

"You were born a tiger, Nix," she said. "And you hid as a lamb, and it was the lamb he loved. But your stripes were always going to show through. You were never meant to be a meek woman who feared the world, who needed to be protected. Maybe he didn't understand that."

I put a hand over her in her holster, the closest thing to a hug I could give her. "Thank you."

"Killian is a tiger," Dinah went on. "That's why it works. Why it will work when this is done."

I swallowed hard. "Nothing is working until Bear is safe. And that means all this shit with the past needs to be pushed aside."

"I don't understand one thing. He loved Bear, didn't he?" Dinah asked the question I didn't really have an answer to. "Why would he risk Bear?"

"I don't know that he knew Bear was at risk. Maybe he just wanted to be free of being trapped in Jackson Hole with us. I don't know." I pressed my hands into my face and then stood, my resolve firming once more as I shoved all the emotions to the back of my heart. I needed to have my focus and that meant I needed to not give a shit about anyone else.

Zee was right, emotions would be the death of me. One step at a time, and then when everything was done, I would deal with whatever the past was. With a lot of therapy. And maybe a lot of chocolate.

"I need that box before we do anything else. We need the ingredients for the bullet." I strode to where the hidden mechanism was that would let me into my stash of weapons inside the barn. I reached up under the saddle and pulled the lever, and the covered doorway swung inward. I found the light and pulled the cord, turning it on with a click. The light bloomed, swaying a little from the force of me turning it on. I lifted a hand to still it.

"Dinah, do you remember where he put the box?" I struggled to speak as my anger ebbed and flowed through my body. I couldn't escape the truths that had been thrown at me, much as I wanted to. Justin had been with me all along. He could have told me what he knew. I paused, struggling to breathe around a particularly tough moment of rage that blacked out my vision. We could have gotten Bear back, and more than that, I would never have grieved for my son. I would have known from the beginning that he was alive. Justin, Simon, whoever he really was had let me suffer.

"Motherfucker." I growled the word under my breath as I fought to keep from screaming it.

"In the back corner on the right-hand side," Dinah said. "Underneath the rocket launcher. I'm guessing he figured you wouldn't be using that any time soon."

I strode to the back of the room and lifted the launcher out carefully. Underneath it lay the metal box with the two stars etched into it, covered with a thin layer of dust. I picked the box up and blew across the top. The stars had rusted since I saw them last, making them rough under my fingers. I opened the box and inside there was a note folded on top with my name, my real name, printed on it in Justin's handwriting.

"He knew all along, Daniel was right about that much," I said. I didn't know if I should have been surprised at that point.

"Makes sense in a weird kind of way," Dinah said softly.

"Didn't you ever wonder at the circumstances of how he met you, of how quickly you fell for him?"

I thought back to that moment I was sure I loved him. We'd been on a few dates and he introduced me to Noah. The three of us had laughed and talked for hours, and by the end of the night, I'd felt the closest thing to love that I'd experienced in years. I wanted to be with Justin, wanted to spend my life with him. To make a life with him. Before that . . . he'd been a fling, a person to hide with for a little while before I moved on to somewhere else. How had I lost my heart that fast, how had I done such a big turnaround?

I shook my head. "It makes sense now. But I was blind to him, Dinah. How could I have been so stupid? I'm trained to pick up on shit like this and yet I didn't. Not for a second."

"I don't know," she said. "But it doesn't matter at this moment in time. What matters is that we are close to killing Romano and that means we are close to getting Bear back."

I drew a breath and let it out. The paper tugged at me, though. I held it in one hand and peered into the box. Inside were the remaining ingredients I needed as part of the bullet—minus the ruby ring for the grindings of a curse. The different herbs would have taken time, some of them rarer than rare. This was going to save us running all over the countryside, at least. I closed the lid and looked at the paper in my hand.

I drew a breath and flipped it open.

DEAR PHOENIX,

YES, I KNOW WHO YOU ARE. I'VE ALWAYS KNOWN WHO YOU ARE. *Strike gave me an offer I couldn't refuse. You see, I belong to him.*

I am his slave for reasons I won't get into here. He offered me twelve years to live normal, to have a wife, and to have a family. He would leave me alone for all that time. But then he would come for me at the end of it. I didn't understand then why he would give me that offer, but I took it. I'd never been free from him, and I doubt I ever will be.

You see, the deal involved you. I was to keep an eye on you, and keep you safe. Strike knew you would be needed if Romano was ever going to be killed—I learned that later. It's taken me all that time to gather the herbs you see here. Some are so rare that they are nearly extinct. Some don't exist on the books at all but reside only in lore. That's what I was doing on all those trips away, hunting them down, finding them piece by piece, putting this together, so we could stop Romano. I thought it would free me from Strike.

Of course, if you're reading this now, it means you think I'm dead. I'm not. I'm an abnormal who can respawn no matter how I'm killed. I wish sometimes that weren't the case. I've lived a long time, and that time has made me very tired.

I had to stop there and catch my breath. He could *respawn*? Did that mean he was alive even now? I wasn't sure how I felt about that. I'd killed him as Simon and taken his head. Surely no one could have survived that.

Could they?

"What does it say?" Dinah prompted me.

"Let me finish," I said, then started reading again.

I love you, Nix. With all that I am. And I love our boy. I didn't think No, I know I couldn't have loved anyone like I love that boy of ours. I hope he never has to see the dark side of the abnormal world. That's why I agreed to this, when Strike came to me ten years ago, after Bear was born. He told me that I could keep you both safe if I helped him put together what was needed for the bullet.

I agreed.

He told me that when Romano was dead, I would be set free. But I knew that was a lie. I'm attached to Strike, he is my creator. I believe when Romano dies and Strike is no longer needed on this plane of existence, he will go back to Hell. And I believe I will go with him.

I closed my eyes and took another breath, unable to keep reading straight through. I needed to gather my strength for the rest of it. Slowly, I opened my eyes and read on once more, no prompting from Dinah needed.

I hope you can forgive me for all the lies. I know you likely won't and that's okay. I know that I am a coward and a fool for letting myself love you the way I did. Because I know you didn't love me back the same way, though I think you did the best you could.

Take this box, you only need two more things to complete the spell and create the bullet. You need one of Romano's ruby rings. And you need a blood-soaked piece of the past. I never understood that part and neither did Strike.

Dinah or Eleanor needs to shoot the bullet at Romano. It will kill him if you hit him between the eyes. Only then will the deal that Bazixal has on him be broken. All the souls of his children will be safe.

I LOVE YOU, NIX. YOU AND BEAR ARE THE ONLY ONES I WOULD die for if the time ever came that I could give my life for you.

JUSTIN

I LET THE PAPER FLUTTER TO THE GROUND. HE PLANTED THIS while we were still married. Since then, I'd cut his head off when he was Simon, and he'd impossibly come back. I'd threatened to kill him, treated him like shit and he'd come back.

But . . . he was right. I never really loved him, not like I loved . . . Killian. And despite his pretty words, I wasn't sure he'd ever loved me or Bear. I could forgive him for not loving me. I couldn't forgive him for not fighting for Bear, for not loving our boy enough to go after him.

"What are you going to do?" Dinah asked, her voice filled with concern. I snapped the box shut. I spoke as I lifted the floorboard for the stashed money I had there. I pulled one of the bigger bags out, knowing it held an even million in it.

"I'm not sure yet. But if I ever see him again, I'll probably see if that respawning deal is real."

Dinah laughed. "Damn, good. See? You aren't going soft."

I clutched the box under one arm, slung the bag over the other, and walked out of the barn, feeling as if I were not truly awake, like this was some sort of strange fever dream.

I walked up to where Killian and Abe stood waiting for me.

Killian took a step and lifted his hand, but didn't touch me. "Did you get what you needed for Brikoff?"

I gave a sharp nod and handed him the bag of money. "Mostly. We need a ruby ring, one of my father's or the boys'." But that wasn't quite right. "No, we need the original one, the one my father wore."

The three of us started toward the truck, moving without truly knowing where we were going, but I knew we had to move. Killian was right about that.

"Where to then?" he asked.

My jaw ticked as a thought coursed through me. There was one place I was almost certain that held the ring. Daniel had been looking for something at Vivian's. Once more my instincts said that was the place to go, to find what it was we were looking for, because she had stolen a trinket from my father. The possibility that it was the ring was high.

The pieces made sense and I nodded to myself. "Seattle. But first we get the bullet as it is from Brikoff. Then we'll fill it when we have everything together."

Killian took the driver's seat without argument and got the truck moving, backing us out of the place that had been the home of my heart, and the seat of so many lies. I shook my head, banishing those thoughts. Forward, I was moving forward because that was where Bear was.

And there was nothing that was going to stop me this time from ending Romano and saving my son.

Not even a guardian from Hell or a husband raised from the dead.

16

BEAR

The Grotto was Shaitan's place of residence, and somehow my grandfather had ousted him and his people when he came to the desert, according to my uncle Tommy anyway.

"The Grotto is protected right now by Strike, the last of my father's guardians," Tommy said. "Shaitan can't take them down because Strike is stronger than him, so at least in terms of that, we don't have to worry. Cooper here knows the way."

Cooper—the driver—gave us a nod, but said nothing.

We bumped along in the vehicle on the desert road, with no seatbelts, and only minimal handholds. My mom would not be happy about that.

I gripped the handhold closest to me until my knuckles ached. "Why would that matter to him if he's immortal? Keeping Shaitan out?"

"That's the question I'd like to know, kid." Tommy's face was grim. "I don't think he's immortal. I think it's a head game to throw us off. Nobody, not even abnormals are immortal. Which means he can be killed. Just like any of us. Which is what I'm going to do with Eleanor here."

A chill slid through me that I had to fight to keep from shaking my legs. Rooster noticed, though, and gave my shoulder a pat.

"It's smart to be afraid, Bear. Fear will keep you alive. Sometimes it's better to run away than to face what's coming."

I glanced at him, then turned away. "That's not what my mom would say."

"Well, she ain't here, is she?" he grumbled back, his face dipping into a frown.

There was something in his tone that made me think maybe . . . "Did you know my mom?"

Rooster let out a sigh. "Yeah, I did. What seems like a long time ago. We were . . . friends."

Friends. "Then why didn't you let me go in New York? I could have escaped easier. I could have gotten farther away. Why would you help my grandfather?" The words came out fast and louder with each syllable.

He held up his hands in surrender. "You can't understand, kid. I'm not the person I was then. Okay?"

I twisted away from him, angry. I'd saved his life, healed his broken face, and he'd sworn to help me. But if he'd been my mom's friend all along, it made no sense as to why he would have helped Romano keep me essentially jailed.

I hunched my shoulders, pretending to fall asleep. After a while, the two men talked in low tones and I listened, storing away their words.

"How exactly are we going to get into the Grotto?" Rooster asked. "Last I checked, it was not circled by fences, men, and guns, but by several abnormals with abilities we do not want to deal with. Like your brother, for instance."

Tommy snorted. "Danny is off searching for what he believes is Dad's ring. Dad told him if he couldn't find it, he couldn't be considered as the first in line for the throne, as it was. He's been looking for years."

"So, we don't have to worry about the necro then?" Rooster grunted and the leather seat squeaked as he shifted his weight. "That's something at least."

"Yeah. The plan is to go in in the early morning, right when the sun rises. He'll be expecting us at night, not during the day. And he's shit on the time difference so I'm banking on some jet lag."

I sat up then, unable to help myself. "Are you sure Luca will be there? How do you know?"

Tommy looked at me and the gun in his hand sniffed, beating him to the punch.

"He doesn't know, Bear. He's guessing," Eleanor said.

My mouth opened wide as I stared at my uncle. "What do you mean he's guessing? Luca was here with us; he thinks I'm dead. He tried to kill Rooster."

Rooster shifted uncomfortably as Tommy's eyes shot to him. "Romano tried to kill you?"

"Shot him," I said.

Tommy's eyes narrowed further and then he launched himself at Rooster. Rooster didn't fight him, just let him slam into his body.

"What are you doing?" I yelled.

"Getting his memories," Tommy yelled back at me. "He just admitted he isn't who we think he is, didn't you?"

Rooster grunted. "I'm not a danger!"

"Pick me up," came a soft voice, barely heard over the noise. I looked at the seat where Tommy had been. The gun, my mother's gun, was on the leather seat. "Switch me out with Linx."

Linx, the tool that could be anything I wanted it to be. "Linx." I touched the weapon that was still strapped to my chest under my shirt.

"On it."

The two men wrestled and Tommy was yelling, oblivious to me.

Or to what I was doing.

Everything happened so fast, I didn't think about why I was listening to a gun, but I did it. I yanked Linx out and he was already a matte-black gun that looked just like the one on the seat. I laid him down and scooped her up, tucking her under my shirt and into the waistband of my pants. Thank God my shirt was big and billowy.

"Good boy," the gun said softly. "My name is Eleanor. Use me, and I will protect you. I will help you aim."

The wrestling stopped as suddenly as it started. I twisted around to see Tommy with his hands locked on either side of Rooster's face. "No fucking way," Tommy whispered.

"Satisfied now? I'm going to protect the kid no matter what," Rooster snarled and pushed Tommy away with a big meaty hand.

"You can't tell him. You can't." Tommy's eyes flicked ever so slightly to me. As if I wouldn't notice.

"Tell me what?" Fear spiked in me. What was it now? What didn't I know?

"I know, that part of my life is over. I understand that, as much as I hate it," Rooster snarled, and he looked almost like . . . like he was going to cry. Which did nothing to help the fear swirling through my body.

"It will be okay," Eleanor whispered. "It will, child." Her words shouldn't have soothed me but they reminded me of my mom, of her certainty in making things happen. My heart rate slowed and eased into a normal pace.

Tommy leaned back in his seat and reached for Linx. He picked the new gun up and tucked it into a holster on his hip. I swallowed hard but he didn't notice the change in his weapons.

"Rooster is here to keep you safe, kid. Never doubt it," Tommy said. "I read his memories to make sure he was on the level. And while there *are* things he didn't tell us, they don't matter now. He's on the up and up."

Rooster's jaw ticked with anger, something I'd seen on a few men. But . . . I swallowed hard, my instincts telling me something I didn't think was possible. "Are . . . you . . . my—"

"No." Rooster shook his head but he wouldn't meet my eyes with his own. "Don't even think it. I'm not him."

But the thing was, as soon as I thought it, I couldn't unthink the words even inside my head. The possibility that somehow Rooster was my *father*. It was ridiculous, impossible, and yet the change in him since I healed his face . . . I'd been unconscious for days. Was it possible to think my dad had switched bodies, or his soul had somehow come into Rooster's body? With everything I'd seen in the last few months, I felt like it was at least possible.

I bit my lower lip to hold back the questions and the sudden onslaught of tears. Wanting something so badly—like having my dad back—maybe I was making it real when it wasn't.

"Here's what's going to happen," Tommy said. "We're going to make camp about thirty minutes from the Grotto. From there, we'll go in on foot, walking through the last hours of the night. I have someone on the inside. They're going to let us in so we won't have to deal with any of the defenses."

"What if Luca isn't there?" I asked. "He could have left already."

"He was headed this way for a meeting with Shaitan and the desert witch. Unless that's already happened," Tommy said with a rueful grin, "which I doubt since I—I mean, we —stirred that ant's nest, which then means we have time. Romano won't stick around once the meeting is done."

"Why not?" I asked.

"Because he doesn't like Shaitan and he doesn't like the heat here. There is something about that desert sheik that even Romano fears." Tommy shook his head. "I don't know what or why, but he does. Which should show you just how bad he is."

The vehicle began to slow and Tommy twisted around. "Here we are, camp."

Camp turned out to be a pile of large boulders with a few tents in between for cover and protection from the desert wind and sun.

Two other vehicles and about six men waited for us, waving or saluting Tommy when he slid out of the truck and stretched to his full height. Every one of them had some sort of weapon slung over their back. I saw a rocket launcher with one of them. That did not bode well.

Tommy strode away and I watched him go. Rooster dropped a big hand on my shoulder and steered me toward one of the clusters of boulders. Once in the shade of the big rock, he turned me to face him. "You still trust me?"

I thought about it a moment and decided to plunge right into the deep end. "You . . . somehow you're him, aren't you?"

I didn't say the word dad, or father; I didn't need to. I already knew. I just wanted Rooster to confirm it.

His jaw tightened and he went to one knee in front of me. "Listen to me. I know you have Eleanor."

My guts twisted, but he shook his head. "No, I'm not going to take her from you. Trust me when I say she will protect you no matter what happens. Tommy does not have everything he needs to kill Romano. I know it, and this is a fool's errand."

I knew it.

"The desert witch said I needed to go with Tommy, to see this through," I said.

Rooster lowered his head so that his chin touched his chest. "I don't know why she would say that, but . . . damn it, I know she hates Romano. So, she won't do anything that would help him."

I thought for a moment. "But it still might get us hurt."

He lifted his head and nodded. "Yeah, that's the problem."

"What do we do?" I asked softly.

Eleanor cleared her throat. "Tommy is going to be killed by his father. He'll go to shoot him and he'll fail. You must know he would have failed if I had been in his hands too. At least this way, Romano won't have me. That would be very bad."

"Why?" I whispered the one-word question.

"Because if he figured out who I really was and what I was capable of, then I'm not sure even Phoenix could stop him." Her words were like stones in my belly as they hit hard with the realization of what she was saying. "No matter what, I cannot come into Romano's hands."

"Agreed," Rooster said softly. "So, we need to go. We need to run away while we can."

I stared at him, knowing who he was, but seeing him through a different, wiser set of eyes. "We can't always run, Dad."

He startled as if I'd smacked him in the face.

"Sometimes running is all you have left," he bit back at me, then stood and walked away.

There was silence for a moment before I felt Eleanor shift a little, gaining my attention. I put a hand over her. "Eleanor?"

"I think you're right to stay. Your mother will be coming for you, and for Romano. If you are together, you can help her. I can help her. If you run away . . ."

"Then she'll be on her own." I shook my head. "I won't run from her. Not like him." I tipped my head toward Rooster.

She sighed. "You have her heart. Fierce like a lion."

A little trickle of warmth slid through me. "Thank you."

"Bear, I . . . I am glad to get to know you. At least, a little. Your mother spoke highly of you always. About how much she loved you. And when she thought you were dead . . . I wasn't sure she would ever come back from that grief."

My eyes welled up. "Same for me, when I thought she was gone. When I thought they were both gone forever." I watched Rooster walk across to Tommy. "Maybe I really only have my mom left."

"He'll still protect you," she said softly. "Even if he isn't who you hoped. That happens with parents sometimes. We don't see what they sacrifice until they are gone."

The truth of what had been shown to me finally sunk in, and with it, I went to the ground with the weight of who Rooster was. That he'd run away, that he'd left me and my mom to fight for ourselves without any thought of whether we were okay. "I wish he'd never come back."

Eleanor sighed. "Let's hope that by the end of this, he figures out what's really important to him. If not, then I don't think he'll survive. Because if Romano doesn't kill him . . ."

I nodded, understanding. "Then my mom will."

"Yes," she said softly. "I think so too."

17

PHOENIX

I stood at the doorway of the fishing lodge, the sound of the Snake River in my ears, Killian and Abe in the truck behind me, waiting. Brikoff, Russian mobster and abnormal with abilities that meant he could make anything with metal, held out a single golden bullet to me. "It's primed, you just have to cap it, and I imbued it with some added strength so it will drive into whatever it is you shoot it at," he said.

I held out the bag of cash—a million dollars—and he took it, holding it limply. As if it meant nothing to him. I lifted an eyebrow and he shrugged.

"You don't seem to care about the money now," I said.

"I wanted to know how badly you wanted this bullet. I want to offer you the money back if you tell me why you think this golden bullet will kill that Romano pig." That smirk on his face from the scar seemed to taunt me.

I rolled the bullet in my hand. "You wouldn't believe me if I told you."

He snorted. "You'd be surprised. Not all the places of this world have such a balanced relationship between humans and abnormals. Russia . . . it is the wild west of that world. I have seen more than I wish to when it comes to strangeness."

"Is that why you're here?" I arched an eyebrow. "Just a vacation?"

He smirked. "Nothing is ever a vacation, and no, I'm not sharing my reason for being here with you."

I thought not.

I didn't need the money, and I didn't want to share more secrets than I had to, any more than he did. "No. My secrets are my own, as are yours to you." I'd only taken a few steps when he stopped me with five little words.

"I know where Emerald is."

Emerald, my niece. I stopped moving, turned and looked at him. That smirk, and the bright blue of his eyes, told me everything I needed. He wasn't lying. The decision was easy.

"You first," I said.

"She's in Europe," he said with more pride than he should have.

"That's a fucking lot of ground to cover for being so damn pleased with yourself." I turned away even while Dinah gasped and shimmied in her holster. I put a hand on her. "Wait."

"She's with a group that works to quiet the abnormal abilities in children. They aren't hurting her but they are keeping her powers from growing."

I kept very still. "She like her mother?"

He grunted. "You wish. She is like her father, able to manipulate the people around her, tampering with their brains."

"What is the group called?"

"The Healers."

I didn't hesitate. "What will be put in the bullet are several things, all which are detailed in the original deal between Romano and the devil that made him immortal. It's the only thing that will kill him."

"Holy shitballs," he grumbled. "Then I wish you luck, killing your father."

My spine stiffened but I started walking again. Our business was done here. That would have to be enough. I got back to the truck and Killian put it in gear, taking us straight to the airport.

Killian didn't say anything for the longest time. Mostly because Dinah wouldn't shut up.

"Emerald, I can't believe we know where she is!"

"We don't," I reminded her as gently as I could. "But she's safe, and that counts for a lot." Though I'd thought Bear was safe too when he wasn't. There was no good in reminding Dinah of that little nugget of truth.

She chattered on and on about how great it was going to be to see Emerald, to see how she'd grown up.

"I'm sure she'll be as beautiful as you," I said in an attempt to slow her down. "But again, we are not going for her yet, Dinah. Not yet."

There was a grinding from the holster. As if her frustration came through the metal itself.

The airport came into view and lucky for us, Killian's plane was still there. Not so lucky, it was surrounded by cops.

Killian put the truck in park and we got out, Abe trotting in between us. As if he could protect us both.

"How are we going to do this?" Killian asked. "I am assuming you don't want to kill them all."

While there were dirty cops in town, the last thing we needed was to add a police tail to this little jaunt. Which meant we had to distract the cops long enough to make this happen.

"Give me your phone," I said, and he handed it over.

I dialed 9-1-1 and waited for the receptionist to pick up before I let out a shout that startled Abe and Killian at the same time. "Hurry, there's a shootout in the center of town! Two gunmen, dressed all in black. They just ducked into the park, through the archway! I don't know if—" I hung up and handed the phone back to Killian.

"They won't fall for that, will they?" Killian's quizzical expression made me smile.

"Small town. They won't realize for a good long time." We kept walking, and then all of a sudden, the cops around the plane went wild with activity.

I'd kicked the ant's nest good on this one, as my brother Tommy liked to say. The three police cruisers peeled out of the airport, sirens and lights flashing as they raced toward town.

"How long?" Killian asked.

"Ten-minute drive each way at that speed," I said. "Thirty minutes or more to realize no gunmen. Rest of the day to figure out that they should have come back to the plane sooner." I smiled at him. "This is what comes from living in a small town like this."

"I see. I could get used to that," he said.

I chose to ignore his words and turned instead to hurrying up. Because while I was pretty sure I was right about the timing, there was always the chance that one of the new cops was smarter than the rest of the pack.

Or, as it was in this actual case, a cop was left behind.

I saw him standing on the far side of the plane as we approached. He stepped around the wheel so we could get a good look at him. Only he wasn't just any old cop.

Noah.

"Noah, what the fuck are you doing here?"

He touched the badge on his shirt, a tight smile on his face. "Official business."

"You were never FBI," I said, remembering that the last time I'd seen him, I'd thrown him out of the helicopter. "And how the hell did you survive that fall?"

He smiled at me, blue eyes sad. "There's a lot you don't know about me. About this abnormal world. It'll get you killed one day."

Killian had slowed. "I don't remember him."

"He's . . . been helpful but also a pain in the ass liar," I said. "Much like Simon."

Noah tipped his head. "Have I been that bad? Here I've been doing my damndest to keep you on the right track. To help you kill Romano."

"Well, you've done nothing but lie your face off and get in my fucking way." I pushed him out of my way to prove my point. I jumped up and grabbed the cord to pull the stairs down for the plane.

Noah reached up and helped me pull it down. "I'm coming with you."

I snorted. "No, you're not."

"I can still help."

I glared at him over the stairs. "You wouldn't survive me throwing you out of the plane at ten thousand feet, and I might just do that."

He grinned. "And I might surprise you."

I had Dinah up in a flash, before the smile could leave his lips. "You're an abnormal?"

"No."

Well, that made no sense. "Then you wouldn't survive."

Martin brushed next to me, his voice quiet. *Demon.*

I stumbled away from Noah, fucking stumbled. "Martin."

Noah frowned. Killian frowned. My heart kicked into high gear. Noah was a demon? How could I have missed that? And was he . . . was he Bazixal? No, he couldn't be that one. I had to believe I would know if I was facing the demon who'd haunted my dreams for so long.

"I can still help you," Noah repeated.

I had to think, and think fast. "Fine. Can you fly?"

Killian stiffened, but otherwise he gave no reaction. Noah frowned. "Yeah, I can. You want me to fly this plane for you?"

"We're headed to the Middle East next. We're flying to the East Coast and—"

He shook his head. "You still need a ruby ring. We both know that so don't try lying to me of all people. You're right, there is one in Vivian's lair, but it's guarded by her friends. I can't cross the threshold or I would have gotten it already."

How did he know this? "Why the fuck wouldn't you tell us this sooner?" I yelled the words because he'd put me so off balance. Gone was my cool as a cucumber routine. "We were there, inside her damn house. We could have gotten it!"

"You wouldn't have thought it a priority then." He shrugged. "Now, hopefully you do. Also, I don't think this plane is a good idea. The police have it marked."

Killian muttered under his breath.

I didn't know what to say. I only knew that I was being pushed in a direction I didn't want to go.

Noah flexed his hand. "Come on, there's a plane leaving for Seattle in a matter of minutes. We can get it."

"I'm not leaving Abe behind." I was stalling, throwing anything I could to stop this from happening. Whatever the hell this was. It felt like ants inside my head, working their way through my brain.

Killian, though, already followed Noah. "It's the best plan yet, Lass."

I wasn't so sure, but I fell into step behind Killian. "Like lambs to the slaughter," I whispered.

Neither of the men heard me.

Noah led the way through the airport. He flashed his badge a few times and pointed to us, and we were let through with nothing more than a cursory glance or two. How the hell was he doing this? I didn't think the FBI had that much say. I was still wearing my Kevlar, guns and knives right out in the open.

Martin's one word came back to me stronger than before. Demon.

"Martin," I whispered. "Stick close."

With pleasure. A cold wash whispered over my ass and I rolled my eyes. What did I care? He wasn't truly touching me, and he may have given me my first understanding of what and who Noah was.

Noah had us in first class, all four of us. The airline attendant didn't even blink at the big, unleashed dog that walked into the cabin, though a few other passengers did before they looked away. Again, Noah just flashed his badge. "Air marshal" was what he said. Another lie, of course.

Abe lay on the floor at my feet, across my toes. Killian sat next to me, and I had the window seat.

"This feels surreal," I said to him, pitching my voice low.

"Let's talk about how sure we are that the ring is at Vivian's. You said we killed her, so it should be an easy toss of the house, right?" His green eyes were serious and I leaned into him a little.

"Vivian's," I said. "I'm not sure it will be so easy. If she left friends to guard her home, then it will be harder than walking in and tossing the place. Don't forget that the house is guarded by Daniel's creations, on purpose or not, they were there. Was he guarding her or what was in the house?"

"The ring." Killian nodded. "Whose, though?"

I thought through it. "She was sleeping with Romano, we know that much. Maybe he . . . maybe he gave her the ring at some point? Or maybe she took it? That would explain why she was able to fly under the radar for so long. Why none of the Magelore hunters ever found her if she could use it for protection. It also explains how Romano knew she was in Seattle. That was where he was going to send me."

Noah leaned back in his seat across from us. "Tell me when we land." He tipped his head back, closed his eyes and promptly went to sleep. Abe did the same, keeping his head on his paws and snorting in his sleep.

The plane took off and we were in the air before we resumed our quiet conversation. Almost like a real couple discussing the day's events while they headed out on a vacation together. The fantasy was there and gone in a flash, because I knew it was just that. A total and complete fantasy. More and more, despite how well we worked together, despite the feelings I had for him.

I could feel the final fights coming, like a growing pressure under my skin reminding me I was not immortal like Romano. I was not indestructible, and neither was Killian. For that matter, neither was Bear. None of us were above being killed.

I closed my eyes as I spoke to Killian. "He sent me after her, when I assume they broke off their love affair." I could still see Romano in my mind's eye.

He strode back in forth behind his desk, far more agitated than I'd seen him in a long time. His dark hair was a mess from running his fingers through it and his eyes were more than a little wild as he stared at nothing. He clenched his fingers over and over again and I stood quietly, waiting.

There was no fear in me anymore, not of him. He'd lost that power over me when I'd learned to kill without feeling. The only worry I had was that he'd somehow discovered my plans to escape, that maybe Barron had confessed our plans to him out of fear.

I shouldn't have worried.

"There is a female Magelore I want you to hunt down and kill." My father bit the words out as if they were poison. "She stole something from me, and I want it back."

I didn't arch an eyebrow, didn't snort at him, though I wanted to do both. Right now, I was all about not provoking him so he wouldn't see what I was doing until it was too late.

"What is her name and do you have a rough location?" I asked.

"Vivian. Seattle." He almost growled her name, which made me wonder at their relationship. I had to fight to keep myself from shuddering. God, who would want to fuck a dirty Magelore?

I nodded. "And the item?"

"You will contact me when you have killed her. I will come for the item myself." He swung around so his eyes were locked on mine. On his one hand, he spun the large ruby ring he wore, the ring that connected him to his guardians. Not that he'd needed them to protect him, not when he had me. I let my eyes shut to half-mast.

"As you like." I was not going to argue with him. Not when I was so close to escaping.

"If it was his ring, then he took someone else's because he was wearing a ring when I took the order from him. And Vivian wasn't terribly surprised by my arrival. She even took Simon to try and use him against me, I think, despite the time lapse between when she took the ring and when I showed up." I didn't feel like calling Simon 'Justin'. In my book, Justin died, and that was going to be that. I refused to think about him out there, just living a life, not caring that his son was in danger, or that his wife was doing everything she could to save their child.

"But a Magelore's home, they are traps in themselves. If they have any treasure they truly love, their lairs can be even more dangerous after they die," Killian said.

"Yes." I closed my eyes fully and let myself reach over to him. He took my hand and laced his fingers through mine. Just like a normal couple.

If you didn't count the weapons on us, the magic in our blood, or the blood on our hands.

Normal.

Right.

"Excuse me," the airline steward said, her tag proclaiming her Patty.

I opened my eyes. "Yes?"

"Would you like something to drink?"

Killian leaned forward. "Champagne. She just agreed to marry me."

My jaw dropped and she squealed and clapped her hands. "Oh, lovely!"

Noah snorted in his sleep and opened one eye, then turned his back to us. Apparently, he wasn't really sleeping.

Patty was gone in a flash and I turned to Killian, spluttering. "What are you doing?"

"Getting us free champagne." He winked and I couldn't

catch the laugh that escaped me. A part of me said I shouldn't be laughing. I shouldn't enjoy this while Bear was in trouble, but the other more logical side of me pointed out the obvious. I'd almost lost Killian, and he'd been right about living in the moment. There had to be moments where the pressure eased or I would end up making a mistake. The intensity at which I'd been running since Bear had been taken was nothing short of insane. Even I knew that.

A few minutes later, we were brought a full bottle of champagne, on the house, of course.

"Oh, can I see the ring?" Patty grinned as she leaned forward.

"It's being sized," I said and held up my bare left hand. Her face was a perfect pout.

"Darn."

Bear would get a kick out of this story one day. How me and Killian boarded a commercial plane, flew with all our weapons, Abe at our feet like a giant lapdog, how the stewardess gave us free champagne for being fake engaged. I downed two glasses of the champagne as if they were shots and let the bubbling alcohol ease my mind enough that sleep stole over me.

The warmth of my hand in Killian's gave me a place to ground myself, but it didn't stop my fears from curling through my dreams.

I jerked and twitched as I saw those I loved killed as I relived the accident that had torn my world apart. As I searched for Bear and couldn't find him in a swamp thick with water and death. And then there was Killian staked out on a crucifix and my father below him. "Well done, daughter. Not conventional, but you made sure he faced me and now he's dead."

But it was Strike that sent the sharp spike of fear through me. His body came into focus slowly, walking toward me.

He said, "Bea thought I would like you, and she was right. I do. I'd hoped you'd turn to me after Justin was gone, but you aren't like that, are you?" He shook his head as he rolled something in his hand. The golden bullet. "You've done well so far. But my master wants you stronger. So please realize I do not want to do this, it is not my choice." His eyes were almost sad as he spoke to me. He lifted a hand to my face and caressed it gently. "Would have been easier if you'd turned to me, Nix."

I woke up hard, my heart beating so fast, it thrummed in my chest. My face and lower back were slick with sweat.

Killian slept beside me, oblivious to my dreams, which was good. I stood and made my way to the lavatory, letting myself into the overly small space. I splashed water on my face and stared into the mirror, something I hadn't done in a long time. I'd lost weight, leaned out even further until there was nothing but the burning of my eyes staring back at me under a fringe of my short black hair, peeking through the bangs.

I splashed a bit more water on me and below my feet the plane shivered. "Strike, you fucking bastard," I muttered. What the hell was it with all the planes I'd been on lately? Perfect traps, that's what they were. And Strike was using the fact that I was forced to travel at a rapid pace against me. As if the thought brought it on, the plane bucked and dipped.

I was out of the lavatory in a flash and Patty was right there, a smile plastered on her face. "Please take a seat, we've encountered some rough weather."

Rough weather, my ass. I hurried to my seat and Killian

didn't so much as blink. In fact, he continued to stare out the window, which did not bode well. "What is it?" I whispered. I glanced at Noah but he was not in his seat. Where the hell had he gone now?

"Not sure, but I wouldn't bet on anyone but you and me to survive them, Lass."

I leaned over him and looked out at the wide-open space. There were no clouds, so my view of what was causing the problems on the plane was clear as a summer day. Still, I struggled to comprehend what I was seeing. Killian unbuckled his seat and stood. "We need to land this plane now or everyone is going to die, us included."

I didn't stop him. I couldn't look away from the things—creatures—that scuttled over the wings of the commercial airliner. They were humanoid with wings, but they were small, and their feet and hands were tipped with claws and hooks that dug into the metal as they scrambled around the plane. Their skin was a solid black that reflected the light into a million different colors, like a crystal. One launched himself at my window, his belly and face flat to the thick plastic. Two of the hooked claws dug through so the tips came right into the interior. There was no screaming, though, from the other passengers. Were they not seeing this? I stood and peered back at the passengers. A few looked back. A few smiled at me.

And then a few teeth fell out of rotten mouths. I scrambled out of my seat. What fresh hell was this? That, I didn't know, but I did know who was the cause of it. "Fuck you, Daniel."

This was my brother's doing then, and I had to give him props on working with Strike. Neither Killian nor I had noticed that the entire fucking plane was made up of dead people. Hell, even Abe hadn't reacted then. Freshly dead, then, they had to be.

"Abe, *hier!*" I leapt into the aisle, Abe with me, and raced to the cockpit where the two pilots were arguing with Killian. Two other humans beside us, then? Where was Patty? I turned around and she lunged toward me, a bullet hole through her head. A bullet? Who had shot her? Noah?

I slammed the door on her face and slid the lock on it. "We have bigger problems than the little rat bastards that are trying to eat their way into the plane."

Both pilots stared at me and then they were yelling at me to get out. For Killian to get out. And then the first body —Patty's, most likely—slammed against the door and the smell of flesh rotting and bursting open slid through the vents.

"Daniel filled the plane with dead people," I said. "Strike helped him somehow."

Funny, I didn't hear Noah asking for help. Yelling to be let in. Maybe he was in the lavatory. I hesitated, thinking that maybe I should help him. Or try to. I put a hand to the doorknob and stopped, slowly drawing it back. No. I wouldn't sacrifice myself for a man I knew I couldn't trust. A man who put us on this fucking plane. A man that Martin said was a demon.

A truth of what was going on tried to work its way into my head but I shoved it away. Not now.

Killian's jaw ticked and he gave me a sharp nod. "Like I said, Captain, we need to land or we are going to die."

"We're not far from the airport, we can land, we can make it," the captain stuttered.

I shook my head and grabbed the edge of his seat as the plane listed to one side. "We aren't going to stay up in the air much longer if those gremlin things start taking out the engines, or we lose pressure, correct?" Even I knew that much about flying.

Killian pulled the co-pilot out of his seat and took his place. "There." He pointed at a long smooth chunk of highway. "That's our landing strip."

"People are going to die!" the captain yelled. "We can't do this."

I didn't look at Killian, I just put the captain into a headlock until his struggles stopped and then I pulled his now-unconscious body out of the seat. The co-pilot yelled at me and I whipped around with Dinah out. "He's not dead."

"Oh."

I waved at him to move to the captain's seat. "Help us land this plane. Now."

Several more thumps reverberated against the door between us and the dead mob. Abe whined and pressed himself against my legs. He'd protect me. I knew he would be scared. I felt it all the way through his lean body.

I recalled all too well the feeling of the dead bison coming for me, of their unwavering desire to end my life. This was not going to be any better than that if we didn't get away from the dead people in the back.

"I really wish I could just get a little airsick and call it a day for shitty flights," I muttered as the two men took the big plane toward the highway.

"Ah, but what's the fun in that?" Killian threw back at me as we dipped suddenly and my feet left the floor for a brief moment. Abe yelped and I grabbed hold of his collar, steadying him and me.

"It would be nice for a change," I grunted as I settled into a crouch. On the other side of the door came several heavy thuds. The dead ones had been thrown off their feet by that move.

A squeal of metal being torn echoed through the cab and the plane dipped on its own.

"The wee gremlins are in, I think," Killian said. "We've lost air pressure."

I agreed with him but kept my eyes on the door. That was where they would come through if we didn't land soon.

"Get us down. We need to be able to get the fuck away from this." As much as I wanted to fight, I knew this was a stall tactic. I didn't understand why Strike's master thought this was a good idea. And did he mean Romano or Bazixal? Didn't matter at the moment, either way it was pushing me to make a dangerous move. One that could end my life.

Nails scratched on the metal door and I took a slow breath. Those nails shot through the three-inch-thick metal as if it were nothing. "Dinah, can you shoot through?"

"Not unless you have some ammo I'm not aware of," she said.

The door began to peel away and the plane listed hard to the left. I rolled with it and ended up against the unconscious pilot, Abe sprawled on top of me.

"We'll be done in two minutes," Killian said.

Done could mean a number of things, so his words were not exactly comforting. I kept an arm tight around Abe's middle. "Stick with me, buddy."

The air pressure shifted and my ears were full of it, making the sounds around us muffled as if I were under water. Killian yelled something, and then the door was ripped off. I let go of Abe, somersaulted across the floor and came up with Dinah in one hand and a knife in the other. The first gremlin that came at me was about the size of a poodle and had hair on the top of its head that resembled that breed of dog.

I slashed at it with the knife and the blade snapped in half.

Well, that was unexpected. I had Dinah up and shot at the little bastard, nailing it in the chest. It flipped over backward, but there was no blood, no kill shot. I'd essentially shoved it back hard, but done no damage. It spread its wings and shot forward. I shot it again, it was all I could do.

And then its friends joined. Like a swarm of angry bees, they buzzed and chittered as a unit, and I could hear them through the pressure plug on my ears.

The nose of the plane suddenly dropped and the gremlins all shot out, away from us.

I spun around in time to see the highway coming up too fast, at too sharp of an angle. There was no sound of engines, and then the plane twisted as if something was lifting the tail over the nose, spinning us. Like a horde of gremlins doing their damndest to slam us into the ground.

There was no time to think. We were seconds from an up close and personal visit from death none of us would walk away from if I didn't do something.

My fire could kill and it could heal. But could it protect?

I managed to get a hand on Killian and one on the pilot. "ABE!" He shot to me, jamming himself under my legs. It was the best I could do. I opened myself to the fire with only one thought: to survive a fall that was meant to destroy us.

The purple and blue flames licked up around me, the heat a warmth that was security, safety and a sense of home. I clung to Killian's hand and he did the same. The co-pilot reached up and wrapped his hand around mine. Of course, he probably thought we were all going to die.

I wanted to believe he was wrong, but as the highway reached for us, as the plane twisted one last time in a death roll, I wasn't sure he was.

18

Free falling through the sky, not for the first time, I wondered if I would see my life flash before my eyes as so many people said they saw as they died. I didn't want that. If I was going to die, I wanted to see only one thing.

Bear's smile.

I wanted to see him as he grinned at me, laughing about something that was funny to only him and me. I held onto him as we fell and the flames shifted around us. The color trembled on the edge of a soft pink rather than the more usual sharp purples, blues, and reds. The color suffused our bodies and the world around us seemed to slow.

The plane's nose slammed into the concrete and exploded, shards of twisted metal and bursts of fire coming for us. But none of it touched us.

We were flipped over and over and I hung onto the men, and kept my legs as tight as I could on Abe, knowing that it was our only chance. Flame and metal, the scream of the plane being pulled apart a piece at a time, the crunch of the concrete erupting underneath us.

And then as quickly as it happened, we were no longer moving and the crash landing was over. There were still flames licking out of the place where the control panel had been, and I had to drag the co-pilot back. He'd passed out at some point.

"Killian, help me."

"On it," he grunted as he scooped up the body of the captain. "He's still alive, but I'm betting he's going to be bruised tomorrow."

I'll admit, my jaw dropped as I scooped the co-pilot under the arm and hauled him out through the wreckage. How was this even possible? I didn't have time to consider anything else. Abe had never stuck so close to my side.

"Martin?" Could a ghost be shoved away from all of that?

Still here. Going to take more than that to get rid of me.

There were bodies stirring even as we stepped over their twisted limbs. The undead were not going to be deterred by a mere plane crash. They reached for us as we passed and I kicked several, snapping more bones. Still they came on, moving toward us with an inexplicable motivation given to them by my brother. It made me wonder if the bison at the bottom of the cliff had risen on broken legs and backs and plodded after us. I shivered, seeing the image all too clearly.

We dragged the two men out and several bystanders rushed forward to help us. We handed the men off and then we were running through the completely stopped traffic. I let Killian lead mostly because my mind was on fire with the implications that Daniel's creatures would not stop. That he was strong enough that distance wasn't an issue at all.

And that Strike had to have helped him, if those gremlin things were any indication.

Killian crossed the highway to where the traffic was still

moving and flagged down a cab. We slid in and then he looked at me. "Where to?"

"Cherry Lane," I said. The house that didn't belong in the outskirts of Seattle, the house that looked like it had been plucked from the Southern bayous right down to the flora and fauna.

The cabbie drove without question. In the distance behind us I could see the flames of the plane burning. I didn't realize I was shaking until Killian touched me on the knee.

"It wasn't the crash that bothers you, is it?" He took his hand from me, giving me space.

"No."

I didn't need to say more than that. We'd survived a crash because of the myst in my blood, the abnormal part of me, and I'd saved two people. But the truth was we weren't out of the woods by a long shot. Daniel was obviously still coming for me and his creations were getting tougher to evade and survive. I managed to pull my shit together.

"Noah wasn't in that plane. How did he get out?" I asked.

"Fuck me. I don't know."

Demon, Martin whispered again, and Killian seemed to hear him this time if his face was any indication, the way it drained of color.

"Please tell me you heard that."

I snorted softly. "That's Martin. He came with us after the professor yelled at him."

"He just said—"

"Yeah, I know what he said. That's what he thinks Noah is." I rubbed a hand over my face, the last bits of my thoughts coming together finally. "If he is . . . I think . . . I think he might be someone else we are dealing with."

"What do you mean?" Killian frowned at me. "I don't understand."

"I dozed and I had a dream that Strike spoke to me again. He said he didn't want to do this—I assume he meant the gremlins now—but that his master asked him to. When I came to, Noah was gone. What if Noah isn't Noah? What if he's Strike?"

Dinah let out a low groan. "Oh my God."

We weren't far from Vivian's place, having crash-landed outside Seattle. I suppose that was good. I started to laugh, and once the laughter caught me I couldn't stop. Killian's rather worried face only made it worse, and then I tried to explain between gasps for breath. I'm not sure he caught what I was trying to say, but in barely a moment he was laughing too. Contagious, who knew laughter could be contagious? Not me.

But maybe that spoke volumes about how much laughter I had in my life before.

"Here you go," the cabbie said, and we tumbled out. Of course, we had no money on us, everything was lost in the crash.

The cab driver followed us and I started to pull Dinah on him, my laughter gone. Killian dropped a hand on my wrist and pulled a hundred-dollar bill out of his back pocket. "Always have something on me, just in case."

The cabbie took it happily and left grinning.

I tucked Dinah away, noting again that she was quiet. At least for her. "Dinah, you good?"

"I just feel like we aren't only running out of time, but chances," she said. "I don't like it. And I think you are right about Noah being Strike. But why would he be helping?"

I nodded. "Yeah, I'm feeling all that too, and I don't

know. He said that he wanted to help us kill Romano. But that makes no sense, he's supposed to be protecting Romano."

That was the thing. Noah being Strike made sense. But then Noah *had* been helpful occasionally.

Oh, shit. It hit me then how much my brain had been affected by Noah all those years. He'd made me love Justin. Every time I'd started to think that maybe I should break it off with him—before Bear, at least—Justin had Noah come around and then . . . then we'd be better.

He'd manipulated me into a life that had made me weak.

Horror and anger swept through me and I stood shaking with the realization. Killian reached out. "Lass?"

"We have to keep moving." I led the way down the long tree-lined driveway that would open into the front of Vivian's lush mansion. I couldn't stop and think about all these things. There was just too much. Too many revelations in too short of a time for my mind to handle.

I focused on the task at hand. Vivian was dead, but that didn't mean her house was safe. Much as I wanted to believe that with her death whatever myst she had created would be gone too, I wasn't going to bet on it.

The gravel crunched under our feet as we walked side by side.

Killian let out a deep breath. "What are we going into here?"

I quickly gave him a rundown of the place, of the security, and the surrounding creatures. "The only one I dealt with was a crocodile that was already dead and had me in its sights."

"You mean alligator," Killian said. "There are no crocs native to the bayous."

"No, I mean crocodile. I had an up close and personal look at that thing." We were at the end of the driveway now and the house and parking area opened to us. The house no longer looked like the immaculate mansion it had been only a short time before.

"It looks like shit," Killian said. I nodded.

"Her myst must have been holding this place together." I drew a breath and started forward. "The ring will be inside."

"How are we going to find it?"

"We could burn the place down," I said, frowning, but I already knew it wasn't the right answer. But searching it from top to bottom would be dangerous and time consuming.

Killian shook his head. "Messy, and it would take time and make it difficult to find the ring."

I agreed, noting that he had not once told me that the ring might not be there. Why did this man of all the men I knew, and of all the times in my life, have to be so damn perfect?

I will help you, Martin said softly. *This is why I am here with you. Or at least part of it.*

"If I could high-five you, Martin, I would," I said. Killian lifted an eyebrow. "Martin says he can help us find the ring."

The house loomed as if it wanted us to come in.

"Let's get this done." I pulled Dinah free and held her at my side.

We stood at the front door which stood on an angle, the hinges partially ripped off. I touched the door, bent and sniffed at the handle. The smell of abnormal was strong, and it was layered with death and blood.

"Magelores," I said softly. "There is at least one here, and something else I don't recognize."

Dinah snarled in my hand. I turned and kissed Killian, tugging him hard to me, biting at his lower lip which drew a rumble from him. His one hand snaked around my lower back, the other up to cup the back of my head. As good and blood pumping as the kiss was, this was not truly about a kiss. I didn't have to tell him what I wanted from him.

His electricity flowed over me and I absorbed it easier than before, not fighting it, but allowing it to course through me, gathering it to me and letting it pool in that spot in my lower back it seemed to like so much.

His mouth was hot on mine, insistent when I moved to pull away. I kissed him deeper, let myself sink into the moment for just a flash, a moment to remind myself that besides Bear, there was another prize waiting for me at the end of this. He let me go, his eyes glittering with desire.

"Into the lion's den," he said.

I snorted softly. "I'd prefer a lion's den to this shit."

He grinned and I grinned back. Other people would call this insane, but I'd never had so much connection to anyone in my life. Which in and of itself worried me because there was still that niggling feeling at the back of my head that told me death was waiting on me to make a mistake.

Death had my coordinates and the bastard was trying to take me and those I loved in one fell swoop.

"Abe, *bewache*." I pointed him to the stairs, guarding our way in and out. He plunked his butt down and watched me with trusting eyes.

With Dinah raised in my left hand, I pushed the door out of my way with the other. The floorboards beneath my feet creaked as I stepped through into the dim foyer of the mansion. There was a wide staircase in front of me that branched off to either side about ten steps up at a landing. Below each branch of the staircases the shadows seemed darker, as if they were being held there. Logically, I knew there should be doors in those shadows.

"Martin?"

There was a whisper of cold around my face and left side. *Wait, I will look.*

"We don't have time to wait. You go down, we'll go up." I didn't look back at Killian but started toward the stairs. Because if there was a ruby ring, it would be somewhere Vivian considered safe. Not in a kitchen or servant's quarters but in a bedroom, in a closet, somewhere hard to find. A hidden safe, something like that.

I made my way up the stairs and took a slow breath. The smell of abnormals was stronger now, which in itself was odd. The weaker the abnormal, the stronger they smelled. But Magelores were not weak in any sense of the word. What the fuck was going on here?

I waited for Killian to reach me and then leaned in to whisper in his ear. "They're setting us up."

His eyebrow twitched. "Plan?"

Vivian, the previous owner of the home and powerhouse Magelore, had nearly killed me. Which meant two Magelores coming for us was not a good thing no matter how I looked at it. "Time to call them out."

I did a slow turn on the landing of the stairs. "I know you're here. I know you want to chitchat. So, either come the fuck out and talk or I'll just burn the house down and wait for you to flee so I can kill you then. Your choice."

Laughter echoed through the walls and a cold wind shot through me as if ice water had been dashed over my head, far colder than the breeze that came with Martin. The hairs on my arms stood on end and seemed to freeze, and my skin rippled with apprehension.

"Killian?"

"Fucked if I know." He put his back to mine, and the heat of his body was welcome as the air around us began to frost, puffs of steam rolling from my mouth. The air was so cold that the inside of my nose began to tingle as the hairs and skin froze. Yeah, this was not Martin.

I reached back to Killian with my free hand. "Hang on."

Without another word, I called up my fire and drew it forward. The flames rippled outward over my body and I wrapped their warmth around the both of us. At the very edge of my fire the ice cracked and snapped as if it was pissed that it couldn't get at us.

"Is this a Magelore trick?" I blinked as the ice in my hair melted and trickled down my face.

Killian tightened his hand on mine. "Look, top of the stairs both sides."

I looked to my right and saw something ghosting toward us. And I mean *literally* ghosting. Martin at least was nothing but a fuzzy indistinct blob when I did see him.

Not this ghost. The person floated along as if there were no connection to his feet, and it was definitely a male. The short-cropped hair, the wider shoulders, the angled jaw. Even if that jaw hung at a strange angle. Even if there was an arm missing from the rest of the body.

Even if the body and face were semi-transparent, gray with the age of death and eyes that ran with a black darkness that was nothing but an empty void.

"Fuck." I growled the word, my nerves reacting to the sight even though we were within the confines of my fire. The ghost—because fuck me sideways, there was no other word for him—floated down the stairs, black eyes empty of any sort of emotion.

"I've got a male on my side," I said.

"Female on mine," Killian said.

I didn't dare look away from the ghost in front of me for the simple reason that if I did, I suspected he would rush me. And I wasn't 100 percent sure my fire would stop him.

There was no thought, I just tightened my hold on Killian. I knew how to fight monsters, I knew how to fight mobsters. But I was no ghost killer. "Martin, some help here would be great."

There was no answer from our friendly ghost. Damn it.

The male stared at me and then tipped his head to one side so far that his face touched his shoulder.

"Where is the ring?" I asked the only question that mattered. "It's mine by birthright."

Where the hell had that come from? I tried not to think too much about what I was saying, letting the words come as they would.

The ghost lifted his head and it wobbled as if it sat on a broken spine. The edges of my flame tightened around us as the cold encroached. Sweat dripped down the sides of my face.

"How long can you hold this up?" Killian asked softly.

I swallowed hard. "Long as I have to."

"She's at the edge of the fire," he said. "I think she's going to try and come through."

A wave of fear I'd never known crashed over me so strong, I was sure it wasn't even my own. More like I was feeling what others had felt when they stood here, when they'd faced these monsters.

There were so many things wrong with this, but I didn't know how to stop any of it.

I didn't know how we were going to find the ruby ring with them on top of us like this either.

"Shit!" Killian snarled, and I twisted around in time to

see a transparent gray-skinned woman wrap her hands around his head.

Electricity arced all over him, sliding through her, but it did nothing. At least, as far as I could see, because the electricity hit me and sent me flying up the stairs and over the head of the male ghost. His head swiveled around ninety degrees to watch me fall.

I landed hard, bounced once and then was up and moving. "Killian, I'm going in! You get outside!"

"No! It's a trap!" he yelled, but I was already moving. I remembered roughly where Vivian's room was, the place she'd taken Simon to fuck and feed on what seemed like a lifetime ago. A feeding room would be a place of safety for a Magelore, a place her victims would be too out of it to do any snooping.

I bolted up the last few stairs as whisper of ice cold wrapped around my ankles and tugged at me. The sensation sent me to my knees at the top of the stairs and I couldn't help but turn and look back.

The ghost smiled at me, showing a mouthful of sharpened teeth inside a black hole. The ghost of a Magelore . . . a truly undead Magelore. That explained some of their power, but it didn't make me feel any better. "Martin, little help!"

Where was he? He'd said he was here for this moment, then why wasn't he actually here?!

I scrambled forward, using a burst of fire on my lower legs to burn off the sensation around my ankles.

With a heave, I was up and stumbling forward, racing down the length of the catwalk that wrapped around the foyer entrance. There was a door partially open near the end of the walkway and I could see the color of the room. The yellow and reds that had been in Vivian's feeding room.

I put everything I could into picking up speed, into

getting to that door and slamming it behind me. Part of my brain tried to calm me, to tell me that ghosts couldn't hurt you. Sure, they could scare the shit out of you, they could haunt you if they wanted, but they couldn't hurt you.

Except I could feel the ice cold burn around my ankles, and the sensation of my lungs slowly freezing as I breathed in the arctic air that the dead Magelore had produced. These were not normal ghosts in any sense of the word—these were the souls of powerful abnormals whose strength seemed not to have diminished in death.

Just what we needed.

I was two steps from the door and I reached my hand out to push it open, to leap through.

The male Magelore flashed in front of me and I fell *through* his body. If I thought the cold was bad before, it was nothing to the sensation that ripped through me now. Daggers made of icicles, of sharp pain, sent me tumbling. Only it wasn't just my body that tumbled down but my mind too.

I saw the first kill I made, saw the horror in my mind as I took the life of an abnormal as he begged for mercy. So many of my kills had been male abnormals. I saw each of them flash through me, one right after another, and I felt my horror lessen as each death happened. I could see how my heart hardened, how my conscience allowed me to do the unthinkable because it meant I was safe; *I* was surviving. There was nothing I could do about the images, nothing I could do to stop them, not even when I got to the very last kill I made for Romano.

My mark was simple, a thug name Hector who thought he was going to start his own mob and step in on my father's turf.

He'd gathered a group of drug addicts who wanted funds for their various addictions and had handed them weapons. The result was that a lot of people were dying, a few which had been my father's underlings. To be clear, my father was not protecting lives, just protecting his assets.

Hector had no idea what he'd put his foot in.

I snorted to myself. "Fool."

I sat on the top of an apartment building, the flat roof giving me a perfect position to see my mark as he approached. The hum of the city flowed through me like a living thing, the lights and sirens, the blasts of a multitude of horns like some sort of awkward symphony. The noise might have been just noise to some people, but the city spoke to me in its own way.

A dark blue sedan pulled up to the curb and I settled into position. Much as I was good at the up close and personal killings, this would be my last for my father and I knew it. And for some reason, I didn't want to see Hector's eyes as he realized who'd come for him. There was no need. There would be no one for him to tell as he'd be dead. Besides, I'd placed the note my father had written on Hector's bed. The note that warned everyone that the Phoenix would come for them if they crossed Romano.

I let out a slow breath. "Not much longer, Father. Not much longer will you use me as a tool."

The scope pressed into the edges around my eye as I sighted down it. Eleanor wriggled in her holster. "You think you can really get away from Romano?"

"I have to," I said softly, something I wouldn't have said to anyone else. "I don't want this anymore. He doesn't need me. He has his three guardians."

Eleanor snorted as if she knew I was stating only the obvious. The deep-down part was that the death and killing was too easy now. The last vestige of my conscience had clawed its way upward and said now was the time. If I ever wanted to be free of this world, to escape my life and all that had been forced on me, I had to do it now or I would never leave.

"*I want out, Eleanor,*" *I said as I adjusted my seat again. Hector was taking his time in the sedan. Waiting was the hard part, pulling the trigger was not.*

"*You're good at this, though.*" *She didn't sound so certain.* "*And what will happen to us?*"

To us. To her and Dinah. I shrugged. "*I didn't say I'd be putting you two down.*"

There was a pair of relieved sighs that made me smile. My mentor Zee thought I put too much stock in the pair of sentient guns, but the reality was they were the closest thing to friends I had. Which was a sad fact in and of itself.

The door of the sedan opened and a man who was not Hector stepped out of the driver's side. He moved around the car, his head swiveling as if he could see the danger before it killed his boss. But he didn't look up to the rooftops. Rookie mistake.

He opened the back door of the car and Hector rose out of the backseat. There was a flash of his blond hair and then his head was in line with his driver's.

"*Two for one,*" *I whispered as I squeezed the trigger of the long-range rifle. A report of the gun and I watched through the scope as the back of the driver's head exploded and he fell to the left away from the car. With him gone, I could see Hector as he swayed on his feet, somehow still standing upright, clutching not his chest, but what he held in his arms.*

I couldn't stop the gasp that escaped me or the words as he twisted to one side. "*God, no.*"

In his arms, he held his son, a child I knew from my research had just turned six . . . blond like his father; the blood on the back of his head was as bright as if I stood there in front of him. They went down then after standing for what seemed like an eternity.

And I sat there, shock slamming through me in waves. I'd killed a child. A little boy who had no reason to die.

I didn't even pack my things, I left them there on the rooftop. Dinah and Eleanor tried to get me to tell them what had happened but I couldn't say it, not even to them. Not later to Zee.

But my father knew. Of course he did, and he crowed it from the rooftops, praising me in front of his men.

"Cold-hearted bitch that she is, she killed the boy too! Three for the price of a single bullet!" He'd hugged me then, the first time I'd ever been hugged by my father as far as I could remember. Because I'd killed a child. There could be no more revulsion in me for him or myself than in that moment, and it was later that night I'd run from my father and everything I'd lived up to that point in my miserable life.

The memory fled and I fell to the floor in a heap just inside the room. I looked back, my eyes one of the few things that seemed to still obey me.

The ghost stood on the threshold, his mouth partially open and those black eyes unblinking as he floated there. I opened my mouth, to say what, I was not sure, and it took me a moment to see through the tears that had filled my eyes. "Like what you see?"

The ghost's mouth moved and words flowed out at a pace that did not match the movement. *"Your soul is torn. Easy to take."*

Once more the cold seeped around me but I didn't pull from it, nor did I call up my flames to combat it. There was a very large part of me that knew a punishment was due for taking the life of a child, and for the first time, I wondered if my rage at losing Bear had some small connection to the loss of that other child's life. As though I'd always feared that I would have my own child taken from me to pay for the loss of that other's life.

I didn't answer the ghost. I couldn't. Instead I pushed to my feet while the ice flowed and formed around me. The fear the dead Magelore had induced had been washed away in a memory I could not escape, the one memory I'd buried deeply and let myself forget so I could keep moving.

I stumbled around the room, my fingers and face numbing under the flowing air that tightened over me. Every time I moved toward the bed in the center of the room the cold went deeper into me, like it was trying to freeze the marrow inside my bones. I had an image of my bones bursting, unable to contain the expanding liquid as it froze. I went to my knees with the pain of my teeth chattering so hard, I thought they might crack against one another. I refused to give into it, though, refused to let it take over my body which meant I kept moving, kept pushing toward the bed.

The ghost Magelore floated to stand—if stand was the right word—until it was in front of me while I was on my hands and knees. My limbs were freezing in place with a cold so deep, it burned. I knew I should stop it, that I should call on my fire, but I deserved to be punished for that last death. The death of a child.

Child. There was something about a special child, but my brain seemed to have frozen along with the rest of me.

I stopped shivering. I stopped feeling anything and that was bad. I knew it was bad. I would be near the end when I stopped feeling the cold. I let it pass through me and I was at peace and I knew I was dying. I was dying and the cold didn't hurt me anymore because I stopped fighting it. Maybe in death, I would find some sort of redemption for my torn soul.

I covered my ears from a screeching noise beating against my skull. A nails-down-a-chalkboard pitch not going away.

It took me a moment to realize that Dinah was screaming at me, that her voice was barely audible through the ice that had formed inside my ears. "FOR THE LOVE OF BEAR, USE YOUR FIRE!"

Bear. My boy still needed me and that meant I couldn't die yet. No matter the cost to my own soul, I could not give up as long as he drew breath.

I sucked down a gulp of air that barely squeezed through my tightened and iced throat, drew that air deeply into me and touched it to the flame that was mine. I gave my flame the last of what I was, whatever it needed to stop this madness around me. For Bear.

The heat burst around me in a wave of purple and blue fire that licked along my skin and melted the ice, thawing it so rapidly that my skin tingled and burned for a second time as the cold left it.

There was screaming then that I could hear, not only Dinah but someone else's. The ghost? No, someone I knew. A man.

"Dinah," I whispered her name.

"Get up, Killian is in trouble!" She didn't turn down the volume for one second.

Every muscle in my body felt as if I'd been beaten with a baseball bat, leaving me limp and weak. But Killian was in trouble, which meant I had to move.

Above me the ghost Magelore writhed as my fire tangled with the edge of his feet. Fire didn't kill Magelores, but it hurt them when they were alive. I didn't think that this dead one was bothered by normal fire. But the fire of a Phoenix, maybe that was something else. I didn't really understand what I was doing as I lifted a hand to the ghost.

"Go." I breathed the word and with it a burst of flame rolled from my body and through his form, the color of the flames soft, like the flames of protection that had wrapped us inside the plane. Pink flames fluttered through him and he arched his back, his arm and the stump of an arm splayed wide. The last thing I saw were his black eyes as they faded from my vision, fury deeply within them.

I let my fire go and stumbled forward. The air around me was still cool but nowhere near the ice of before. It took me a moment to spot Killian at the front door, the female ghost circling around him. There was no more electricity around him and he was on his knees, his body encased in ice.

Time, it all came down to time, and I had none left.

I held my hand out, palm facing the Magelore ghost, and let my fire race out of me. A long burst of brighter pink flames flickered and shot in a perfect line, connecting me with the Magelore's form. She reacted the same as the other, arching her back with her arms spread wide, her black hole of a mouth and eyes swiveling toward me.

"Go to hell," I whispered.

And then she was gone, as if she'd never been. But I knew better. These were no ordinary ghosts. Sure as shit, I'd banished them, but there was no doubt in my mind they would be back. And I wasn't sure I could do another round with them. I stumbled down the stairs and ran as fast as I could to Killian. His head was bowed, thick with ice. I grabbed his face in my hands and tried not to think about the way his skin was waxy and cool, as if he were already dead.

I poured my fire over him, melting the ice as quickly as I could. As it left him he slumped forward into my arms.

His words were slurred and filled with a pain I understood all too well. "Lass, I didn't mean to kill her, you have to believe me."

I closed my eyes and just held him. "I know." I helped him to his feet and onto the front porch, down the stairs and onto the gravel of the driveway. "Wait here." I pointed at Abe who danced around us.

"Abe, look after him. *Bewache.*"

Killian groaned, but I made myself get up and leave them both. Because the reality was, as I stepped back into the house, I could already feel the ghost Magelores ramping back up for another round. And this time they would come at me together. I had only a limited amount of time before they were back full force.

I ran up the stairs, slower than before but at least not dragging my ass completely. "Dinah, you saved both us back there."

"Fuck, don't do that to me," she muttered.

"Might not have a choice. It's getting cold again," I said as I approached the bedroom, the one that I thought held the ruby ring. There was nothing Vivian would have protected more than a ring that in turn protected her from three guardians from Hell.

It hit me then why Romano had sent me after Vivian. Because she couldn't be hurt by the guardians because she held the ring, and he wanted a way to kill her off so he could get the ring back. But then why wasn't he here now?

My feet stuttered then and my ears strained at the sounds within the house. There was a creak somewhere, like that of a footstep. Then another and another.

I bared my teeth and sprinted for the door of the

bedroom, sliding through as I heard the roar of anger from something . . . big. I pushed the dresser in the room across the front of the door, buying myself time, and then started to toss the dresser drawers.

"Dinah, any ideas?"

"About what exactly? The thing that's coming for you next, or where the ring is?"

"Fuck, Dinah, be helpful!" I yelled at her.

"Floorboards are too obvious. But the bitch liked her bed," Dinah said.

She had a point. I abandoned the dresser and moved to the bed. I stripped the linens off first and flipped the mattress over while I cursed Martin for not being more helpful. There were no cuts or stitched places in the mattress or the box spring.

The door to the bedroom shuddered and the dresser screeched as it was pushed open an inch. A set of claws the size of bear paws slid through the edges of the door. I glanced at them only long enough to realize they were like the creatures that had pulled the plane apart, only sized up.

Did that mean Strike was here? No, I didn't think that was the case. Gut feeling, this was someone else.

I turned away from the creature making its way in and grabbed the headboard of the bed. Padded and stitched. I ran my hands over it.

Nothing.

Wrong way, you are going the wrong way!

"Martin, it's about damn time!" I yelled. But it was too late, we were in the room and rather trapped.

It took me a long time to find it. His cool breeze tugged at me, pulling me forward.

I had no words for the frustration that poured through me. The door creaked again and I spun, yanked Dinah from her holster, and fired into the spindly finger claws that wrapped around the edge. The thing on the other side howled as we took off two pieces of him.

The injury would either slow it down, or hurry it up.

I was banking on slowing it down.

I was wrong.

19

The roar of the beast on the other side of the door told me everything I needed to know. There would be no more time to try and work my way out of this problem. I had to kill whatever it was, and then Martin could show me where the ruby ring was.

A voice called out to me. "Dear sister, you've wounded my pet."

"Daniel." Dinah breathed his name.

The beast on the other side of the door roared again and threw itself with renewed vigor against it.

"Dinah," I said softly as I stepped away from the bed and moved so my back was to the open French doors that led onto a small balcony. "We're going to kill him. We have to."

The thing was, Daniel had been Bea's favorite brother. She'd been kind to him, and treated him better than she'd treated anyone else.

"I don't want to," she whispered.

"Well, he's going to kill me if I don't kill him." I kept the words calm even though they were the truth. "He's not here to play tiddlywinks."

She choked a sob. "Use the other gun then. I don't want to do it."

Fuck, this was not what I needed, but I would do what I could to keep her out of this. I jammed her into her holster and pulled out my backup gun. Eleanor would have had no problem shooting Daniel.

I didn't say it out loud, but the words and truth were there in the air. The real reason I'd always chosen Eleanor to kill over Dinah was that I'd known deep down that despite her bluster, Dinah didn't like the deaths she caused. It made sense now; Bianca had been in her day the most squeamish of us.

The door shattered in half, and the creature stuck the upper part of its body inside. Built just like the gremlins on the plane, the body was lanky and yet heavily muscled with wings that protruded out both sides and a mouth that gaped wide as if the jaw was unhinged. I pulled Dinah back out and aimed her at the beastie. "Smoke bomb."

"Please don't use me to kill him!"

"DO it!" I snarled.

"Not until you swear not to hurt him!" she screamed at me and I bared my teeth and shot at the oversized gremlin with the other gun. The bullets just seemed to irritate him more than anything.

"Fine! I swear I will do all I can not to hurt him."

Dinah's inner workings shifted and I squeezed the trigger as the giant gremlin launched across the dresser at me. Dinah shot straight down into his mouth. He clamped his teeth shut around the smoke bomb and it exploded inside. Teeth went flying in every direction and the smoke burst out around his head, blinding him as his eyeballs were pushed out with the pressure.

I ran toward the creature as it flailed and roared blindly,

finding my last reserves of strength and clinging to them. At the final second, I leapt up on top of the dresser, stood, and spun into a roundhouse. I slammed my foot into the side of the gremlin's head, toppling it over. Its claws reached for me, swiping across my right arm from shoulder to hand. The burning lines ran hot with blood. I didn't stop, just hopped off the dresser and stalked down the hall.

I saw only one thing, one person standing on the landing of the stairs.

Daniel.

"Bea wants me to let you live," I said. "Why the fuck, I will never know."

"Because he is like you, Nix," she said softly. "Broken before you ever really knew what being whole was."

His eyes widened and then narrowed rapidly. "She's not alive."

I smiled, and let the smile turn into a smirk tainted with my anger. "She's alive. She asked me not to kill you. Unfortunately, that's not going to happen." The words were doing their magic, throwing him off his game.

Dinah gasped but I didn't care. He was going to die. I would shoot him with the other gun. But if that was the case, why the sudden need to talk to him?

I didn't need him to talk. I didn't need information from him, so why was I stalling? I should have just shot him in the head right there. Killed him and been done with it. I had the aim for it even without Dinah. There was no magic bullet needed to end his life. One ordinary one would do the job.

An image of the child in Hector's arms, the child I'd not meant to kill, swept up through me and I knew in that split second why I didn't want to kill him. In his own way, it was not his fault he was a monster. In his own way, there was an innocence about Daniel, maybe about all of us Romano kids. Because none of us had been raised to be anything but killers, to be monsters in our own right, tools to be used so our father could further his rule.

Tears caught me off guard but I let them come because I understood suddenly what Dinah meant about Daniel being like me.

I lowered the gun and stared at him. "I wish our family wasn't so fucked up."

If I thought I'd confused him before, it was nothing to what that line did. He frowned at me like I'd lost my mind. Maybe I had. Maybe I was the fool for not just blowing his brains out and ending this right here.

I was at the top of the stairs looking down at him. His monster still snarled and roared in the other room, crashing through everything in an attempt to get away from the smoke and to find a way to see. I took a step down.

"I wish I'd played tag with you when we were little, that we'd wrestled and fought like normal siblings. I wish we'd played in the forest, pretending to be the monsters instead of actually becoming them."

Dinah let out a soft cry. I went on as I took one step after another. "Daniel, we never had a chance to be normal. Even being abnormal we never had a chance living in that house, with monsters surrounding us. We either became like them, or were eaten by them. I didn't want to be eaten, so I became one of them."

His eyes were wide with something akin to fear which I didn't understand. I was in the middle of the stairs now. "Bea was kind to you. I never knew why," I said.

"Because Gabe raped me." His words seemed to slip out of him, surprising him as much as me.

Gabe, the first brother I'd killed, the one who'd been

there at the time of my own rape. If I let myself, I could see him over my thirteen-year-old body laughing at me as he tried to kiss me.

My whole body seized up and I stared at Daniel, my own body trembling as if the ghosts of the Magelores had come back. I said words I'd never spoken out loud, that I'd never allowed myself to admit to.

"Me too."

He swallowed hard and our eyes locked. Understanding that probably neither of us could have found anywhere else flowed between us. And then he shook his head, breaking the momentary spell. "Father wants you with him. He'll reward me. I have to take you to him. But I don't want to be the bottom of the pack. Which means I have to kill you."

"I know," I said. "And I want him dead. He stole my son, he destroyed my life. He destroyed all our lives. Tommy knew it. Bea knew it. I know it. I don't really want to kill you, Daniel, but I will."

Daniel trembled on the spot as he shook his head harder and harder as if fighting something only he could hear. Finally, he put his hands to his head. "*No*. No, I won't go back to being afraid!"

"You don't have to." I took another couple steps. "You don't have to, Danny." I used his childhood name for the first time in years, and he staggered as if I'd hit him. "We can look out for each other. That's what siblings do. Tommy . . . he's gone after Romano."

"He'll never stop coming for us, you know that." Daniel lifted his eyes and I saw the denial in them, the fear, and the need to feel safe. I couldn't fix any of those things.

"I'm going to kill him," I said.

Daniel shook his head harder and then I saw the ring on his finger. The ruby ring that kept him safe from the guardians' control. I pointed to it. "Give me the ring and I will kill Romano. You'll be free. We'll both be free and safe."

"Danny, please," Dinah said. "Please listen to her."

Daniel's eyes shot to my holster. "Who . . . who is she?"

I gave him just her name because I wasn't sure he could handle anything else. "Bianca."

His eyes rolled and then closed and he pressed his hands into the sockets. "I tried to find her body, to bring her back. I could have raised her but not without her soul. Why the fuck would you put her in a gun?" He launched himself at me and I stepped to the side, avoiding him easily. Without thought, I raised Dinah and put her to the back of his head.

She sobbed. "No, no, you promised you wouldn't hurt him."

I drew a slow breath and let it out, all the tension in my body going with it. "This was her choice. A way to escape Romano."

He took a deep breath that turned into a shudder. I went on. "Danny, there are two ways to never be afraid again. You can help me and we can face him together, we can free ourselves. Or I can end things for you right here, right now. There can be no in between. I can't risk my son. I won't risk him being raised like we were by Romano."

Daniel turned to look at me, tears streaming down his face. "You must love your boy very much."

"More than anything," I said softly. "More than my own life or anything that scares me."

He swallowed hard. "I can't help you, Nix. But I . . . I don't want to be afraid anymore."

Dinah was crying and my own face was wet with tears. "This would be easier if you kept fighting," I said.

He gave me a lopsided grin, and for a flash, I saw the boy who'd been my brother. The quiet one who'd hidden in the library, the one who'd slumped whenever our father came in. He slid off the ruby ring and handed it to me.

"The other ring is here somewhere. The original one, but it's hidden better than anyone could have guessed," he said. "Don't bother with it."

I stuffed the ring into my pocket, feeling it and knowing it wasn't the ring we needed. Yes, it was one of the rings, but the moment he said the original ring was here I knew . . . that was the one we needed. "Daniel. Are you sure?"

He slumped on the stairs. "I couldn't do it myself. Strike kept me from ending it. He sent me after you, you know. Father made him. I don't think Strike wanted to come after you."

My jaw ticked as I went to my knees beside him. "I believe you."

I moved to lower Dinah and she trembled in my hand. "No. I can do it. I can do this much for him."

I reached out for Daniel and he fell into my arms. I hugged him tightly, wishing I could do something else other than end it for him. My lower lip trembled as I raised Dinah and rested her on the edge of his ear. I closed my eyes.

"Brother, find your peace, wherever it may be."

He sucked in a deep shaking breath. "Find your boy, Nix. Keep him safe the way no one ever kept us safe."

I couldn't speak around the lump in my throat. The pain in my heart was something I didn't fully understand. To discover one of my siblings like this, so broken that death would be the only peace he could understand, shattered something deep in me that I didn't realize was still there. A bit of hope that somehow, I could find a way to bring some of my family back together.

Foolish, a child's hope that had been buried so deeply, I didn't even realize I still held onto it, yet there it was.

I squeezed the trigger and Dinah cried out as the bullet left her.

A splatter of blood hit my face as Daniel slumped against my one arm. I let him slide to the floor, his body limp.

I stared down at his face, his eyes still seeing for just a split second before his brain caught up with the fact that pieces of it were missing. Dinah sobbed, shaking in my hand and I tucked her into her holster. No point in making her see more than she had to.

"Dinah, I need you to pull it together," I said as I did a slow turn away from Daniel's body. "We are not out of the woods, not by a long shot."

"I can't believe . . . that I . . . that we killed him." Her words hiccupped out of her. I frowned, blocking the emotions.

"He didn't want to go on. We gave him a clean end, Dinah. That's more than you or I are going to get if Romano or Bazixal get their hands on us." I moved away from Daniel's body and headed toward the stairs. The air was still cool, the ghosts were still active, but they seemed quieter now with Daniel gone.

At the top of the stairs, I looked back at Daniel's body. The two Magelore ghosts stood next to him, staring down at his body with what I thought maybe was a form of sadness . . . or hunger? The male Magelore turned his eyes to me and grinned a split second before he dove into Daniel's body. My brother's limbs jumped and jerked as the Magelore did whatever the fuck it was doing to him.

"Shit." I bolted along the upper hallway once more to the bedroom that I was certain held the real ruby ring.

"What's happening?" Dinah's worry came through loud and clear.

"Nothing good." I leapt through the door to the bedroom and over the dresser. The clawed gremlin creature was gone, its ties to Daniel severed so it was free to go where it pleased.

Thank God it didn't feel like sticking around. I wasn't sure I could handle the monster, and my brother's Magelore-possessed body at the same time. *Downstairs. The other ring is downstairs.* Martin's voice floated to me, his presence damn near warm after the Magelore ghosts. Damn it, that information would have been good about a minute earlier.

I whipped around as laughter floated through the air. My brother's voice, but not his voice, as if he were trying to affect a voice that was not his own. I knew in my head that the Magelore was trying to scare me, to make me slip up and make a mistake that would allow him to take advantage of me. I'd done it to enough marks to know the tactics of a hunter.

"Nobody scares the Phoenix." I growled the words and anger as hot and clean as the fire I carried inside me cut through the garbage that the Magelore was putting on me. It was then that I saw what we'd walked into.

A trap, for sure, but more than that. A spell that brought out the worst fears.

And spells were something I was getting pretty fucking good at dealing with.

20

Rather than wait for the body of my brother, inhabited by a demonic Magelore, to come to me, I grabbed the edge of the dresser I'd just pushed against the door and yanked it out of the way.

Dinah gasped. "What are you doing?"

"Facing him. Dinah, something's going on here. It's made you afraid and unable to kill. It set Killian on his ass and it sent me running like a child afraid of the dark. That isn't any of us. That is the myst that Vivian imbued this house with."

I grabbed the door handle and swung it open just as the Magelore reached it. His eyes widened and for a split second, he looked shocked.

I let a slow smile whisper over my lips even though the fear in me grew once more. I wasn't going to let him use his wiles on me.

"Do you know who I am, Magelore? I hunted your kind. I killed Vivian."

Daniel's mouth moved at a strange angle as the

Magelore spoke through him. A weird facsimile of my brother's voice, and I had to fight the urge to shiver. I would not give this Magelore the satisfaction of seeing me afraid of anything, most certainly not him.

"We will eat your soul."

"Not much of that shit left." I lifted one hand as I called up my fire, let it burn hot along my fingertips. "Plus, you'd need my permission. That's the deal with souls. You can't just take it. I'd have to give it to you and that isn't going to happen. Not ever."

"I can." He growled and reached for me. I caught his hand and my fire crept up over his arm. Of course, he couldn't feel it. He wasn't really alive.

I smiled at him. "I've danced with the devil in the flesh, Magelore. And for you to take a soul, there must be an agreement. You've given me nothing."

His eyes flickered and Dinah gasped. "What are you doing?"

"Anything I have to do to save my son." The knowledge flowed through me and with it came a sense of peace I'd not expected. "You can have my soul, Magelore, *if* you give me what I want in return."

His eyes flickered once more. "You want the ruby ring that protects from the guardians of Hell."

"You got it, big boy." I nodded once. "You give me that ring and you can have what's left of my soul."

Dinah screamed, "Phoenix, don't do this!"

"Dinah, of all the people I know, you should know best that we are capable of giving up everything to protect those we love. This isn't about you and me anymore, but our children. Bear. Emerald. Our lives for theirs."

She went quiet and the beats of time between us were as

heavy as I'd ever felt. The Magelore stood there, using Daniel's eyes, blood still streaming from the gunshot wound to the head. The sound of the blood dripping to the floor was the only noise.

"Okay," she said softly. "I'll do what I can to remind you of your humanity once your soul is gone."

"Thanks."

The Magelore—I didn't want to think of him as Daniel—turned away from me, away from the bedroom.

Martin brushed close to me. *They can't see me. They don't even know I'm here. If I find the ring for you when we are close, the deal won't count. He won't have shown you everything.*

I gritted my teeth to keep from grinning. "I might have to marry you, Martin."

He chuckled. *Much as I like you, there is someone else waiting for me.*

Another time I would have laughed at the thought of a ghost waiting for a lover.

"This way." The Magelore waved a hand that flopped in a terrible, loose-limbed way that looked so very wrong.

He led me down the stairs, across the landing and up the other side. I glanced at the doorway, and couldn't see Killian or the female Magelore. I grimaced against the desire to go and check on him. I didn't know how long this Magelore would lead me along. For the moment, Killian was on his own.

"Dinah," I touched her grip, "if something goes wrong, you make sure Killian finishes this. Bear can do what I was meant to do. He can take my place."

"You don't have to do this," she said softly. "There's another way."

"There is no other way."

"There is," she said. "My soul is in this gun."

I swallowed hard and then shook my head. "Dinah, you've given up everything already. And I need you to be the weapon who shoots Romano. You know that."

"Eleanor is still—"

"No, we don't know that she is going to be found. We don't know what will happen to her when Tommy fails to kill Romano." I bit the words out as we followed the Magelore. He led us up the stairs and then to the left at the top. Right to a dead end in the wall.

Don't worry, Martin said, *it's a hidden door that leads down to where the ring is.*

The Magelore lifted a hand and pushed on the wall. There was the hiss of air releasing and then four darts shot out and slammed into his body. I took a step back and he glanced over his shoulder, his head lolling as he grinned. "This way."

There was only one way to do this, to keep going forward and to hope that Martin was right. I followed the Magelore into the empty space. The darkness was absolute and I didn't hesitate on using some of my abnormal ability to light our way. Steps led down into the belly of the house, winding 'round and 'round so many times that I wasn't sure we weren't going to end up in the pits of Hell.

After fifty feet, the walls fell away from us on either side and there was nothing but empty space beckoning.

"Watch your step," the Magelore chuckled.

"He's happy now; he's getting a soul," Dinah whispered.

"How far?" I asked him.

"Moments and you'll have your prize, and I'll have mine." He didn't look back but lifted his hands in the air and danced them around like he was starting to rave.

His movements and the lightness in his voice helped to dispel the last of the fear that had risen in me. A tricky trick, to make someone so afraid that they couldn't think straight. I'd used it myself, but had never had it used on me. Mostly because I'd never had anything to fear. Death didn't bother me. I'd seen it enough times to know that it would come for me one day. Probably sooner rather than later. I frowned as I let my mind go in that direction. What was it that had frightened me then?

I stared at the back of Daniel's mangled head, the bits of gray matter visible in the flickering of the flames I held in my own hand.

He turned and his eyes were dead, nothing in them. No soul, no heartbeat, and yet he moved, he existed to a degree because of the creature that had taken over his body. I blinked a few times and the truth of my fear came home to roost.

There had been only one other time that I'd been truly afraid on a level that I'd never been able to fully escape. The deal Romano made with the devil, I'd been there. I'd felt those flames of Hell lick along my skin and the evil that had crept around my father and tried to creep around me. I was a very bad person by then. I'd killed a lot of people. But . . . there was no need inside of me to kill. No true desire to it.

Death was my job. I was good at it. But I didn't lust after it. The evil that had touched me that day lusted for death, for pain, for never-ending torture. It wanted to bathe in the blood of the innocents of the world, to take the souls of those who'd done no wrong. The devil had tried to get me to hold his gaze and I'd done it, for a short time before looking away. As if that would have saved me.

That same feeling had overcome me in the house, that sense that if I didn't make eye contact, then perhaps I would be able to bluff my way through. Stupid, but perhaps that was the core of a survival instinct when it came to souls. The fear had triggered that years-old sensation that one day I wouldn't be able to look away. That I would have to stare into that abyss and try to find a way to keep from falling.

Sweat popped out along the edge of my face as my memories got the better of me.

Under the stone, the ring is under the stone. Say it out loud!

"The ring is under the stone," I said.

The stairs ended abruptly and the Magelore bent to one knee, his fingers clumsy on the stone below him. I moved to the side so I could see what he was doing. The stone flooring was done in slabs and the one that the Magelore dug at was about three feet wide, oblong and looked like it hadn't been moved in years. He drove his fingers under the edge and several fingernails snapped. Or maybe the fingers themselves, I wasn't sure.

He got a grip and lifted the slab.

"Get it," he said.

I had to come around to the side of him and crouch. The slab would break my spine, or whatever other parts of my body happened to be under it, if he let go.

I reached in quickly, swept the area with my fingers and grabbed hold of a small velvet bag. I pulled out, the bag gripped tightly, and the Magelore dropped the stone.

"Give me your soul."

"Let me make sure this is the ruby ring," I snapped.

He snarled and stood up, blood flicking all over my face.

I did my best to ignore him and opened the bag. I tipped it over my open and waiting palm and a fat ruby ring tumbled out. I rolled it over once. There was a flicker in the depths and I swallowed hard with what I was going to do next. I hoped to all that was holy Martin was right.

"This is it," I said. "This is Romano's ring."

"Give me your soul," the Magelore snarled. "You swore you would."

"Did I? But you didn't tell me where the ring was. *I told you*. I said it was under the stone and you helped me get it out. That's not the same thing as you telling me where it is." I tipped my head to one side and carefully slid the ruby ring over the thumb on my left hand. "Which means you . . . get nothing."

The Magelore roared and I spun on my heel and bolted up the stairs.

"Are you fucking kidding me?" Dinah screeched. "You can't double-cross a Magelore. They'll make it open season on your head!"

I didn't answer. There was no time to explain what Martin had helped me with. Instead I focused on the stairs below my feet. I was a desperate woman. I had nothing to lose and if a lie was going to be the worst of my sins, then I was doing pretty good as far as I was concerned.

My thighs burned as I leapt up the stairs one after another. There was nothing but the raging screams of the Magelore below and I knew why. He couldn't make Daniel's body work easily, which meant he either had to give up the body and go back to his ghost form, or try and force the dead body to obey him.

And if he gave up the body, his ability to take my soul diminished even more.

"Martin, I hope you are right!"

I am, but hurry, just in case.

Oh fuck.

I hit the top of the stairs out of breath and stumbling forward. I didn't stop, though. I didn't look back. Just bolted along the top hall and down the next set of stairs, using the railing to pull myself along faster.

Across the landing, down the final set and then I was sprinting across the open foyer of the mansion.

I leapt across the threshold from house to outside and ended up on my knees, sprawling forward onto my belly. But I was out. I was out and that was all that mattered. Abe was not there waiting as he should have been. There was no welcoming woof.

Breathing hard, I pushed up and looked around. Night had fallen in the time I'd been in there. I'd known that was possible but had hoped it wouldn't be the case.

I looked around. "Killian?"

There was nothing but the sound of the night birds, and the occasional croak of a frog. The cold brush of Martin and the jabbering of Dinah to keep moving if I wanted to keep my soul intact.

But where the fuck were Killian and Abe? At the foot of the stairs was the box with the herbs and the journal in it. He wouldn't have left it behind, it was too important. Certainly, he wouldn't have left it out in the open.

I yelled for him again as I pushed to my feet, gathering the box to my chest. "Dinah, I have a bad feeling." I let out a long whistle for Abe, but there was no answer.

"You think he's dead?" she asked.

I shook my head and forced myself into a jog that would take me out to the edge of the driveway.

My heart pounded out of control, not because of what I'd just survived, and not because Killian was missing.

But because of what it could mean. I rolled the ruby ring on my thumb. "He wouldn't have left, Dinah. Which means someone took him."

"But who could take him? He's strong, far too strong to

go without a fight. And Abe would have fought to protect him too." She sucked in a sharp breath. "You mean . . . Strike, don't you?"

"Yeah." I looked around at the house, and the gravel road. No sign of struggle, no spots of blood. "I mean, Strike has Killian and Abe."

21

BEAR

The walk to the Grotto was quiet except for the occasional squeak of a strap holding a gun, or the crunch of a boot on the hard sand. I said as much to Tommy.

"You didn't think we'd go in there shooting and yelling, did you?" He grinned down at me, his mouth a veritable jack-o'-lantern smile in the bright moonlight. I looked away, uncertain of a lot of things. Like maybe it was a bad idea to come with my uncle. There was no need to look to my right, Rooster was there blocking my view. Only . . . he wasn't Rooster.

I had to bite my lower lip to keep it from trembling. Because my dad had been my hero, and now . . . I wasn't sure what to think about him.

"Why didn't you come back?" I whispered the question, more to myself, but he heard me.

"No choice." His voice rumbled through me and I wrapped my arms around myself. I wanted him to hug me. To tell me that it would be okay. But he'd done none of those things. He'd not even said he loved me.

A tear slipped down my cheek and I moved away from him, to the other side of my uncle. Tommy put a hand on my shoulder and gave me a squeeze. A sigh shuddered out of me, but his hand tightened further and he tugged me down to the sand.

I dropped with him, my eyes finally taking in what was in front of us. No longer was there a spread of desert with nothing seemingly out there in the dark except us. From out of the ground there had sprung a huge wall that went on for a long distance to either side. It was the same color as the sand under our feet, and there were no lights around it, which explained the fact that I hadn't noticed it before.

"There's the door. Stick close to me, kid," Tommy said. "I'll tell you if we need some of your fire."

"He can wait here with me." Rooster reached for me. I flinched away from him.

"I'm going with my uncle." I threw the words at him. His jaw ticked but I didn't look down from the locked gaze. "I can help him."

Eleanor wiggled a little. "Be careful."

Tommy put his hand on the gun he thought was Eleanor but was Linx. "Time to go, bitch."

Of course, Linx said nothing. He couldn't and keep the charade up. Tommy snorted. "Now she shuts up. Figures."

He crept forward and I stuck to his side. I didn't care if Rooster came with me or not.

No, that wasn't true. I wanted him to come. I wanted him to prove that he cared. But I wasn't sure he would.

Tommy and I swept across the open space between us and the wall. He pressed himself against it, keeping his gun up. There was a creak of wood and the click of a lock and then a portion of the wall opened and a hand beckoned.

Tommy scooted forward and I followed. I was going with him, as the desert witch had said.

I looked over my shoulder. No Rooster. My heart clenched.

He'd been dead for months, maybe I had to just let him go completely. No more hope.

"Your mom will come," Tommy said as we crept through the door. "Forget about him. He's not the man you think he is."

I nodded, but I wanted to cry. I wanted to sit and bury my head in my hands and sob because for one flash of a second, I thought . . . I thought I'd have my family back again.

I reached out and put a hand on the back of Tommy's belt so I didn't lose him in the semi-darkness. There was the sound of water running, and the flicker of lights here and there, but not enough that I could count on it to guide me.

"Close." Tommy breathed the word. My heart picked up speed as if it realized why we were here. To kill my grandfather with a gun that wouldn't kill him. I put a hand to Eleanor and she whispered to me.

"No. He would have failed no matter what. You must keep me hidden until your mother arrives. She will come. She is not like your father; she will not fail you." Her words soothed me and the tremors in my body slowed.

A part of me couldn't believe I was doing this, deliberately putting myself back into my grandfather's clutches. But between the witch and Eleanor, I knew there were not many choices. And if my mom was coming here, then I would be here waiting. Ready to do whatever I had to do to get back to her.

Tommy reached back for me and I took his hand, thinking that was what he wanted.

"Fire," he whispered.

Right. I held a hand up and the blue and green flames danced across my skin, lighting the recesses of a tunnel. "Come here, in front of me, and I'll be right next to you with Eleanor," Tommy said, gently pushing me out ahead of him.

"Idiot," Eleanor whispered.

I smiled and took a step, and then another into the darkness that was lit only by my flames. The tunnel wove around and around like a twisting snake. Not down underground, just around. Maybe it was a maze. That would make sense, a challenge to get inside the fortress.

From one second to the next, the tunnel was there, then gone. I stumbled out onto what was a dance floor. I knew because there were people dancing, spinning slowly to a drum beat that tugged at my own feet.

I dropped my hand and the flame was gone in a flash.

"Stay here." Tommy swept up past me and started walking, cutting through the crowd.

The people continued to dance with only a few eyes darting toward Tommy as he strode between them, even going so far as to push a few of them out of the way. At the head of the dance floor sat Luca Romano on a chair that could have been called a throne, it was so big and fancy. Surreal, the whole thing felt like a strange dream. I looked closer at the dancers. None of them smiled, and many had sweat running down their faces. They were no happier to be there than I was.

"The prodigal son returns." Luca didn't stand, but instead swept his hand at Tommy. Next to Luca was a man I knew and my jaw dropped.

"Noah?"

The best friend of my father stared passed Tommy to

me. "Shit." I saw his mouth make the word even though I didn't hear it.

Tommy, though, had my attention now. He raised Linx. "You need to die, old man."

He pulled the trigger.

Nothing happened.

"Eleanor!" he roared at the gun.

Of course, she said nothing. Linx said nothing. But he transformed into a knife, at least giving Tommy something to work with.

Tommy stood there, shaking, with nothing but a knife facing a man we both knew couldn't be killed. I didn't know what to do, so I held my ground. I had to be here. I had to be here for my mother.

The world had gone so still that even the music had stopped. It wouldn't last. I felt it in my bones.

"You must run," Eleanor said. "Or they will know you want to be here."

I spun on my heel and tore off, not the way we had come but toward the other doors that led out of the dance hall. I pushed my way through several couples, sending them scattering to either side of me.

"Faster," Eleanor urged me, and I pumped my arms and legs as fast as I could, running through halls, following some intuition that would lead me outside.

Only I needed to be caught. I saw a doorway up ahead and grabbed the knob, turned it and slipped inside. The room was dark and I crept in, keeping my body low and my movements careful.

Slowly my eyes adjusted to the dim light that came through a small window. A rustle of cloth froze me in place.

"Who's there?" a voice called out. I wasn't even sure if it was a man or a woman, just a voice.

I flattened myself to the floor and scooted toward the bed frame, sliding under it. The bed creaked and feet landed right in front of my face. "Romano!"

The door opened and then shut again. I closed my eyes and breathed through the fear that caught hold of me. "Eleanor, what if you're wrong? What if my mom is hurt or can't come for me?"

She let out a sigh. "I would know if she were dead. She's not. You have to trust me, little Bear."

"You sound like her," I whispered.

There was a catch in her voice before she spoke again. "I know. We've been together a long time."

I lay on the cold tile floor waiting to be caught, knowing it would come. "You really think she's coming?"

"She is not like your father, Bear. You know this in your heart, I think. Phoenix will never stop fighting to find you. Death might not even stop her." She laughed softly. "You are her heart and soul. You saved her, you know that?"

"I did?" I whispered the question as my body shook. The waiting was the hard part, but talking to Eleanor helped.

"Yes. I do believe you did. You taught her what love was again. She'd lost it for a long time." Her voice again had that odd catch in it. "One day, you'll know the whole story, but for right now, I want you to only have faith in your mother. She will come. She will save you if it is the last thing she does on this earth. She will make sure you are not afraid anymore."

I took a breath and let it out, letting go of the last of my fear with it. I was like my mom. I was strong. I was capable. I would not go down without a fight. "Thank you, Eleanor."

"You're welcome. Maybe one day I will be your gun."

"Nah, I have my fire." I whispered the last word because

the door had opened and several sets of feet came tromping in.

"Back to bed, old man. The boss is looking for a kid, not a miserable excuse for..."

I made sure the toe of my one boot peeked out from under the bed. If I didn't help them, they were never going to find me.

A hand latched onto my foot and yanked me out so fast, I felt Eleanor slip. My shirt started to slide untucked and that would have revealed her hiding spot. I grabbed the edge of it and held it to my waistband while the blood rushed to my head as I was pulled out fast, upside down.

"Looky here, the old man wasn't kidding. He did hear something." The voice was not one I knew, but obviously belonged to one of my grandfather's thugs.

I was dropped unceremoniously to the floor. I crumpled and curled in on myself, making sure Eleanor was secured in the waistband of my pants. One of the men grabbed me by my ear and yanked me to my feet, propelling me forward and out the door. Down the halls and back to the dance floor I was shoved until I was pushed to my knees next to my uncle Tommy. I glanced at him.

His face was beaten and bloody, and his one eye was swelling right in front of me. "I'm sorry," I said.

"Not your fault, kid." He growled the words, then spat a gob of blood to the side. Guilt twisted through me, but I reminded myself that Eleanor had said the bullet wouldn't work anyway. I'd saved her, and kept her out of Luca Romano's hands.

I found myself slowly looking up to the man who sat in front of us. My grandfather.

He stared right back, those dark eyes of his bottomless. "How did you survive?"

I shrugged, thinking fast. "I don't know. I was picked up by a desert sheik. He said I almost died."

Luca's eyes narrowed fast. "Shaitan picked you up and then let you go?"

I took a gulping breath and shook my head. "Tommy came through. I saw him and got away."

"You . . .got *away*?" Luca did not sound convinced, and I didn't blame him. Apparently, I wasn't a very good liar.

"There was a lot of gunfire, and explosions, and stuff," I said, hearing just how lame the excuse was to my own ears.

"Shaitan does not just *let* people go. Especially those he deems worthy of saving." Luca leaned back. "But for now, that doesn't matter, he cannot enter here. What does matter is I have my leverage back." He smiled then and my blood ran cold all the way down my spine.

"What do you mean?"

He laughed. "You'll see. Your mother is on her way here. Now I have you, and I have Tommy. Who do you think she'll let die first?"

Tommy shuddered. "Kid, he's playing his games again. Don't fucking listen to him."

I wasn't listening, I was looking. "Where's Noah?"

Luca's eyebrows shot up. "You recognized him, did you? Well, I'll leave that little surprise for later. For now, enjoy the dancing." He raised a glass to us in a salute and took a drink of whatever was in the cup. The dancers wove around us as though we were part of the ornamentation, and not captives.

"Just hold. She's on her way," Tommy said. "We'll get out of here yet, kid."

I didn't look at him. I wasn't sure we both would.

22

PHOENIX

I stood in front of Vivian's house trying to figure out just what to do next. Killian and Abe were gone, most likely taken by Strike. Leaving me to figure out the rest of this on my own.

Around me, the night birds and bugs called to one another. I heard the sound of water splashing here and there, and then the sound of footsteps running. There was a woof in the distance. It could be Abe, but I wasn't sure.

I clutched the gray metal box so hard that the edges of it bit into my chest and hands. Pain had always helped me center myself, but not this time. I was frozen, for the first time uncertain of what to do or where to start.

"Had we been in there too long?"

"What do you mean?" Dinah asked.

"Magelores' lairs can twist time. They can make it so you walk in, are there for hours, but when you walk out only a minute has passed."

"Oh shit, do you think it happened the other way around?" Her voice was husky with emotion. "Like years?"

Fuck, I had no way of knowing until I found a newspaper or someone to ask. "I have no idea." No, that wasn't true. The trees looked to be in the same shape and the house wasn't any more run-down. "No, I don't think it's been that long. The house would have fallen down around us by now."

"Then snap the fuck out of it," Dinah yelled at me. Her words cut through the ice that had formed on me.

Her words helped me breathe again. That was when it hit me that I was hearing running feet. I yanked Dinah from her holster and spun as Killian burst out of a chunk of bushes.

He stumbled and fell to the ground at my feet, Abe with him, his tongue lolling out and his sides heaving. "Lass, it's about damn time you got out of there."

I dropped the box and grabbed him by both arms. "How long was I in there?"

"Just over a day. The door shut and I couldn't get back in. I've been dealing with dead things since you booted me out. All of a sudden, they just stopped coming for me." He was breathing hard and I just stared at him. He'd stayed. He hadn't left.

I wrapped my arms around him and hugged him as tightly as I could. Abe stuffed his face in between us, getting in on the action. "I thought Strike had gotten you both." I whispered the words, my fear spilling out of my mouth.

"Nah. I'm a sight tougher than a dirty old guardian of hell."

His confidence brought a smile to my mouth. "Smart ass, Irish."

"Of course." He gave me a last squeezed and released me.

I helped Killian stand and hurried us both down the long driveway, away from the Magelore's home. He was limping, bruised and battered but alive and with me. Behind us there was a crack of wood, the moaning of timbers as they fell. I didn't look back. The reason the house had stood was to protect the ruby ring that had belonged to my father. The original ring.

Now that it was gone, the spells holding the house together slipped away.

We managed to flag down a car that took us almost all the way to the airport. The older couple who picked us up had water and granola bars, of which I gave most to Killian. As exhausted as I was, I needed him to be able to fly.

Because there was no fucking way I was getting on a commercial plane again.

The nice old couple let us out on the road that led to the airport with a wave and wishes for a better day. I could barely lift my hand in response.

"You don't really want to get on a plane again, do you?" Killian asked as we headed toward the airport.

"No. But unless you have a better way to get us all the way across the world to the Arabian desert, I've got nothing else to offer." I had my arm around his back, partially supporting him.

"The ring," Dinah said softly. "Use it to call Strike."

"Why the hell would I do that?" I stared down at the ring on my left hand. The stone sparkled up at me in the dying light of the night before morning struck and the new day rose.

"Think about it. For all that he's been pushing you, it's all been to make you stronger. Don't deny it, your fire has gotten faster and deadlier with each challenge."

What she said, I already knew, but I didn't like it.

"If Strike really wanted you to end Romano's life, this is going to be his chance to prove it then," I said.

"Not a good idea." Killian shook his head. "Remember the gremlins? He brought those on the plane. Pushing you or not, we could have all died."

I did indeed remember the gremlins. But that was when he'd been sent for us. This would be different. His master—whoever that was—wouldn't be the one sending. We'd be calling him.

"Let me think this through." I let go of Killian and paced in a circle, thinking fast. Abe sat next to Killian, watching me closely.

I rolled the ring around so the ruby sat in my palm. I had a sensation of something missing, and without letting myself consider what I was doing, I grabbed my knife from my boot and put the tip to the palm holding the ring. Blood welled up and the ruby seemed to glow brighter from it. I clamped my hand around it. "Strike, you bastard, if you want Romano dead, you need to show the fuck up to this party."

There was a tugging sensation in my hand as if the wound was being stitched closed and then a flash of brilliant red light spread around me. I squinted my eyes against it and for a moment I thought I saw the Stick Man and beside him the Shadow. Then they were gone and . . . Noah stood there.

I just stared at him.

Martin whispered in my ear. *Demon.*

"You really are him," I said.

Killian had his hands up, lightning arcing between them. "What do you mean?"

"Strike and Noah . . . they are the same person. He can make us see what he wants us to see, right?"

Noah nodded.

Dinah let out a soft cry, but said nothing.

I did not want to get into the past, not now. "I need to get to the desert. You know the one. Wherever Romano has Bear."

"You don't want to take a plane?" He arched both eyebrows high and I glared at him.

Abe let out a long low growl and hunched his back as if he were going to leap. "*Nein.*" I held a hand out, stopping him. "Not yet."

Noah just stood there. "You called me. Very clever. You know none of the men ever figured out that trick?" He smiled and there was a warmth to it I didn't like. Like he saw me as more than a tool but as a woman he'd like to fuck. He'd said as much, that I should have turned to him.

I stared up at him, almost not caring who and what he was, and I knew that was dangerous. Not caring would put me in a bad position to negotiate. "You want Romano dead. This is the price you pay to make it happen. You need to get all of us to where Bear is."

He grinned then, and the image of him as Noah wavered, showing me the other man, the one I knew as Strike sliding through the façade. "There is a price to pay when you call on a demon, Phoenix. I could just keep Bear to myself for the next ten years, train him and then have him kill Romano. Bear has the same abilities you do, stronger in some ways actually because of his father's blood. He will have talents from both of you as he ages."

I could only imagine the kind of training Bear would receive from a guardian from Hell. What kind of life would he have? Nothing, he wouldn't have a life, and he'd be twisted into a monster worse even than I'd become. Killian let out a growl that mimicked Abe's.

"No."

"I didn't think you'd like that." He tipped his head to one

side. "I want something from you, then. Like I said, a price to pay."

"Name it then so we can get this show on the road," I snapped. "Time is of the essence last I checked."

He smiled again and took a step toward me. "I want Bea when we are done here."

Dinah gasped and I took a step back, putting my hand over her. "So you can torture her?"

He closed his eyes then and a twist of pain slid over his face. "I still love her, and that love is killing the dark in me. I won't be a guardian of Hell much longer."

"Yes," Dinah said. "Yes, I'll go with him."

"Dinah, you don't know what that will mean," I said. I wasn't worried about losing her as a weapon but as my sister for a second time. "There is no guarantee you'll end up human again."

"That's true," Strike said. "But I'd like to have her with me just the same."

"Bad idea," Killian said. "Better that it be money."

"Yes," she said again. "I'll agree to those terms. Now help my sister end Romano."

"Done, my love," he whispered and a heavy sigh slid from him. "I need you to take my hand, Phoenix. Then you take Killian's."

I looked at Killian who let out a big breath. "Abe, *hier*." He snapped his fingers and Abe launched into his arms without a moment's hesitation.

But I hesitated. "With or without blood?"

"With." Noah held a hand out to me.

I paused. "You made me love him, didn't you?"

He snorted. "You wanted to love Justin, to fit in with the normal world, but you didn't. And you never would have without me. I gave you the push you needed. There was no way I was going to let you out of my sight. I promised Bea I would do all I could to protect you."

I shook my head and took a step back, suddenly uncertain. "Then why not just give us the answers? Why make me jump through all these hoops?"

He grinned then, surprising me. "I'm still an asshole demon, Phoenix. I answer to my creator, as you will answer to *yours*. My boss wants Bear. And he wants you. I will do what I can to help, but I am bound by the chains I carry too."

I didn't like that his words made sense. But did they make sense, or was he manipulating my mind once more? Sweat broke out along my spine, but I pushed on. "You're a guardian of HELL. How can you love?"

His grin was lopsided and I saw more of the Noah I knew in it than ever before. "We—all of the guardians—were human once. We made a deal with the devil and the price we pay . . . well, this is it. Or at least, it's mine. What is more torturous but to still have your emotions intact, to have them play out in front of you but be unable to act on them?"

Human once, then. Not abnormal. He reached out for me and I offered him my hand once more, reaching back for Killian. His fingers tightened on mine. "God, I hope you be right, Lass."

"Me too," I said.

For Bear, I would take the hand of a demon and let him lead me. Strike turned my wrist so my palm stretched out in front of him. With the tip of one finger, he drew a line along and blood welled up through the skin. Not a cut. But *through* the pores of my hand.

I locked eyes with him and he just smiled and winked as if . . . as if this were a game to him. Which I was stupid to think my life would be anything but a game to a demon.

Strike clasped his hand over mine and there was a blast of heat that ripped from his hand through mine and up my arm. On some weird instinct, I tried to grab at it for my own, to make his fire mine.

"Don't do that," he growled.

I didn't say anything but did try to stop drawing his heat to me.

Strike tightened his hold on me. "You might want to close your eyes for this."

"Not a fucking chance," I said. There was no way I would close my eyes and not be ready for wherever the hell we popped into. Because if he took me anywhere but the desert, I was going to kill him on the spot, his help be damned.

The heat between our palms intensified and I let it burn through me, breathing it in and out. Between one breath and the next the world around us fuzzed over. There was no jerking sensation, no sense of moving in any direction. Just a fog that closed in around us and made the world indistinct as if we walked in a dream world. Strike let my hand go.

He turned and walked away from us. "Follow me."

"We're going to walk all the way there?" I barked the words at him, anger suffusing me.

"This place here is not like the real world. The time is slow here. We'll walk and be in the desert in a matter of minutes in the real world." He didn't look back once.

I looked at Killian who slowly put Abe down. I called Abe to me with a simple hand gesture and he hurried to my side. Killian's eyes were tight.

"Lass, this is dangerous. I've heard of stories like this, people being trapped inside a void with a demon. I thought they were fairy tales."

"Nope," Noah threw over his shoulder. "Not at all."

I broke into a jog to catch up to him, all the while my fingers itching to hold Dinah. But I wasn't so sure she would shoot him even if I asked her to. I suspected she would hold back even if it meant her actual death.

I was going to make the best of this time with a demon who was trying to help us, even though he'd tried to kill us.

"Tell me about your boss."

"He's a demon. You've met him, if I recall correctly." Noah didn't look at me but continued to navigate his way through the clouded terrain. I could see that each step we took jumped us forward far more than a single step in the real world, but still, we weren't exactly going at light speed.

There was a strong chance he wouldn't acknowledge any of my questions, but we had the time so I was going to try. "Why does he want me and Bear?"

He surprised me by answering in detail. "You are the Ascendants from a long line of abnormals with great power. Demons crave power, they want to control it, to make it their own. It's the only way they do things. Ascendants are rare, only coming through one or two in a generation."

A few more strides and we were across half the country by what I could see, the landmarks I knew flickering in the blink of the eye. This was going to go fast indeed.

"There could be another abnormal like me then. Why not go after him or her?" I stepped over a rock and we were in the middle of a highway, cars going by us so slowly they might as well have not been moving at all.

"You are correct. In your generation, there were three born to the Ascendant lines. To your mother's generation only two. Her and another male."

My eyebrows shot up. "Three in my generation. What happened to the other two?"

"One died in a robbery gone wrong, when he tried to rob Mr. Mancini. What powers he had were being used as a two-bit thief and Mancini didn't realize what he was until it was too late." Noah glanced at me. "The other of your generation is unfound. My boss has looked, but all he knows is that it's a man around your age. No actual information other than that."

Something niggled at my mind. "Are the Ascendants born usually men?"

"Yes. Women are rarely born into this line. The emotions they have naturally make them more likely to burn up within the flames of their own power. Natural selection has created a bloodline that is primarily male."

He spoke so casually, but also with such certainty that I believed every word.

"So, I'm abnormal even for a rare abnormal is what you're saying?"

He did look at me then. "Something like that. There is a chance you could burn the power right out of you if you use too much."

Lie, that was a lie and it lay heavy on the air between us. I didn't call him out on it because I didn't need him to know I could pick out the lies on his tongue. I smiled to myself. "Good to know."

Step, step, step.

Dinah cleared her throat. "We still have to finish the bullet to end Romano. What's the plan for that?" I tightened my hold on the metal box.

Noah glanced at me, but really he was looking at my side where Dinah was. "That will be up to Phoenix. It is her flames that must melt the products together."

I snorted, not willing to tell him we had the bullet and that it was primed. It needed only the ingredients and to be capped and it would be ready. "Sure. Because I've done that shit before. I am *not* going to put my son's life on the line with something I've never even tried."

"Then you will have to figure it out. I cannot hold your hand through every step," Noah said.

We were over an ocean now, and each step I took, I expected to fall into the water. Killian was on my left and Abe was glued to me, panting hard as we moved along. No doubt his brain was saying *run away*. I didn't blame him.

"Here." Noah stopped, and around us I saw nothing but open sky and desert sand.

I had one more thing to say, knowing what I knew about Justin now, how he'd been Simon, how he'd fooled me so deeply with Noah's help.

"You knew all along what was needed to kill Romano, didn't you?" I asked.

"I did." He nodded and the air went out of me as the realization struck.

"Justin felt like he was truly going to be free, didn't he?"

"He did." He nodded again, his eyes unblinking.

"But he was never going to be, was he?"

Noah shook his head. "I needed him to be fully invested in you and your son. To protect you. And he needed something to do to keep him busy and out of trouble. As you've seen, on his own he finds trouble rather easily. This task kept him busy for years. Now . . . I am not quite sure what to do with him."

"What do you mean?" Killian asked the question that was on the tip of my tongue.

Noah looked at him. "I own him. He is my creation. And he is down to his last life. Re-spawning is not infinite."

He spoke as if he were a parent speaking of his teenage son who needed to be manipulated into the right path.

"All along you had the ingredients." Not a question, a confirmation. All those trips Justin took away from us. The first when Bear was just days old. I did close my eyes for a moment, seeing the sadness on Bear's face whenever his father left, the worry that he wouldn't come back. A father he would never see again even though he was still alive. Fucked up, this whole world was royally fucked up.

The metal box in my arms suddenly felt very heavy and I lowered it to the ground between my feet. "I'll finish it here."

"Do you not want to know what's missing?"

"The curse," I said. "That's the part you could never find, wasn't it?"

He snorted. "Too smart. I should have brought you in on this years ago."

"Why didn't you?" I rolled the ruby ring on my hand, thinking about how many times I'd been duped by Strike, Noah, whatever name he went by.

"Boss didn't want you in on it. He wanted you weak. I told him that would never be the case, not a sister of Bea's." He shrugged. "Not my call, Nix. It was never my call."

I didn't feel bad for him. He'd made his choice and become this demon for whatever reason.

Killian put a hand on my arm, carefully. "Out, we need out now."

I twisted around. He was pale, his face so white it blended in with the fog around us. "Noah. Get us out now!"

"Finish the bullet, make sure you've got it," he countered.

I spun, kicking out and catching him in the knee. Abe barked once, leapt forward and bit into Noah's other ankle, yanking him off balance further. I reached back for Killian even while I scooped up the metal box. We had everything. We were in the desert. We just needed to get out.

Dinah screamed as Noah went down. "Don't hurt him!"

"He's not on our side, Dinah! It's a trap!" I yelled back. I didn't know why I believed that, not until the heat started in around us. The pull and tug of flames, the call of a demon I'd met once before.

I shoved the metal box at Killian and spun, snapping Dinah up and firing right into the mouth of Bazixal as he strode toward us.

Noah groaned behind us. "I'm sorry."

Killian started to slump, shaking his head. I stared straight at Bazixal and aimed for his eye. "Go to hell."

23

Facing down the demon from my past, the demon who'd made the deal with my father, was no small thing. The heat rolled off his body in waves and lifted my hair, the same as he had done before.

A cool breeze brushed over me. *I am still here.*

Martin, bless him, kept the worst of the heat at bay.

I put myself between Bazixal and Killian and Abe. "Get ready to run, boys."

Bazixal laughed. "I have you now. You don't think I'm going to let you go that easily, do you?"

I still had the electricity pooled in my spine from before we went into Vivian's house. I tapped into it and sent it shooting down my arm, and through Dinah as I pulled the trigger. There was no thought as to whether it would work or not—it had to.

The electricity and her bullet slammed into his eye, which sent him tumbling backwards with the force of a Mack truck ramming him. He roared, royally pissed even as he pushed back to his feet.

"Time to go." I jammed Dinah in her holster and yanked

a knife. I cut my hand, the blood dripped into the ground at my feet and the fog around us faded. I reached for Killian but he was already stumbling through, out into the real world and the cool night air.

I spun as I stepped across the threshold and looked back. There was nothing behind us, no void, no Noah, no Bazixal.

"That . . . could have been worse," I said.

Killian laughed and shook his head. "No, it couldn't have been."

Abe whimpered, his body shaking where he pressed against me. I dropped a hand to him and he flinched before he relaxed again. I knew how he felt. Jumpy and uncertain, ready to run, fight, or fall depending on the situation at hand. I refused to let my mind think on what had almost happened. Why the fuck did Bazixal think he had any right to me?

Nope, I couldn't go there. We were too close to Bear.

"Noah, Strike, whoever he was is right about one thing." Killian handed me the box. "Finish the bullet. Can you get it ready to be used?"

I nodded and flipped the box open as I dropped to my knees. "I have to." The sand cushioned me, cool from the night, but I had no doubt the grains would super-heat in a matter of hours.

I made myself focus on the task at hand, to not think about what was coming.

The herbs were all there. I lit a small fire in the palm of my hand and let it heat the bottom of the box until the items were on fire, burning. Even as I took this first step, the next bloomed in my mind, each step forming behind my eyes a split second before I needed them.

Burn the items to ash, put them into the bullet. I used

the edge of my knife and ground off a few bits of the ruby ring for the grindings of a curse and put them in too. I pulled out the diary and cut off a piece of the original deal, and put it into the metal box. The smell was sweet like a heavy rose perfume. I grimaced but kept the heat up, kept moving the box so the ingredients meshed. They pooled together as though they were attracted to one another. They were a powder so fine, it looked like a liquid. Killian helped me pour them into the empty casing.

Finally, there was that last bit of gold at the bottom of the box. I heated it into a puddle and poured it into the top of the bullet, capping it, trying not to think about how my hands had become a crucible for my father's death. I smoothed the edges out as best I could.

"Not pretty," I said as I held the bullet up, still warm from my flames. "Dinah, can you shoot it?"

"Put it in, and let's find out," she said.

I did as she asked and there was a clicking noise, not unlike the sounds she made when shifting to a smoke bomb.

"Yes, I can shoot it, but there is a *but*," she said.

"Tell me."

"You need to be close. It has zero trajectory. Without a proper tip, I can't guarantee where it will end up if you shoot from a distance." She shivered in my hand. "I'll hold it back, shoot as you wish and—"

"How close?" Killian asked.

"Like, an inch from his head," she said. "There is no other way."

Of course not. I shouldn't have been surprised, but I was a little. I'd hoped to be able to just shoot Romano and then walk away.

"Let's go." I walked toward the glowing orb of the moon that hung low in the sky.

"How do you know what direction?" Killian asked.

"I don't. I'm following my feet," I said. "All this Ascendant shit is supposed to bring us luck, and some sort of path to follow when we need it. I'm letting it happen." Because there was no other option.

Killian was beside me, his hand brushing mine as we walked—trudged really—through the loose sand. An hour passed in silence before he cleared his throat.

"I remember most of our time together now."

I flicked my eyes to him and then back to the sand. "Okay. Is that important?"

"Aye. It is." He took my hand and stopped me, pulling me around to face him. "It's important because I believe you are right. Death is stalking us." He kissed me gently, a flash of electricity slipping through him and into me, giving me some of his power.

"Thanks."

He grinned. "I think I love you, Phoenix."

Dinah let out a soft sigh. "Say it back, please say it back to him."

I couldn't, though. Love was a tool to be used against me, and it had been used effectively. "I can't."

He gave me a wink. "I understand. I can say it for both of us, Lass."

I opened my mouth, not sure what I was going to say because there would never be a right time to tell him I loved him. Instead of words, though, I tipped my head toward the sound of feet pounding the sand.

I flashed a hand movement at Killian and Abe, and the three of us flattened to the ground. I counted five men wearing guns, and then a sixth... a sixth that I knew. A man who'd been at the school where Bear had been attending, a man who had been his bodyguard.

"Abe, *fass!*" I pointed at the big guy and Abe hesitated. I put a hand on him gently, and gave the command again as I got up. With more confidence, Abe stood and I ran with him toward the man who'd been set to guard my son. Abe was the only one fast enough to get to the bodyguard and take him down before we lost him in the desert.

The dog shot across the sand in a blurred streak, silent as he raced after the bodyguard.

The big man twisted in mid-stride, sensing something in that split second before Abe tackled him from behind. They went down in a flurry of cursing and flailing limbs. Abe snarled and then let out a yip as he was booted in the side. But I was there a moment later and I leapt on top of the bodyguard.

I had Dinah out and a knife pressed to his throat as I knelt with one leg on his chest. "Where is Bear?"

His eyes flicked to me and away. "You can't save him. Let him go, Phoenix."

I pressed harder with the knife. "How do you know?"

"Because I tried, Nix. I tried to save him. I got all the stuff. I got all the secrets and it still wasn't enough. Romano can't be killed. Tommy failed." His words came out louder with each one until he threw me off him.

I rolled away and came up in a crouch breathing hard, realizing as I stared at this man who he really was. Who he'd been. "You . . . were Justin. You were Simon?"

His shoulders hunched as if I'd hit him. "I was."

I swept to my feet, anger and hurt propelling me. "Where is Bear, *Justin*?" I said as I drew close.

He hunched further. "With Romano, at the Grotto."

My jaw ticked hard and I struggled with every shred of

willpower not to blow his brains out right there. "I have . . . *my* . . . son to save. I will not deal with this emotional shit until that happens. Are you going to help? *Can* you help or are you too tied to Strike?"

Justin turned and stepped toward me. I didn't move, so he kept coming until he was right in front of me. I knew he wanted to touch me, but I didn't make any sort of motion to indicate it would be a good idea.

Dinah helped me out there. "Don't you fucking touch her, you idiot. Dumb fucking idiot. You left her to grieve her boy, and you fucking well better believe she will never forget it. Because I'll remind her if she ever for one second softens toward you."

His eyes never left mine. "You forgave Dinah for not telling you the truth about her. Because she wasn't able to. I am bound by a similar spell. There were and still are things I cannot tell you, things I couldn't do to help. When I respawn there are rules. Can you not do the same for me as you did for Dinah?"

"Not now, not ever." I stared him down. "You are not Justin. And I was never Bea. But you knew *that,* didn't you?" I didn't know how else to say it. "That was a fantasy we both let ourselves believe. But Bear's life is not a fantasy. Help me save him, or fuck off and *never* come back."

He nodded again, slowly. "That's why I'm leaving. Strike can find me anywhere, and he always knows who I'm with. And he isn't done with you, Nix. Once you kill Romano, and I have no doubt you will," his fingers brushed against mine, sending a sharp tingle through my skin, "Strike and his boss want you for your power. And if they can't have you, then they will take Bear."

My heart clenched. "That will not happen."

He lifted his hand enough to touch his fingers to mine, a

pain-filled goodbye I never thought I'd have. "Your love saved me, Nix. Even if it wasn't all of your heart." His eyes flicked to Killian. "I have always been a coward. I know that. But for Bear, I can be brave a little while longer. I'm going to get as far away as possible, so I won't be used against you. If you see me again, kill me. I won't come back of my own choice." He stepped back as a single tear trickled down his face. "I'm sorry I couldn't tell you the truth sooner. It's why I left the note."

He took a few more steps and I shook my head, raising Dinah on him. "No. You're coming with us. Being brave means facing this for Bear."

He sighed and I strode to him, shoved him ahead of us. "Lead the way, brave one."

"You can call me Rooster if that helps. That's what this body goes by."

"Fine, Rooster. Get the fuck moving." There was only so much I could take when it came to revelations. This shit was hitting my threshold.

"How far?" Killian asked.

"Five minutes," Rooster said. "I heard gunfire and Romano laughing. I saw Strike leave, which told me he was going for you. So, I left."

I could not for the life of me understand how he could leave our son—willingly leave him with Romano. "Why is Strike helping us?"

Rooster was quiet a moment before he answered. "He wants Romano dead. But it's only so he and his master can get to you and Bear free and clear. I think that was always the end game."

"Free and clear?" I said.

"What the hell does that mean?" Killian asked.

"Means that the deal her daddy made ties her into

things too. I don't know exactly how." Rooster shrugged and flinched as if something hurt him. "But it means they need Romano dead first. Which is where you come in. You kill him and then they have you."

I swayed in between steps, watching Rooster who'd been Simon, who'd been Justin, who'd been my husband and the father to my child, walk in front of me.

There was a brush of cool air, and then Killian put his hand on my lower back. "Keep going. One step at a time."

He was right. I made myself pick up my feet again and put them one in front of the other. Rooster's words wouldn't have affected me so much if I hadn't just heard what Bazixal had to say to me. That he wasn't going to let me go that easily.

Except there was no reason to why he would have me at all. I'd made no deal with him.

"Here," Rooster said and I blinked, so lost in my own thoughts that I'd let the wall of the Grotto sneak up on us. "I don't know how you'll get in. Tommy had an insider let him in."

"I'm going to start a fire," I said softly. I walked up to the wall and placed my hands on it. Wooden, it would burn, and burn hot, in this dry desert air.

I called the fire up through me and let it pour out of my hands. The blue and purple flames mixed and raced along the wood, eating at it like locusts on a field of grain. I stepped back ten paces and waited quietly.

There was a calm in the moment I knew all too well. The calm before the death toll began to rise. I welcomed it.

The crackle of the flames on the wood grew louder and the smoke drifted high and suddenly there was shouting on the inside of the wall. A door swung open and I let out a slow breath as I raised Dinah.

There were no innocents here.

I walked toward the door as men poured out, men with weapons. I shot them one by one, never slowing in my approach, nor speeding up.

The report of the gun in my hands and the fly of the bullets was my world narrowed to just a small focus, one I understood. Rooster was to my left, and Killian was to my right. He had a gun and picked off men as they topped the wall with their sniper rifles.

"We should be running!" Rooster yelled as a body went down right in front of us, a spray of blood splattering my face.

"No. This is the end game. No more running." I reached for the door and held it open, sweeping the inside tunnel. "Abe, find Bear."

The Malinois had his nose to the ground in a flash and he let out an excited bark. I followed him, trusting that the two men would follow me. My world had one thought now. The truth of who Rooster was, the words of Bazixal, the power flowing through my veins . . . none of it mattered. Bear was going to be back in my arms in a matter of minutes one way or another.

Even if I had to burn the Grotto to the ground and kill every last soul within its walls, I would get Bear back.

24

BEAR

The bark of a dog snapped my head up and I twisted around, my knees grinding into the stone floor painfully. Romano shoved my head back down with a booted foot. "Stay there, boy."

He'd put me at the edge of his throne, so he could literally keep his foot on me. Tommy lay on his belly, flat out and unconscious. I could still hear his bones breaking, and his skin tearing open as Luca Romano's men beat him into a bloody pulp. Eleanor dug into my belly and I reached for her.

"Not yet," she whispered.

I stilled my hand, listening for another bark. How it could possibly be Abe, I didn't know, but it was him. I was sure of it. And where Abe was, my mom wouldn't be far behind. My throat tightened and my eyes prickled with tears. Eleanor was right, my mom would always come for me.

There was a sudden onslaught of gunfire and then what sounded like crackle of electricity.

My heart gave a funny thump. Killian had come with her

then? My own father had left me behind, but Killian had come for me. The tears fell down my cheeks. I was not alone, no matter how awful this all had been.

I drew a deep shaking breath and embraced my flames, ready to use them.

Luca Romano grabbed me by the scruff of my neck, his fingers digging in as he lifted me off the floor.

"Is this what you came for?"

* * *

Phoenix

THE SCENE IN FRONT OF ME WAS NOTHING SHORT OF CHAOS. Bodies were strewn, fire caught at the edges of the dance floor and my father stood on what could only be called a throne, holding my son up high enough that his feet dangled.

"Is this what you came for?" Romano roared the words at me.

I tucked Dinah into her holster. "Switch it out, Dinah."

The metal inside of her made a grinding snarl as she shifted the golden bullet into place. "Ready," she said.

"I came for my son," I called back. "And for your life."

His hands tightened on Bear's neck and he cried out, reaching upward to stop him, digging his fingers into his grandfather's skin to no avail.

"I think it's time for you to see your boy die. Perhaps then you'll understand why you will never win. Why you are better off doing as you are told."

Abe had been slinking closer to the two of them. "*Fass!*" I gave the command knowing that it would cost Abe his life, but save Bear. This was his moment, the reason he'd been with me all along.

To save my son.

He shot forward, low to the ground like a streak of Killian's lightning.

Abe leapt and grabbed at the arm holding Bear up, hanging off Romano, twisting and fighting to make him let his boy go.

Romano smiled and his hand shot around Abe . . . toward Bear's shirt. He yanked a gun out—a gun I knew all too well—and pointed it at my dog.

"Eleanor, no!" I screamed the words but it was too late. She howled as the bullet left her.

The blow flipped Abe over, sending him sprawling backward, a wound deep in his side, dead before he hit the floor, the bullet taking him right in the heart. I knew it by the lack of blood—his heart had stopped before the bullet had finished passing through. Eleanor never missed. Never.

Bear's eyes were wide, and his whole body shook as he crawled toward his dog. "No, no, not Abe."

Romano laughed and kicked Bear, flipping him over. "What are you going to do about it?"

I took a step, and then another and another until I was running, the same path as Abe.

Bear got his hands on Abe and screamed. I slid to a stop as flame burst around him, blue and green and brilliant. Romano snarled and backed away from him. Bear grabbed Abe and dragged him back, away from Romano.

My heart hurt for Abe, but he'd done what he'd been trained to do. Save his boy.

Romano held Eleanor and pointed her at me as I sidled toward Bear. "You see, Phoenix. You cannot beat me."

I didn't pull Dinah. I dropped to my knee beside my son. The flames on his body were gone, but even if they weren't, I would not have changed course. I gathered him up into my arms into a hug. The weight of his body, the feel of his skin on mine was like having a piece of myself back. I let the flames glow around me, soft pink and suffused with warmth instead of the harsh heat of the flames that caused so much destruction.

Bear looked up at me, his wounds healed, and I laid him back down. "Don't move. Stay with Abe."

All the while I'd kept my eyes locked on Romano's. His had turned thoughtful and calculating.

"An abnormal? You *lying* little bitch, you hid it from me all these years?" Of course he'd be angry, thinking I'd kept power from him.

I didn't answer him. He deserved nothing from me.

"I'm going to do more than beat you," I said softly. "I'm going to break you into pieces, and then I'm going to kill you."

"I can't be killed." He waved a hand to encompass his body. "I am immortal."

I smiled at him and laughed in his face. "Your master, Bazixal. He was right, you are a mewling pawn. I told you not to make that deal with him, but you didn't listen, did you?"

Romano's face drained of color. "What did you say?"

"I have the bullet, Luca Stephan Romano," I intoned his full name, echoing the night of the deal, "the bullet that will end your immortality and your life. I have it and I am going to use it. And you will be no more. The deal will be no more."

"Then he will use you if you are so stupid to do it, but I don't think you have a bullet, or you would have used it by now," Romano snarled, but I saw the fear on his face mixed with the uncertainty. "Maybe I've changed my mind. Perhaps I'll kill you now and keep Bear."

Killian laughed from behind me. "No. The boy be coming with me if she dies. He won't be used by you again."

"I took him from you once," Romano shouted at Killian. "I'll do it again."

"No, no!" Bear shouted. "Don't hurt my mom!"

I didn't dare look back, but by the direction of Bear's protests, I knew he was with Killian. That was the plan. Killian would take Bear and get the fuck out of here. I would catch up.

If I could.

Eleanor snarled in Romano's hands. "You always were a fucking monster."

Romano flicked his eyes at her as he pointed her at my head. She never missed. Fuck, I was going to have to be fast.

"Dodge to the left," Dinah whispered. "She's sloppy to the left."

"Shut your mouth and do your job." His finger squeezed the trigger on Eleanor. I knew I should have dodged, or tried to, but I knew Eleanor.

I knew her and I knew that if there was ever a time she would miss, it would be now.

The report of the gun echoed through the room and the bullet slammed into the top of my left shoulder, spinning me around. I went to one knee, and grabbed at the wound.

Eleanor was crying. "Phoenix, I'm so sorry. I'm so sorry!"

"It's okay," I said. "It's okay."

"No, it's not!" she screamed as he squeezed the trigger again. This time the bullet caught my left arm in the bicep. He was shooting for my heart and she was doing all she could to not hit me in a vital area.

"Fucking shoot her!" he roared.

Eleanor sobbed. "No, I won't. I love her. It's my job to protect her. I won't hurt her again."

Dinah started to cry.

I stared at the gun in my father's hand, the gun that held my mother's soul. "It's okay, Eleanor. Don't fight him."

"I can't do this!" she screamed. "I can't kill you!"

Romano cut the distance between us and put Eleanor's muzzle a foot away from my head. "You can't miss now."

This was going to be close. He squeezed the trigger and I swept my right hand up. Eleanor roared and a boom sounded like a bomb had gone off, the concussive force of the explosion sending me back a half step even while shrapnel and heat ripped across my skin. Romano let out a howl and I took the moment to my advantage. I had my hands on him as he dropped Eleanor. I slammed a fist into his jaw, snapping his head back. My fists might not be able to kill him but it made me feel better.

"Where is your guardian now?" I yelled as I drove a knee into his balls, sending him to the ground in a sprawling heap. "Where is your pet to protect you?" My eyes blurred from the kickback of Eleanor's shot.

"Strike." He groaned the name. But there was no Strike coming to his rescue. I hammered at him, but there was no blood, and I wanted his blood, goddamn it. I wanted him to hurt for everything he'd done. For all he'd taken from me, for the damage to my life and all those lives he'd made me take.

I was panting, out of breath with the anger and the rage, with the blows I rained down on his body.

He began to laugh. "Here he is. My guardian will finish you now."

I spun to see Strike standing ten feet away, watching us.

His eyes flicked from Romano back to me. "If you shoot him in the belly, the bullet will steal his immortality, then you can kill him however you like."

I spun back to Romano, drawing Dinah in a smooth motion. I had her an inch from his navel, right over his liver. That same instinct I'd followed my whole life whispered that I needed more than just the bullet. I called up my own flames and the electricity that Killian had given me. The two powers writhed around one another as they shot down my arm and into Dinah as I pulled the trigger.

The percussion of the shot echoed and spread like a shockwave had been released. I was blown backward from the force as Romano screamed, the boom going on and on, battering at my ears. Breaking glass, breaking bones, breaking walls, the world around us seemed to shatter on the force of the deal he'd made going to pieces.

I hit the ground with a grunt, rolled and was back on my feet, my hands up against the wind that swept out and around us. Slowly, the pressure died and I lowered my hands.

"Is he dead?" Dinah asked.

I took a step toward him. "Not yet. But he's dying."

Romano still lay on the floor panting, his hands cupped around the wound in his belly and the blood pouring out of him. Human, he was human and his life ran red as the dying sun.

I walked to over to him and stared down at the man whose blood ran in my veins. The same blood that now coated the floor. "You are going to die, Romano. Any last words?"

He stared up at me, his eyes glazing with pain and with death as it crept up over him. "You . . . are just like me. A killer. A monster." He smiled, blood coating his teeth as he coughed.

I bent down and whispered back, "No, I'm like my mother. A woman who would do anything to save her child."

I took my knife and pressed it against the side of his throat, nicking the jugular. Not enough that he would die fast, but enough that he would bleed out faster than the wound in his belly would cause. Seeing him bleed, seeing him dying at my feet removed the need to wound him further.

I stepped back, watching him shiver and convulse, dying alone in a foreign land without a single person to grieve him. His body gave a last tremble, his chest rose and the final breath went out of him. Dead, without any fanfare, the way he deserved.

"The deal is broken then." I turned to face Strike.

His face twisted with something akin to discomfort. "No, it's not." He stood over Tommy, a ruby ring in his hand—the one I'd dropped out in the desert if the rough edge of it was any indication. He pressed the ring to the back of Tommy's head. "My master wants the souls he was due."

"The deal is broken with Romano's death!" I yelled the words because fear had caught hold of me. Two of Romano's children were to be offered in the deal. Two. Tommy's soul counted as one and there was only one other child left of Romano's.

Me.

No, I would not go down without a fight. I was not going to let Bazixal have me.

Heat began to pool around us, the heat of a devil's fire.

"Mom!" Bear called for me and I turned to him. There were times to fight, and times to run. This was a time to run, to regroup and figure out what the fuck was going on. Abe stood at his side. I tried not to think about how that was possible.

I bolted for him, scooping Eleanor up as I went by and tucking her into her holster. Or trying to put her in, at least. I couldn't seem to get her to fit but I didn't look to see why. We were too busy running through the burning Grotto. I jammed her into the waistband of my jeans, under my belt.

Killian and Bear led the way, Abe sticking close to his boy. They'd found a way out then.

Behind me, I could hear laughter and then the rising of what sounded like screaming of people, only people was the wrong word.

Souls, Martin whispered. *There are souls being tortured and taken.*

His words were enough to make me go a little faster.

A few more corners and we were outside. There were no vehicles left that I could see.

"This way." Bear waved at me to follow him. "We have to ride out."

We slid to a stop on the cobblestone at the front of the stables. Four horses were saddled and ready to go. Rooster stood with them.

"He found them," Bear said, hope in his voice. I knew that hope all too well. The belief that maybe your dad wasn't the fucking asshole you knew in your heart he was.

"Let's go," I said.

I didn't question anything or try to break Bear's happy bubble. I just leapt astride the horse closest to me. The four horses picked up on our excitement and fear and bolted into the desert, Abe racing alongside as though he hadn't just been shot. Hadn't just died.

Rooster pointed out the direction back to the city closest

to us and we galloped away, the night hiding us as the Grotto burned, lighting up the sky like a beacon.

I rode beside Bear, reached out to him and he reached back. We held hands for a few strides and then let go. It was enough for now. He was here, we had him back.

Except that I knew this fight for our freedom was not over yet. We still had one monster to face.

Bazixal.

25

The Arabian desert stretched around us as we galloped through what was left of the night, the horses slowing as fatigue set in.

I finally allowed them to walk. We slid off the horses' backs, one by one, and walked with them, stretching our legs. Abe was panting hard, but still with us. I moved around to the far side so I was next to Bear. I grabbed him in a hug and picked him right up as if he were a toddler and not a ten-year-old boy. He didn't protest a bit, just hugged me tightly with legs and arms. I buried my face against his neck, breathing him in.

The son I'd thought I'd lost, the boy I thought I'd never get back was here with me. "I'm sorry it took so long."

"S'okay," he mumbled. "I knew you would come for me."

I didn't look at Rooster, but could feel the weight of his eyes on me. "Rooster helped—"

"I know who he is," Bear said softly. "And I know he ran away."

I let him down so he could walk next to me. But I didn't

take my hand from his. I couldn't for fear he would be snatched from me once again.

"Tell me everything that happened," I said.

Bear began his story with the jail and the Ikimono myst, how the antidote had gotten into him and how he'd been so sick that he'd been dying. He talked about how Rooster had tried to save him, and how they'd both been tossed from the car. Then there was Shaitan, and the desert witch, Tommy coming to rescue him and from there they broke into the Grotto.

I looked at Rooster. "That was when you took this body, isn't it? When the real Rooster died from the gunshot wound."

Rooster nodded. "Yes."

"I took Eleanor from Tommy, Mom." Bear's eyes were full of guilt. "She told me the bullet he had wouldn't work and I believed her. Did you really kill him?"

"I killed Romano," I said. "Someone else killed Tommy." I didn't need to fuel what were sure to be nightmares for years with the thought of Tommy's soul being stolen away in the last seconds of his death.

A thought trickled through me. "This desert witch, you said she trained you a little?"

"Yes, and she thought pretty highly of you." Bear's hands tightened on mine. "I know I was supposed to be afraid of her but I wasn't. She didn't scare me."

A woman with knowledge of the arcane would be rather handy right then. "Any idea how we might find her?"

Killian twisted around to me, looking at me across his horse's back. "What are you thinking?"

"That there has to be something about this deal we are missing still if Bazixal thinks he has any sort of hold on me."

Much as I wanted to shelter Bear from the truth of our world, I knew the time for that was long past.

"There!" Bear shouted suddenly, snapping my attention around. "There's her tent!"

I stared in the direction he pointed, somehow not surprised that indeed there was a large tent standing in the middle of the desert off to our right.

"She doesn't like men, though," Bear said. "I think Killian and Rooster should stay behind with the horses."

I nodded and reached for Dinah. "You ready?"

"Check Eleanor," she whispered. "I can't hear her."

I frowned and reached for Eleanor still stuffed in my belt. I hadn't even thought of her in the flight from the Grotto. I was too wrapped up in wondering what the hell Bazixal was up to.

I touched her handle and pulled her out. The muzzle of her gun was peeled back and the chamber was completely blown open. Which was why I'd not been able to get her into the holster.

"Eleanor?"

There was no answer.

Emotions swirled around me, more than I could deal with when we were still facing so much danger. I held her out to Killian. "Here, take her."

He did, his eyes worried but he said nothing, just let his finger brush over mine in a silent show of support. "We'll be waiting on you, Lass. Be careful. A desert witch is still a witch, no matter that the name sounds a little prettier."

I nodded and held my hand out to Bear. He took it and I pulled him tightly against my side.

We were maybe fifty feet away, but we walked slowly.

"Mom?"

"Yes?"

"Abe was a good dog. There will never be another one like him."

I looked back at Abe who was following us still. His eyes were locked on Bear. I bit my lower lip, realizing he wasn't really there. He'd died, saving his boy.

He will stay with your son until he finds a new protector. Martin's voice was gentle, the pressure of the wind around me cool and soothing.

My throat tightened and the tent wobbled through the sudden tears for a companion I thought had survived. "Yes, the best. He was the best dog. You're right too, there won't be another like him, but that doesn't mean you'll never have another friend like Abe."

Bear leaned his head into my side. "What are we going to do, Mom?"

I tightened my arm around him. "We're going to talk to this desert witch and then we're going home."

He lifted his head. "Home, like the ranch?"

I shrugged. "For a little while. Then we'll figure it out from there."

I didn't want to tell him that there was a chance he would be without me. I didn't want him to worry, but I should have known better. He was way ahead of the curve.

"What about this Bazixal guy? He's a bad one, isn't he?"

I looked back at where Rooster stood a little apart from Killian. "Yeah, he is."

Bear turned with me. "He's not like my dad, at all, anymore. My dad died in that truck, didn't he?"

A sigh slid from me. "Yes, Bear. He did. That man . . . is not your father anymore."

"Good," he whispered. "I'd rather think of him as a brave man, than a coward."

His words were so grown up, so true, and they hurt my

heart. He shouldn't have had to grow up so fast. "One day we'll talk about all of it, but not now. Okay?"

He agreed with a bob of his head.

We were at the tent and the bottom of the doorway flapped. Through it I could see a pair of feet covered in rings and the toenails were painted a bright blue. I arched an eyebrow. "Nice polish."

Laughter spilled out of the tent and the flap was lifted. "You were not impressed by the jewels?"

Her face was partially hidden by a veil, but her eyes were striking enough on their own. Violet eyes rimmed in thick black lashes. I shrugged. "Money means nothing to me."

"Good. Then we will discuss your current situation." She opened the flap farther and Bear scooted in first, going to the far side of the tent and sitting cross-legged.

I didn't know what she thought we were going to discuss, but it surely was not going to be the stones on her toes.

"Bazixal still thinks he has a hold on me. Any idea why?" I pulled out the diary from under my shirt and from there I pulled out the deal written on the demon skin.

Her eyes flicked over it. Reading it. A sigh slid from her.

"The deal should have been broken," she said. "Romano is dead, I felt his spirit sucked down into the depths of Hell."

Well, that much was good.

Her fingers flicked over the deal, brushing it here and there. "He has signed it in his own blood . . . ah. This is why." She pointed at the signature at the bottom.

I stared at it. "You're going to have to paint a clearer picture."

"Your blood is on this deal."

Her words were like a gong inside my head.

"Dad, this isn't a good idea," I said, moving toward him. My

job was to protect him, which meant I had to get him out of here. Now.

I reached his side and put a hand on his shoulder. He backhanded me, catching me off guard. I took a step back, tasting blood.

"He hit me, my blood was on his hands," I whispered, horror flickering through me. My blood was signed into this deal.

"But you didn't sign it!" Bear cried out, reaching for me. I let him come, let him crawl into my lap.

The desert witch watched us. "Bravery will only take him so far. He is still a child. It is good that you let him have that place of safety."

"He's right. I didn't sign it." I pointed at the words. "So, what does this mean to me?"

Her fingers coursed the paper again. "I think it means you must find a way to challenge Bazixal. To face him and force him to let you go. It can be done, but it is not easy." Her eyes were flickering, burning lights. "You have great power, but can you stop the pain when it comes? Or can you ride it through, can you bring the pain into you, making it into power?"

I frowned. "I don't understand."

She handed me the paper and I folded it, put it back in the diary. I wasn't even sure why I kept it still, only that I thought I should hang onto it a while longer.

"Go back to the beginning, Phoenix," she said. "That is where you must face him, where it all began."

I closed my eyes, exhaustion catching up to me. "What do you want for this knowledge?"

"A favor, one that will cost you nothing," she said, and I thought she smiled under her veil. "We are powerful women, and we must stand with one another if this world will ever see change. There is another woman, a powerful woman like you and me, waiting in a cargo plane not far from here—to the south. She needs help. That is my price."

A woman with a cargo plane in the desert. A plane that could take us off this continent and get us home. I stood and Bear moved with me without me having to say anything. "It sounds more like this is a way out for us."

"That too. I like this man child. He has great things coming for him." Her eyes crinkled at the edges.

Bear and I took our leave, walking quickly back to the horses. He grabbed my hand and gasped. I turned to see there was no tent behind us.

"Mom, she's gone."

"Yeah, get used to it. Abnormals can do some pretty freaky shit when they're strong." I tugged him forward. "Just roll with it for now."

He nodded, but kept turning to look. I knew the feeling, but I didn't give into it.

I boosted him into the saddle even though he didn't need help and then leapt onto my own horse. "We head south. There's a plane that can get us out of here."

Killian arched one eyebrow, but he said nothing. The four of us headed at a steady clip to the south, the sun still climbing on our left.

"How far?" Rooster asked, his voice husky with the need for water. The horses were sucking wind too, but we had no choice but to push on.

"I don't know." We were at the bottom of a sand dune that climbed high over us. I got off and held onto the edge of the saddle, letting the horse pull me up the steep incline rather than carry me. Bear followed suit as did the two men.

At the top of the dune my horse blew hard, its legs trembling, but my eyes were locked on the scene in front of me.

A massive army-green cargo plane with two people buzzing around it and a windstorm headed straight for them.

I squinted at the windstorm. "That is not natural."

"That's Shaitan." Rooster gasped for breath at the crest of the dune. "He's dangerous, like as in a desert demon dangerous."

"That plane is our way out, which means we have to stop him from taking it." I took a step and then another, leading my horse down the steep side of the dune. "At the bottom, mount up and ride hard for the plane, Bear. Rooster, you stay with him and protect him."

Killian jogged down the hill with me. "You and me going to do some damage?"

"That's the plan." I smiled at him. "It's what we're good at."

He laughed and then we were at the bottom of the slope and mounting. The horses were exhausted but they gave us everything they had left as we raced across a hard-packed ground, their hooves clattering on the stony bits.

We were maybe two hundred yards from the plane when I caught sight of one of its occupants. The powerful woman that the desert witch wanted me to help.

Her red hair stood out against the sand and the dark green of the cargo plane. I'd met her once and she'd cleaned up a rather messy death in a hotel room for me.

Easter Willis.

I didn't have time to wonder what the hell she was doing this far out of her territory. The windstorm slammed into us, a scream of fury within it spiking through my ears. The horses skidded to a stop, and they all went up, rearing, striking out with their legs at the awful noise. I slid off, so did Bear. Rooster was dumped on his ass and Killian went off to one side.

"Bear, get inside!" I yelled at him, pointing to the ramp. He grabbed the horses on either side of him and ran. Damn it, I hadn't meant for him to take the horses.

Behind you.

I spun with Martin's warning in time to see a sword slicing through the swirling sand and dust.

I bent backward, watched the blade slice through the air in front of my face and then I snapped back up, Dinah in hand. I squeezed the trigger and she ... choked.

"I can't. Something happened," she cried out.

Awesome.

That left the flames. I called them up and they raced down my arms and legs, over my entire body. Hotter and hotter, I wanted them to burn this motherfucker to ash. The sand around me began to drop, tinkling to the ground in little shards of glass.

"Ah, so *you* are the Phoenix?" a voice called to me from within the whirlwind. "Then come, let me have you."

I laughed. "You must be Shaitan?"

"I am."

"A coward then who cannot show his face? No surprise there." The flames made me bold even without Dinah.

The heat was intoxicating rippling through me and with it came a desert song on the wind. There was music in the sand here, music that filled my ears and whispered of the power I could be if I let myself train, if I let myself sink into Shaitan's arms and bed. He would hold me up for the world to fear, for my life to be molded to his vision.

A part of my brain screamed at me to snap the fuck out of it, but the other part was so drugged I couldn't do more than obey.

I let the fire douse and took a step, my mind fogged with the potential. Someone was shouting, someone I should listen to, but . . . I didn't want to be weak. I wanted to protect those I loved from the monsters.

I took a step, then another and another. A hand was held out to me and I reached for it.

"Not a good idea." A woman's voice cut through the fog and something slammed me to the ground. A body then?

I didn't even know. There was a flash of light, followed by a bolt of electricity and the arc went through me, snapping me out of the fog like nothing else. Killian was on top of me, breathing hard. "Time for you to go, Lass." There was a heavy strain in his voice as if he were holding back.

He scooped me up like I was a child and my limbs didn't protest. Hell, I couldn't protest. I was limp as a fucking wet blanket.

There was a scream of rage and then we were inside the cargo plane and the sand was blowing in. Killian hit the lift button for the ramp and it shut on the raging weather outside. Though weather would make you think that it was natural.

"What happened?" I mumbled like I'd been drinking heavily. I touched my mouth, tasted blood. My fingers were cut, probably from the shards of glass my flames had created.

"We need a jump!" Easter yelled out as she ran past us. "Lightning boy, can you do it?"

Killian put me down, took a limping step and then put a hand on the metal panel closest to us. I crumpled to the floor. "Bear." His name slipped from me and I twisted around.

A split second later he was there, wrapping his arms around me. I hugged him back. Killian jump-started the plane and the engines turned over, once, twice and then they caught. The propellers began to move and Easter let out a whoop as she bolted by, toward what had to be the cockpit.

"Dietrich, get us going!"

"On it, boss lady!" a man I assumed was Dietrich yelled back. I just sat there and watched it all happen like I'd been smacked on the head.

Repeatedly.

"What happened?" I repeated as Killian crumpled next to me, breathing hard, one arm wrapped around his middle. My legs were wobbly, trembling like I'd been sick for weeks.

"I am hoping our new friend can tell us." Killian slid his other arm around me. "You walked into the storm on fire and then the flames were just gone. I couldn't see you. Three men attacked from the other side."

I leaned into him, my head drooping to my chest. "I feel like shit. And you're hurt."

Killian groaned. "I'll be okay." Except his voice did not sound okay. I tried to turn to get a closer look at his wound.

Bear curled in tighter to my side. "We've got you, Mom."

There was a snort from behind and I didn't bother to look. Rooster was pissed. Let him be. He missed his chance for making things right.

Footsteps turned all three of us around. Easter strolled our way, her face a mixture of disbelief and suspicion. Her eyes shot to Killian. "Oh, that is bad. Did you get hit with one of their pig stickers?"

"Aye." He groaned the word and lay back on the floor. "Aye, I did, and they are curved."

"Fuck." I had to push back the spike of fear that caught me off guard. "I can close the wounds, but I can't get them out. You got a healer on board by chance?" As much as I wanted an answer to my question, it would have to wait. Killian was in trouble and I had to focus on him. I pushed the fog in my brain back.

Easter dropped to a crouch beside me. "No. If he can hold out, there will be one in Ireland."

Killian sucked in a breath and grimaced, his face paling. "Why not Heathrow?"

"Because that's an international airport and we've been smuggling things, fool," she snapped. "Ireland has a great airport for people like us."

He grunted. "Aye, I'm aware of it. When we land, we'll stay in the plane. They don't like me so much there. We'll get a healer in the States."

"Worse than your family?" I managed to quirk an eyebrow.

"Worse than me family." He grinned but it was tired. He closed his eyes. I peeled his arm away from the wound. Deep, bleeding and riddled with foreign objects if I was seeing this right. This was not good. "Killian?"

He didn't answer.

I put a finger to the pulse in Killian's neck, slow and unsteady. "He won't make it that long. I think he's bleeding out."

"Then he'll die." Easter stood and walked away to a set of seats screwed into the wall. I looked around the space while I struggled to find an answer to this new problem. I would not think of Killian dying, not now. I'd healed Bear. I could heal Killian. But I couldn't get the hooked blades out. Which meant this was just a stopgap.

"Easter, I need you to hold him down. Bear, get back," I said. "I'm going to cauterize the wounds so the bleeding stops. That will get him through the next few hours." At least, I hoped it would. I could feel the edges of blades that had been broken off inside of him and I knew that the blades would be hooked and curved. I knew because I'd used some just like them in one of my hits years ago. They were meant to kill slowly, and meant to be placed so if they were removed they would take half your innards with them.

"We have nothing to cauterize with." Easter approached slowly, her eyes narrowed. "So, what in the . . . name of sweet baby Jesus . . ." Her words trailed off as I lifted my hands and called my fire to them.

"Yeah, I doubt Jesus has much to do with this," I muttered. Dinah snickered, but I heard the anxiety in her laugh. She was worried too. Killian was family now.

Easter crouched beside his head, took both his hands and raised them to her where she could kneel on them. "He's got electricity. That may go off," she said, concern in her voice.

"He should focus it on me." My hands tingled with the blue and purple flames. I didn't know how to temper this, so I was going in hot in the most literal of senses.

I glanced up at Easter. "Ready?"

"I don't think there is any ready when it comes to lighting a man on fire who could fry us both like a high voltage electrical line."

My lips quirked and I nodded. "Point taken."

I straddled his hips so I could hold his bottom half down, then dropped my hands to the first two wounds and pushed the flame into them. Killian's body arched upward under me, and a scream ripped from his throat. The sound made the hair on the back of my neck stand, like that of a wounded and raging lion who was cornered and knew it couldn't escape. That image was so strong, I closed my eyes and just fed the flames.

"They're done," Easter said.

I lifted my hands and stared at the first two wounds. Blackened with lines of purple and blue racing from them, they were indeed closed. But those two were not the ones that truly worried me. The one under his heart, cutting through several ribs, was going to be the bad one. If I used too much heat, it was close enough that I could heat up his heart.

I blew out a breath and nodded. "Let's do it."

Killian let out a groan. "Enough."

"Not yet," I said, "and try not to fry us, please." I pressed one hand over the wound below his heart and carefully fed my flames into it. This time I didn't let the fire do as it wished but tried to hold it back, to rein it in, and keep the heat to a minimum. Just enough to cauterize. Killian roared and I pressed my free hand into his shoulder just as a tingle of electricity tripped along my skin, an early warning.

"Let him go!" I yelled at Easter a split second before the lightning ripped through him and into me. Easter was thrown back, but I got the brunt of the electricity and I took it in, let it pool in my body even while I screeched. The pain was white hot and it seemed to go on forever and ever, as though I were caught in a loop of neverending agony.

As fast as it hit me, it was just as suddenly gone and I flopped backward. I hit the deck of the plane hard and lay there twitching, my limbs dancing and jerking like I was a marionette on someone's puppet string.

"Nix, you okay?" Dinah yelled to me from her holster. At the same time, Bear scrambled over and grabbed hold of me.

"Mom, are you okay? Is Killian going to be okay?" He grabbed my face and forced me to look at him.

I managed a groan, but my throat was raw as if I'd been

screaming. I didn't think I had, more likely it was the path of the electricity that had burned its way through me.

Easter bent over me, her eyes wide. "You took that like a champ, right on the chin."

I laughed, but it sounded like a hoarse bark. "Not my intention. And we will be okay, Bear. We both will." His face was an open book.

He didn't believe me, at least not completely.

Easter did laugh as she held a hand out to me. "You must really like him."

I stifled another groan as she helped me to my feet. "Something like that."

We all turned to look at the still-prone Killian. "We can't move him now," I said. "If we do, it could wiggle those blades and set off the bleeding again."

Easter nodded. "I'll grab a couple blankets to toss over him." She walked across to the back of the plane and pulled out a couple of green army blankets. She handed them to me and I limped over to Killian. My entire body was bruised and twitching. But I moved toward him, bending and checking his pulse first. Steadier now, even just that bit of stabilization would be enough to get him through to Ireland and a healer, no matter what he thought was happening. I laid the two blankets on him, careful not to move him so much as an inch.

My shoulders slumped, but I couldn't rest, not yet. There was still shit going down that I had to deal with. "Easter, what were you doing in the Arabian desert?"

I turned to see her drop onto one of the benches. "Making a run for it. Mancini is cleaning house, killing his contractors left and right."

I arched an eyebrow. "Any particular reason?"

She shook her head and scratched at the side that was

shaved. "He's taking out the powerful ones for sure. I slipped through his noose with barely a minute to spare."

I moved slowly to sit beside her, grimacing as I slid into the seat. "Why the desert?"

"There's a powerful shaman here, though I doubt she's actually called a shaman. She's put a call out to any powerful female abnormal to come to her and band together against the men. She said it's always been the men who ruled the abnormal world and that needs to change." Easter looked at me. "I don't want power, but I don't want to die either."

I grunted. "I think we met her. Powerful, yes, and she sent me to you. Said I could help you. Though, I don't know that I did much seeing as we are headed back the way you ran from."

"Your man did help. I'll count it. Any longer there and Shaitan would have had us all." She grinned at me. Bear stood at my side, his arm around my waist. He didn't say anything else but I could feel the fear rolling through him. I tugged him a little closer.

"You've got some new tricks since I saw you last," Easter said. "What's with the hot hands?"

"Latent abilities showing up," I said.

Easter squinted at me. "You remind me of someone."

"I'm a Romano by blood."

"No shit!" She blurted the words. "I hate that man."

"Well, he's dead now, as are all his children except me." That truth was harder than I thought to say.

"Not really," Dinah said. "I just stuffed my soul into a gun."

Easter's eyes went wide and her face paled. "Did that *gun* just talk? Holy hell, then . . . you're *the* Phoenix?"

A sigh slid from me. "I am. Though, right now, I feel like

a pitiful sparrow that's been caught in a tornado and had its ass kicked repeatedly."

Easter snorted a laugh. "Well, I might just come along with you then. Just to see what trouble we could get in together. The Phoenix," she shook her head, "who would have thought it?"

I turned my head to look at her, but Bear tugged on me. "Mom, I have to show you something."

I glanced at Killian, my heart twisting. There was nothing I could do right at the moment for him. "Easter—"

"Yeah, I'll watch him." She nodded. Weird that I could trust her, even though we knew very little about one another.

We moved away from the open door and deeper into the cargo plane, Bear leading me along.

When we got into the hold, the smell of horses assaulted me. "Bear, want to tell me what happened?"

"I couldn't leave them behind," he said softly. "I just couldn't, not after leaving . . ."

He didn't say Abe's name, and I knew why. It was too soon, and the thought of his body still lying on the dance floor inside the burning Grotto was too much pain. I kissed the top of Bear's head. Even though I could see Abe's spirit there, brushing against Bear's legs. I ran my hand over the image and could have sworn I could feel him there.

"I get it. I do. And it's okay."

All four horses were bedded down with straw and had water and hay. But the pens they were in were far bigger than they needed, which made me wonder just what Easter and her partner were doing, what they were shipping out into the middle of the Arabian desert. There was no way she was just making a run for it. A woman like her did nothing for nothing. Money was involved somewhere.

I had more questions that I needed answers to if I could. Like what had happened back there in the desert, but I wanted Bear out of the way for them. As much as I could, I needed to give him a semblance of normal.

"Bear, get their tack off, make sure they have something to drink, okay?"

He bobbed his head and shot off to do as I asked. I didn't want to leave him alone, but I knew that there would come times like this that he would need to be on his own. To know he could still stand without me next to him.

A fine balance I wasn't sure I could walk well, at least right away. Reluctantly I went back the way we'd come, settling on a compromise. I stood in the doorway between the hold and where Killian lay.

Easter saw me and walked toward me. "I gotta ask, what made you think you could take on Shaitan anyway? I mean with the fire and everything, I would have thought you'd have run from him." Her eyes narrowed as she spoke.

I leaned against the door frame. "I thought I could deal with him, and why would my fire make it harder?" Pride got in the way there. I'd killed my father and thought I could take on a demon. I was an idiot.

Easter shook her head. "No one can deal with him. He's a demon, Phoenix. And not just any demon, but a fire demon. He has control of the flames that light in the desert. You'd have been better off to use your boyfriend here to zap him."

A breath slid out of me. "You're saying anyone who has fire could be controlled by him?"

Bear tugged on my arm. I looked past him. The saddles were all off the horses, but he had to have done it at light speed. Apparently, I wasn't the only one having separation anxiety. "He was looking for the Phoenix. He thought it would be a man and then he thought it was me."

"He didn't try to control you?" I stared down at him, concern arcing through me.

He shook his head. "No, I got to the desert witch before he could do anything. And I wasn't fighting him either. Maybe that made a difference."

I didn't think we were done with Shaitan . . . call it my Ascendant sixth sense, but that desert demon would be trouble.

The plane rumbled through some turbulence and I put a hand on Bear for what looked like balance, but was really so I could make sure he was still there. It would be a long time before I let him out of my sight.

I had to admit that the cargo plane made me nervous. How many times had planes failed me now? Three? Four? I'd lost count.

And this time, Bear was with me. I wanted nothing more than to strap him to my side with a large safety harness. Just in case. I grabbed another couple of blankets and set him up next to Killian. He fell asleep, his head in my lap. From the entrance into the cargo hold, Rooster stood watching.

I scooted out from under Bear and stood, walking over to the body that held my husband's soul. There was no other way to put it. This man was not my husband, but . . . he had been.

And it was time to have a discussion that was long overdue.

26

Rooster stared at me as I walked toward him, the cargo plane bumping in a bit of turbulence and then settling once more. We were only a few hours from Ireland. Killian was holding steady, but I wasn't going to push it.

He would stay in Ireland and someone would have to get him to a healer.

"Do you have something you want to say?" I stopped a few feet from Rooster.

He sighed and lifted a hand as if he would take mine.

"Don't you dare," snarled Dinah. "Don't you touch her."

"She is my wife," Rooster said.

"No," I fired back. "You died, not once, but twice. Till death do us part, remember?" I stared hard at him, seeing only an echo of the man I'd lived with for more than ten years. "And you ran away."

"I didn't have a choice. I told you that in the note." His plea fell on deaf ears. I leaned in so we were a hairsbreadth apart.

"I would have found a way."

"You think that now, but you wait. You wait and see what happens to you when you face Bazixal. Or Strike. You can't stand up to them, Nix. You can't." He shook his head and a shudder went through him. "I've been running my whole life from them and just when I think I'm free, they pull me back in. If I could die, I would have let it happen already."

"You're truly immortal?" I arched an eyebrow. "I doubt that."

He put a hand over his face. "No, not immortal. But I don't know how often I can re-spawn. I assume not indefinitely."

I just stared at him, hearing the lie. He did know, even if he wasn't telling me. So many emotions rushing through me, so much hurt and pain and loss. And love ... yes, even a little love still. "He was the best thing we ever made. I could forgive you for hating me, for running away from me. But not from him."

Rooster's eyes snapped up to mine. "Strike can find us even now through me. Do you understand that? I need to get away from you both. You might not think that I care, but I do. I love you both."

He took my hands and Dinah let out long hiss but I said nothing.

"You were the best of any of my lives, both of you. And if I thought that staying would help, I would stay, but I don't think it will help. I think it will only end this faster. Maybe you can find another Hider, someone like Zee who can tuck you away."

I pulled my fingers from his hands. "You will get off the plane with Killian in Ireland. Get him to a healer. Let your son have at least one man to look up to."

The words were meant to hurt and they did the trick.

"You think he can't look up to his real father?" he snarled, his fingers curling into fists.

We were nose to nose, anger snapping between us. "I think the man he knew as his father is dead. That man would have given his life to save his son. But not you. You'll run and that will be that. So, run away again, *Justin*. Only care for Killian first. It's the least you can do."

He stepped back, breathing hard. "I still love you."

I turned my back on him. "Words, Justin. Those are just words. Without actions behind them they mean nothing."

"And you think Killian loves you? He's known you for weeks, a month at best." He spit those words at me. I didn't answer him. I didn't have to.

I knew Killian loved me. I'd seen it in every step he took beside me, facing horrors that he could have just as easily walked away from, even after his memories were messed with. He could have let me go it alone, but he hadn't. I moved toward where he lay, Bear's head on his thigh.

Killian's eyes were closed, but he lifted a hand and placed it on Bear's head, and Bear reached up and placed his hand on top, hanging onto him. I turned to see Rooster staring at the scene. No, I didn't need to say anything. The love and care Killian had for me and Bear was clear to the naked eye.

Rooster turned and walked away.

"Goodbye, Justin," I said softly. I could never truly hate him, even knowing that he'd become Simon and killed Zee. He'd given me Bear. And that was worth every other shitty thing he'd done.

I sat beside Bear and put a hand on his side, feeling the rise and fall of his chest under my fingers. The time ticked by and I let my body rest, though my mind was anything but still.

This battle for our freedom was not over yet, and I had to do everything I could to keep these two safe. We'd lost Abe, we'd lost Eleanor. I put a hand on Dinah and stood.

"What is it?" she whispered.

"We have to talk," I said softly.

"You have a plan?"

I sighed and slipped her out of her holster. "Yes, but no one is going to like it."

She laughed. "Sounds like my kind of plan."

* * * *

IRELAND WAS AS GREEN AS KILLIAN'S EYES. WE LANDED ON A strip that was deep in the countryside and there was only a single vehicle waiting for us. A dark green van with a lift on it.

"I radioed ahead that we need a healer." Easter stomped out of the cockpit and glanced at Killian. "Is he still alive?"

"Aye," he whispered. "Though, I wish right now I had a stiff glass of whiskey."

"Later," I said.

We moved him with the help of the van attendant. Rooster said nothing as I directed him once more to stay with Killian. My heart hammered in my throat as I made sure Killian was settled. The healer, a young man with bright blue eyes, got to work on him right away, muttering under his breath in what I thought was Gaelic.

"Killian," I leaned over him and pressed my mouth to his ear, "thank you."

"Still can't say it?" he asked.

"No, not till this is done." I brushed a hand over his, then took a step back and turned.

Bear stood there, watching me, watching us. "You want me to stay with them, don't you?"

I went to one knee and he rushed into my arms. I didn't try to hold the tears back because I knew this was likely the last time I would ever see him. God, I had to let him go again and again. Would it ever be enough? Would I ever be allowed to just have a life with my son? The only hope that remained was that if I faced down Bazixal, that this would be the last time we were separated.

"Listen to me, Bear. I want you to take Dinah." I slipped off my holster and adjusted it as small as I could, sliding it over his shoulders and tightening it around his waist. He looked down. "Who is she?"

God, he was too smart for his own good.

"I'm your auntie," Dinah said. "And I won't let anyone hurt you, kid."

His eyes flooded with tears and he shook his head. A child. He was just a child and I was asking him to be a man. "I don't want you to go, Mom. Please."

"I don't want to go either," I managed to speak around the tears. "But I have to. I have to face this demon and I have to stop him from hurting us."

"Then you should take Dinah. You need her." He fumbled to get her out of the holster.

I put my hand over his. "No. You need to keep her with you. She won't be able to damage a demon."

Sobs rattled his body and he leaned toward me, pressing his forehead to my shoulder. I hugged him as tightly as I could, breathing him in. "I love you, Bear."

"I love you too," he whispered back. "Please don't die."

I stroked a hand over his head. "I'll do my best."

I didn't have to tell him that Killian would look out for him, or that Rooster would stick around at least to make sure they were safe.

"We're fueled up," Easter called to me. "We should go."

I kissed Bear on the forehead, stood and walked away. Walked away from the boy I'd fought so hard to find, that I'd killed to protect.

One more time. One last time. One way or another, I would end this.

27

BEAR

I stood there watching the cargo plane take off in a burst of speed that swept my mother away from me again. Tears tracked down my cheeks but I didn't bother to wipe them. I understood why she was going. I understood why she left me behind. But my worry was that without me there, something would go wrong. I couldn't even place why that feeling wrapped around me, but it was persistent enough that my feet took me in the direction of the plane before I could stop them.

"She's strong enough," Dinah said. "She'll take care of the demon and then this will be all over."

"I think she needs me there," I said. "I think without me, she won't be able to kill him."

Dinah sighed. "She'd only worry if you were there."

"No, it's not that." I rubbed a hand across my cheeks. "I can't explain it. I need to be there."

"It's too late now," she said. "You stay here, we'll make sure Killian is safe."

Dinah was right, it was too late, but I couldn't dodge the feeling that I should have gone with her. For right or for wrong, my gut feeling was pushing me to find a way to stand with my mother.

I bit my lower lip, turned and hurried to the back of the van. As I stepped around the corner, the healer pulled a piece of knife from Killian's belly. He flicked it behind him and it spun, end over end. Hooked and split in several places, blood dripped through it as it flung through the air.

"That be that, lad." The healer bent over him. "You look familiar, do I know you?"

Killian had said the people here didn't like him.

"He can't speak," I said.

The healer shot a look at me. "I heard him speak to his lady friend."

Killian groaned and pressed a hand to the wounds. "I'm from here, but it's been years. Mayhap you know a cousin or two of mine? Think you can finish the job now?"

The healer nodded. "In a minute."

I twisted around to see where Rooster had gone. He stood about twenty feet away speaking to someone. I frowned and narrowed my eyes. It was hard to see past Rooster, to see who he was speaking to because he was such a large guy. I took a step to the left and sucked in a sharp breath.

I hurried to Killian's side. "We have to go. Noah is here."

Killian groaned. "Fuck." I tried to help him sit up while the healer yelled at him to lie down.

Everything was happening so fast. I twisted around to see Noah push Rooster out of the way and start toward us. I only knew that he was with my grandfather, that he was working for him. I put a hand on Dinah.

"Dinah, what do I do?"

"Pull me out," she whispered. "I'll protect you."

I did as she said and pointed her at Noah as he strode toward us. He slowed and held up his hands.

"Bear, I'm your friend. Why don't you put that down?"

"No. You aren't my friend," I said. "You were working for my grandfather."

Noah shrugged. "Yes and no. I work for a lot of people."

I clutched at Dinah's grip with both hands. She was heavier than I expected. "I don't want to shoot you."

"But I kind of do," Dinah said and she went off in my hands, sending me backward right onto my butt.

The concussion filled my ears, and for a moment, I didn't hear anything. And then Noah grabbed me by the arm and put Dinah back into my holster. I wanted to find my fire but I couldn't any more than I could reach for Dinah. It wasn't there.

"Don't you hurt him!" Dinah screeched. "Strike, don't you hurt him!"

He ignored her. "You were right, kid," Noah said, his words trickling through to me. "You are meant to be with your mother right now, and I'm going to make sure of it."

I fought him, I did, and I saw Killian fall off the bed and crawl toward us but I knew it was already too late. Noah snapped his fingers and Rooster was there, as if he were a trained dog and the pieces fit together. They'd been in on this together all along.

And then my world went black.

Phoenix

THE FLIGHT BACK TO THE STATES WAS REMARKABLY QUIET except for the rumble of the cargo plane's engines and the occasional mutter from Easter and her co-pilot. She'd agreed to circle around NOLA and I would take a parachute and jump. Not ideal, but I understood her not wanting to land when I was going in to face a demon. I'd explained that much to her.

"You're shitting me." She stared at me like I'd lost my mind.

"When you have a child, or someone worth fighting for, you'll understand," I said. On me, I had only a few weapons left, knives mostly. I felt naked without Dinah and Eleanor.

Eleanor, I still had, but she was quiet, of course. Dead. I sat in the back of the plane with the parachute on, holding the remnants of my gun. Of my mother. I snorted softly and ran my fingers over the broken pieces. A brush of cool air brought my head up. "Martin, I thought I'd lost you somewhere back there."

No. But my journey ends here. I found my woman.

I chuckled. "Easter?"

Yes, she is a myst maker from an old line . . . I've been searching for her.

I nodded. "Then go with my thanks, Martin."

There is one last thing I wish to tell you. Her soul is within the gun still.

The cool breeze brushed down my arm and over my hand holding the gun.

If you fix what is broken, she may come back.

He said nothing else and I felt him move away from me, toward the cockpit. I didn't want to hope for something that was likely not going to happen. I knew that facing Bazixal was going to be deadlier than anything else I'd ever done. No job, no hit, no kill was going to come close to the danger

I was willingly putting myself in. I heated up my hands with my fire and smoothed it over the metal, bending some of it back into place. But it was far from healed. "Brikoff, I'll get Brikoff to fix this, Eleanor," I said softly.

"We're here," Easter called out to me. "I'm going to open the ramp and circle around. Choose carefully, don't forget this is bayou country."

I glanced back at her. "You've helped me when you didn't need to."

"I have a feeling we're going to meet again, Phoenix. I'd rather be on your good side." She grinned and saluted.

I blew out a breath and turned toward the opening ramp and the wind rushing in around my legs. There would be no good way to do this. The mansion where my father had made the deal with Bazixal had been on the north side of New Orleans proper. I waited for the plane to head that direction and then ran down the ramp and leapt off the edge.

The wind caught me, tugging tears from my eyes as I fell. From not only the wind, but from everything . . . for Bear and Killian, for Abe and Eleanor, for Zee, for Dinah . . . even for Tommy and Daniel. So much pain and destruction because of one man's lust for power.

Now, it was up to me to try to make it right. To fix this mess.

I pulled the cord on the parachute and I was snapped out of my freefall. My trajectory was good as I was headed for a clump of trees over what looked like solid ground.

My parachute tangled in the trees and I was snapped through the branches. I closed my eyes as I was slapped in the face and my body swung hard against the tree trunk. The wind was knocked out of me and I hung there a moment struggling to get it back. Finally, a breath swept in and I opened my eyes.

"I know I'm supposed to be lucky, but this is fucking ridiculous." I stared at the mansion that was across an expanse of water from me. The mansion that this had all started in and where Romano was supposed to end it. I looked into the sky, to see the crescent moon hanging directly over the mansion. Luck, this was crazy luck.

I grabbed a knife and cut away the cords so I dropped to the ground. Only it wasn't ground but sloppy mud that sucked all the way up to my knees. The sounds of the bayou hummed in my ears, the frogs and the birds, the splash of water. I took a step and then another and another. There was no point in taking my time now.

If Bazixal didn't know I was coming, I'd have been shocked. I made it across the chunk of mushy bayou with only one encounter with a large snake that really had no interest in me at all.

Stepping out of the muck and onto solid ground, I stood there for a moment and gathered myself. I reached for my fire and felt it humming under my skin, waiting for me to use it. That was all I had, and yet . . . I knew it was right. Dinah would have done no damage to a demon like Bazixal.

She was better off protecting my boy.

I blew out a breath, anxiety rolling through me for the first time in a long time. This was not my kind of fight. I had no idea exactly what I was going into, or just what Bazixal would try to do to me. What he might try and trick me into signing or doing.

I swallowed hard, my mouth dry, fear chasing me.

The walk to the door was over far too fast. I didn't knock on the big double doors, I just pushed them open and let myself in. I strode through the house leaving a trail of mud and water behind.

All the way to the main eating hall, I went. The same table was set up, and all the chairs were as before. I glanced to my left at the fireplace but it was just a place for a fire. For now.

A squeaking grind snapped my eyes around to the head of the table. The chair turned and I expected a monster. What I got was Mancini.

"What the fuck are you doing here?" I barked the words at him, throwing them out before I thought better of them. Before I thought at all.

He smiled at me, those jigging and dancing eyes bobbing away. "You can't guess?"

"You wanted Romano dead. He's dead. But that doesn't explain . . ." I trailed off as I stared at him, at his eyes. Different than the demon's eyes but . . . close enough. My heart began to hammer out of control as he stood.

"You see, I am bound by rules I do not like." He trailed his fingers on the table as he worked his way toward me. "Demons must always be bound by rules. Mine were that I could not directly interfere with Romano's failure. I could help him succeed but I could not actively work to kill him and end the deal."

I struggled to find enough moisture in my mouth to speak properly. "It was you pushing me all along then."

"It was. I needed you to be strong enough." He smiled at me, his teeth not pointed but blunt, squared off. "You see, two of my guardians were coming to the end of their punishment with me. Their time was up. You killed them, which meant they lost their souls to me." He tipped his head at me as if thanking me.

I continued to stare at him while the words poured from his mouth. Like he was proud of himself for his deception.

"I knew you would be an Ascendant from the time you were born. I tried to take your mother, but she slipped away from me with your sister's help. So, I waited for you to come of age, whispering to your father that you would make an excellent killer. That you would want to prove yourself. And then I helped to set you free of him."

"Why?" I couldn't help the one-word question.

He held up a finger. "Because there is no better driving force than that of a mother's love. Did you know that? I did. I've seen it in action before. Seen mothers throw themselves off cliffs to save their children, seen them throw themselves into a raging fire, seen them lie, steal, beg, kill and fight for their children. You were strong before, but I knew if you had a child, you would be a force like no other."

I was shaking. I couldn't stop. "You used me from the beginning."

"Well, to be fair, I used your father. He was nothing but a tool. His life and death were and are nothing. You will be my guardian now. You will be my finest creation."

I gripped the edge of the table, only realizing then that I had moved with him, keeping it between us. "No. You have no hold on me."

"Your blood is on that contract." He smiled. "Your father helped me out there."

"That contract is null and void. He's dead." I snarled the words. The fire in me began to flicker upward, curling around my body. Mancini—no, Bazixal—grinned and shrugged his shoulders. The image of Mancini fell away from him as if he'd brushed off a coat. His body elongated, growing and stretching into the demon I remembered from that night so long ago.

"Shall we compare flames then?" He grinned and the skin on his face tightened, his eyes enlarged and the dancing in them . . . I knew what it was now.

Souls. He had souls in his eyes and I do not mean his own.

I gripped the edge of the table and stared him down.

He laughed. "No different than before. I like that about you, Phoenix. You are stronger than you even know. But you are a killer. Your soul is tattered and torn, and I want it."

He snapped his teeth at me and they cracked like boulders being smashed together.

I pulled the diary out from under my shirt and peeled it open until the deal was in my hands.

"It won't burn." He smiled at me. "You cannot burn it. And with it still intact, you have a tie to me. There is on that paper a demand of a certain number of souls. I have two of the three."

He snapped his fingers and Noah slid into the room. He handed Bazixal the ruby ring. "Ah, Tommy and Luca. Lovely."

He closed his eyes and tipped his head back, then popped the ruby into his mouth. Horror slashed through me as I watched his throat bob and dance. When he opened his eyes again, I could have sworn that there were more objects in his left eye.

The fire in me rose higher, my fear driving it. Bazixal tipped his head. "Your soul, or your son's?"

I opened my mouth to deny him both.

Noah had gone to the doorway and reached through.

My eyes had to be deceiving me. They had to be. Bear stood there, his dark eyes wide but defiant. Dinah was still in her holster attached to his body.

"Your soul, or your son's."

Noah shoved Bear toward me and I caught him with one arm. This was my worst fear come to life. That I would be forced to leave him. Death was one thing, I could accept that I might die, but to give up what was left of my soul, to live as Noah and Justin were living? No, that I could not abide.

But there was no choice. There was no way I was going to let Bear's soul go to this demon.

"No," I said. "No."

"No, what?" Bazixal tipped his head. "The blood on that piece of paper means you have an agreement with me. I am owed a soul."

Rooster stepped out of the shadows. He moved to the other side of me and took the skin paper from my hand. "Then take mine."

Before I could stop him, he cut his finger on the tip of a knife and smeared it under Romano's signature.

Bazixal laughed. "You think that will save them? You are a fool."

Rooster looked at me. "Blood of an abnormal."

The blood of an abnormal was an accelerant and burned like nothing else. It had burned through the Stick Man when no other fire could touch him. Justin had been with me then as Simon, he knew. Hell, Noah had been with me then too. I shot a look at him. He blinked slowly as if . . . he knew now.

I grabbed the paper and called up my fire. It lit the blood on fire while Bazixal reached for Rooster.

Justin looked back at me, eyes full of sorrow. There were no words. There didn't need to be. We were fighting for our son together—finally.

"What are you doing?" Bazixal stopped his grab for Rooster, as if he felt the skin curling away in my hands, the words disappearing in a bloom of fire that could eat through anything.

"Ending this," I said.

"Strike, stop her!" he yelled.

Noah came at us fast, and had his hands on my arms in a split second.

Pain rocked through me, instantaneous and powerful, a crushing wave that hammered me to the ocean floor. Pain was not even a word for it, too mild, too nothing. My bones and skin were being peeled apart, I was going to be nothing but flopping limbs when he was done with me.

I fought the agony as it coursed through me, fought it . . . and a voice whispered to me.

Eleanor.

Don't fight the pain. Let it flow through you. Be the vessel, my girl. Let the pain pass. Stop fighting it, embrace it.

I didn't want to give in, to give up. But her words . . . they made me think of the day Bear was born. Of the immense pain, the thought that I was going to die in childbirth because he was breech, that he would be orphaned before he was even breathing on his own.

This pain was far worse now, but . . . it was the same too. Filling me, pushing me to the brink of my control, to the brink of my conditioning.

I drew a breath and stopped fighting the swells of agony that rolled through me. I let them pass over my body and let my mind pull away from its connection to my nerves.

I opened my eyes. Noah's hands were still on me, Rooster was still in the clutches of Bazixal and the skin paper had stopped burning. I called my fire up once more but this time there was no anger in it. No pain.

Just light and healing. The flames dulled to a pink so

pale that they nearly went out. Bear's eyes went to mine and I smiled at him. "Call your fire, Bear."

His body flooded with greens and blue as his flames flickered over his skin. He picked up the deal at our feet and held it out to me.

"Together."

Our combined flames raced over the deal and met in the middle with a flash of heat so intense it created a blast of air. Noah was thrown away from me, and Rooster was thrown away from Bazixal.

The demon roared as the fireplace began to shift and widen, flames reaching up for him. "You cannot kill me!"

"But we can banish you," I said. "You have no hold on us, Bazixal."

He roared as he reached for us, scrambling at the table and chairs, flinging them out of the way even as he was dragged back.

"Strike. Grab her!"

I looked over my shoulder and reached for Dinah out of the holster still attached to Bear with my free hand. I brought her up and fired twice, right into his head. She did not cry out. She didn't try to stop me.

Noah's head snapped back, but he didn't go down. I sidestepped, pushing Bear ahead of me with my hip. The deal was still burning.

"It needs to be ash," Rooster yelled. "It needs to be ash!"

His words were cut off and I spun Dinah back toward him. Bazixal held him over his head, one hand wrapped around his throat. "Will you save him too?"

"No," I said. "I won't."

The demon clenched harder, cutting Rooster's neck clean through with his bare hand. "Then he dies for the last time."

I didn't dare say that was what Rooster wanted. Bear trembled at my side, but his fire never wavered.

Behind us, Noah stumbled. "I can't grab her. The flame is too hot."

"No such thing!" Bazixal screamed. "It's not possible."

"You need a third Ascendant," Noah said. "You need a third to make this happen."

Bazixal roared, rage twisting his features. "Traitor!"

Eleanor shivered where I had her tucked against me. "Me." She whispered the word.

I pulled the gun out.

"Tear it apart," she said. "Finish the breaking so I can be whole again."

It was as if she and I were alone. "Mom."

"It's okay, Nix. Let me go, this was why I did what I did. I always knew that it would take three Ascendants to burn the deal. I wanted to be here for you."

I let the fire in my hands consume the gun, melting it away until it dripped into a puddle of molten hot metal at my feet.

A wavering image flowed beside me and then she was there. Her face was like mine in shape, but otherwise she was fair to my dark. My mother smiled at me and raised her hand.

"There was never any bringing me back. This is the last I can stand with you," she said.

Tears streaked my face and they seemed to feed the flames. Her hand swept out and laid over mine and Bear's. "Hello, grandson."

He stared up at her. "Hello."

"I told you she would come, didn't I?"

He smiled up at her. "You were right. Thank you."

She reached down and brushed a hand over his head, then her eyes came back to me.

"I have always been with you."

"I know that now," I whispered.

Bazixal screamed, but it was distant. He would be banished, but I knew it would not be forever. This was a moment I wanted to hang onto for as long as I could.

Her flames were orange and white and they danced in between mine and Bear's and the world grew dark around us while our fire ate up the danger in our hands.

"It's ash now," Bear said. "It's all gone."

He put his hand in mine, the ash gritty between our palms. My mother stood there a moment longer, her smile sad, but . . . proud. She was proud of me.

"Zee is waiting for me."

I choked on a sob. "Go then. Be happy."

She smiled at me as she faded away, her last look for Bear. She blew him a kiss and gave him a wink.

He smiled back. "Goodbye, Eleanor."

28

The old mansion on the bayou didn't seem as deadly as it had only moments before, despite the fact that we were not alone. Noah shifted behind us and I spun around, Dinah raised once more. Dinah didn't say a word, and for a moment, I thought she'd left me too.

"You can't kill me," he said.

"I don't know that I can trust you enough to let you go without trying." I pushed Bear behind me and started to work our way out of the house.

His eyes were hollow, the brows drawn. "I have done all I could to help you save your son."

"Why?"

"Because my daughter is out there and I am forbidden from finding her," he said. "Find her, Phoenix. Save her as I helped you save Bear. Keep Dinah. I release her from her promise."

He turned his back on me and walked toward the still-raging fire and stepped into it. He was engulfed and then he was gone. Just like that.

"We won't see him again, will we?" Bear asked.

"No, I don't think we will." I gave him a gentle push and then paused. Rooster's body lay on the floor. His chest was still.

I bit the inside of my cheek. "I don't want anyone to face this place again, Bear. Will you help me bring it down?"

"Yes." And then . . . "Dad?"

"He'll burn here, and no one will ever bring him back and hurt him again," I said.

"Good."

We raised our fire at the same time and as we walked through the house, set it ablaze.

With an arm around Bear, I walked away from the place that had been the beginning of my fate to become the Phoenix in truth. To have a son. And to love him more than anything I'd ever had in my life.

"I want to go home," Bear said. "But I don't think that means what it used to."

"I want to go home too. And home is wherever the people you love are," I said.

Bear looked up at me, a smile just whispering on the edge of his lips. "I guess we need to find Killian then, right?"

I laughed as we walked down the hard-packed road, the sound of the bayou around us. "Yeah, I think it does."

I WATCHED FROM A DISTANCE AS KILLIAN AND BEAR SPARRED in the fresh-fallen snow at the edge of the barn. Killian had been frantic by the time we'd tracked him down in Ireland. He'd managed to gather a number of his distant family to help him find us. They came along for the ride when we flew back to the States. They were the start of his second gang to get the abnormal world back under some semblance of control.

Funny to think that winter was upon us, that Christmas was just around the corner. That a year had gone by and I was back in Jackson Hole with Bear. We'd managed to build a new house, different than our log home from before on a different part of the land we owned. Backed against a bit of the mountain, it was far more defensible and we liked it that way. Killian had settled into the life of a part-time rancher like it was second nature to him.

Of course, he still ran his people, but it was different now. We knew we were targets and we took steps to protect ourselves and Bear. With my father and Mancini gone, there were whispers of other men who would take up their hold on the underworld. But for now, it was quiet.

We'd heard nothing from the Arabian desert and Shaitan, but I didn't think that quiet would last.

Dinah . . . had mellowed some. Her anger and desire for blood had eased with all the fighting. And with the knowledge that I knew who she really was.

"When are we going after Emerald?" she asked.

I sat up from my spot at the desk. "Today, if all goes well."

She gasped. "Really?"

"Yes."

In my study were a few things to remind me never to let my guard down again. The ruby ring Daniel had worn. The casing from the bullet that had killed my father—Bear had picked it up without me knowing. And the broken remains of Eleanor. I touched the melted puddle of metal that had been the gun that held my mother's soul for so many years.

Dinah sighed. "I don't think you ever stop loving your mother."

"Or missing her," I said. "I wish . . . I wish I'd had a chance to tell her all the things before she died."

"I know," Dinah said.

I turned at the sound of a motion detector going off, telling me someone had driven through the main gates of the ranch.

A motorbike pulled up, and a woman all in black leathers slid off. I stood in the doorway to the house as she pulled her helmet off and a swath of red hair slithered out from underneath. I grinned at her. "Cold enough?"

"Like a pair of witch's tits," she grumbled. "Tell me you have coffee going."

"Come on in."

Easter stomped her way up the stairs. There were parts of the house not yet done, but that was okay. We had time. And Killian and I wanted to do it right. Make it as safe as possible.

I went to the kitchen and Easter followed. "What kind of a job are we talking about here, then?"

Right to the point, as always. A cold breeze fluttered against me, as if Martin had brushed the skin of my belly. "I see Martin is still with you."

She frowned. "Who?"

I started to laugh. "Martin, you're a tease."

She's not quite ready for me yet. Soon.

I shrugged. "Never mind." I took a sip of tea and set it on the counter. "Look, I have money, and I want you to find a kid for me. Her name is Emerald."

Dinah gasped again. "Nix, I want to go!"

"You are going." I pulled her from her holster and slid her across the table to Easter.

Easter shook her head. "I don't need your talking gun."

"You do," I said. "And it's my right as the person hiring

you to determine any extra things I may require of you. This is one of them. Dinah doesn't miss. She comes with smoke bombs, electrical charges, and unlimited rounds of traditional ammo."

Easter sighed. "I have no aim."

"That's fine. I have perfect aim," Dinah said. "Just point in the right direction and shoot."

A pair of red eyebrows climbed. "Fine. But I should warn you, you aren't the only mouthy thing around."

It was my turn for eyebrows to climb. "Do I want to know?"

She laughed and shook her head. "It's a long story. Maybe another time."

"Deal. When you bring Emerald back, we'll discuss it." I stood and went to the kitchen sink. I hit a button and the false sink flipped up revealing stacks of cash and a few weapons. I pulled out three hundred thousand and hefted it to Easter.

"To help in finding her. Anything you don't use will go toward your fee."

"You don't want to sign something?" Easter frowned. I leaned forward.

"You think double-crossing me is a good idea?"

Most people would have cringed, started sweating, looked down. Easter just laughed. "Yeah. I guess not."

I handed her a small stack of papers with the little bit of information I'd been able to gather on Emerald.

"Here's the intel, such as it is."

She took the papers and tucked them into her jacket. "You going to tell me why you aren't going?"

"No," I said. "I'm not."

Dinah wriggled in her holster. "You didn't tell me why either."

"No, because you might not go then." I laughed at her. "And you need to do this with Easter. You'll come back to me when the time is right. Now go." I stripped off my single gun holster and handed it to Easter. She stripped off her jacket and put it on, then tucked Dinah inside.

"All right then. See you in a few days."

She turned and strode through the house, out the door, to her bike. I stood in the doorway of the house and watched her go.

From where I stood, I could see Bear and Killian starting their way back to the house. I went in to the back bedroom where I'd been keeping a surprise for Bear. I touched the winged necklace at my throat, the one Bear had given me the previous Christmas.

I opened the back-bedroom door, bent and scooped up the dark-haired puppy. "What do you think? You want to be the next best dog ever?"

The puppy whined and wormed toward me so he could lick my nose. I put him on the floor and he scampered out into the living room just as Bear stepped into the house.

There was no squeal, not shout of joy from Bear. I walked down the hall until I could just see Bear, kneeling on the floor, his face pressed against the fur of his new pup. My eyes filled with tears. Beside Bear was the ghost of Abe, and the minute he saw the puppy, he faded, his eyes closing as he sunk down. The puppy scampered through him, oblivious.

Killian stepped around Bear and came to stand next to me. "I thought we were going to wait, Lass."

"I couldn't," I said.

"What about me? Don't I get something?" he whispered in my ear.

I smiled to myself as I took his hand. "You want your present early?"

He grinned at me, green eyes flashing. "I think I've deserved it, haven't I?"

I grinned back. "Okay, you can have it early too, but I want no complaints that I got you nothing under the tree."

I held his hand up, palm facing me, then slowly lowered it and pressed it to my belly.

"I love you, Killian Fannin. Merry Christmas."

AFTERWORD

Thanks for reading all the way to the end! I hope I managed to surprise you with some of the twists. I'll be honest . . .I didn't know that Simon was Justin either until I hit that part of the story. But as you can see, my brain new better as it had given clues in the second book without tipping me off until this one. Sneaky!

I hope you are looking forward to Easter's storyline, its going to be a doozy! The first book is called (at the moment) "A Savage Spell" and I am planning on it releasing fall of 2018.

Need something else to read until then? I've got a shit ton of books (no, seriously) I'm not going to list them all. Lots of strong, kick ass women wielding weapons and magic . . .

You can find them all at:

www.shannonmayer.com

AND you can sign up for my newsletter if you want. Or not. Whatevs ;)

NEWSLETTER

Made in United States
Orlando, FL
03 December 2021